Invisible River

Invisible River

A Novel

Helena McEwen

BLOOMSBURY

NEW YORK · BERLIN · LONDON · SYDNEY

Published by Bloomsbury USA, New York

All papers used by Bloomsbury USA are natural, recyclable products made from wood grown in well-managed forests. The manufacturing processes conform to the environmental regulations of the country of origin.

LIBRARY OF CONGRESS CATALOGING-IN-PUBLICATION DATA

McEwen, Helena, 1961–
Invisible river : a novel / Helena McEwen. —1st U.S. ed.
p. cm.
ISBN-13: 978-1-60819-266-3 (pbk.)
ISBN-10: 1-60819-266-0 (pbk.)
1. Women art students—Fiction. 2. Parent and adult child—Fiction. 3. Children of alcoholics—Fiction. 4. London (England)—Fiction. I. Title.
PR6063.C425I58 2011
823'.92—dc22
2010027887

First U.S. Edition 2011

1 3 5 7 9 10 8 6 4 2

Typeset by Hewer Text UK Ltd, Edinburgh
Printed in the United States of America by Quad/Graphics, Fairfield, Pennsylvania

To my parents,
with love and thanks

Part One

1

I just wanted him to turn round and wave as the train went out, instead of walking up the platform with that gloomy stooped back. Turn round and wave and say, 'It's all right, you can leave, I'm all right.'

But he didn't, because he's not.

And when I walked along the moving carriage to look out the open window, the train threw me around against the knobs, like it was angry.

He didn't turn round, so part of me went with him up the platform. Went with him up to the house, where he'd be bound to get the bottle out, doesn't matter it's before breakfast.

That's why he didn't turn round. So part of me would go back with him, up to the house, into the kitchen.

And I saw St Michael's Mount slip away behind the hedges, with the sun glinting on the sea.

'Let me go!' I shouted at the sea, and then at the hedges, and into the marshes at Marazion.

And all the way through Cornwall past Redruth and Cambourne and Bodmin Moor and St Austell I could feel the pull of my father left alone.

I was halfway into Devon before it happened.

It was because of those tunnels cut in the red rock; you plunge into them after the miles of sealight, and the tentacles couldn't hold on. They had to let go, and then the city of London began to hum like a magnet, pulling me towards it.

It was telling me my future with promising feelings.

I arrived, and London splashed me all over. A big wave. Lots of experiences all at the same time, colours and loud noises. Women in patterned headscarves asking for money, and men in dark jackets calling out words, and many signs pointing you along bridges and upstairs and down walkways, and old ladies looking bewildered and men in uniform having an argument, and blaring traffic noise and electric skies shining dark and light at the same time and lights changing colours, and so many faces.

And after a lonely night in the hall of residence, at the end of a long grey corridor lit with striplighting that flickered and made the air tremble, and the strange dislocated not-here feeling in that little room that smelt of gravy, I walked out into the autumn morning and smelt a bonfire behind the exhaust fumes. I only had to cross the road to walk into the tall glass cube that would be my art school for the next three years.

I've brought my canvas bag with my brushes wrapped up in a tea towel, sticks of charcoal wrapped in tissue paper, a bottle of linseed oil and twenty-two tubes of paint, as though I am going to start painting straight away. But the girl who consults a list, and tells me we have been specifically told *not* to bring materials on Induction Day, sends me up in the lift to the third floor.

I find my way along the corridor to my name on a piece of paper taped to the wall, and put my bag down next to an easel. I am gazing at my white space.

4

'Who are you? I am Bianca,' says an Italian voice.

I turn round.

'Hello, I'm Eve.'

Bianca has also brought a canvas bag full of materials, gold paper and different coloured glass pots, which she begins to unpack.

'They have forgotten the TRO! In-TRO-duction,' she says. Her voice has a bell in it, a ting-a-ling sound. She is unusually thin, but she has a glitter about her.

'It's because they're inducing us, like babies being induced into the world of the art school,' says a voice from the corridor.

Bianca laughs.

'I'm Roberta,' she says, coming into the studio and putting her basket on the locker and two plastic bags on the ground, which both fall over, so paint-spattered tubs of acrylic roll over the floor. 'But call me Rob.'

She has a round face and dark curly hair.

'Hello, Rob.'

'I recognize you from the interview,' she says to me.

'Yes!' I say. 'What was yours like?'

'Oh, hellish. One of them was drunk!'

'I didn't like the head of painting much.'

'Oh, the small one who kicks your pictures about?'

'Yes!'

'No, me neither.'

'Where are you from?'

'Near Nottingham, and you?'

'Cornwall.'

'I'm from Rome,' says Bianca.

'Have you come all the way from Italy?' says Rob.

'I am escaping.'

'What from?'

'Bad people.'

'There are bad people here, you know.'

'Yes, but I don't know them!'

In the lift we discover that Rob's boyfriend, Mick, is doing metalwork at Camberwell.

The induction tutor glares at us, tapping her clipboard with her biro, as we join the first-years at the bottom of the stairs.

We are divided up. In our group there is a blonde girl from Ulster, a pretty and delicate-looking girl from Liverpool, slender as a bird, with pale skin. She wears a pair of enormous boots so she looks like a doll. Two girls from Manchester who titter together, a girl with long red hair, a Japanese boy and a young man with a black beard but no moustache who says 'fuck this' and 'fuck that' all the time.

'We will begin in Sculpture!' says the tutor, pointing her biro.

We walk through the doors into the noise of banging and welding and the screech of the circular saw. Sparks are flying, there is a smell of metal, sawn wood and plaster. A student in a blue overall is cutting through metal.

'Fuck this!' shouts the young bearded man into the noise.

We are shown how to use the lathe, what precautions to take with the welder, where the plaster of paris is kept, and how to use the glue-gunning machine.

We walk away from the screeching sound, past partitioned spaces with drawings taped to the walls and stacks of sketchbooks, into a room that is quiet.

Five people are in a kind of meditation, putting layers of white gauze soaked in plaster of paris on to armatures made of wood and wire. Their hands and fingers are white, and I like watching the white fingers smoothing the soaked gauze. They stand back patiently while we look at the ghostly forms.

Outside, next to the enormous kilns, are sheds full of bags of clay, huge pieces of stone, tree trunks, prams, bicycles, bits of rusty wrought iron and some old windows.

'Isn't it beautiful!' says Bianca.

We walk through large studios where students stand about in the midst of their work, gathered round kettles, smoking cigarettes, or look up from their absorption as though we are barely visible.

Rob says 'Hello!' to a blonde girl, who looks at her blankly and turns away.

We walk into the ground-floor studio for enormous canvases, large as the side of houses. 'Fuck that,' says the young man, with admiration.

'Who was she?' asks Bianca.

'She goes out with a friend of Mick's,' says Rob. 'She's a third-year and, well . . . I'm a first year. That's Suzanne! Stuck-up cow.'

'Porca miseria!' says Bianca. 'I can't bear these cool English cucumber types!'

Rob and I both laugh. 'What? What is funny?' says Bianca.

2

We are shown round the lecture theatre on the first floor, the art history department and the secretary's office. We are introduced to Miss Pym, the secretary, and Tom, the first-year tutor.

At last it is time for lunch.

Roberta and Bianca and I sit together with the red-haired girl, and discover things about each other. One wall of the canteen is made of glass, so we are in the courtyard along with the pigeons.

Cecile is a ballerina who has been dancing for the Royal Ballet, but received an injury and decided to change her career. She sits with a perfectly erect spine.

Rob is going to marry Mick. He is a blacksmith and they've known each other since they were five. We all say ooh! because childhood sweethearts make people say ooh! along with the vision of horseshoes, and cold autumn mornings, and a young man with a pinkish face holding the hind leg of a horse and tapping it.

We find out that Rob lives near London Bridge with Mick, that Bianca lives in Brixton with two Italian girls who are doing textiles at Goldsmiths, and the ballerina lives in Kensington with her husband, who is twenty-two years older.

'And I live in a soulless room down a long corridor in the Halls of Residence,' I say gloomily.

'I will ask around for you,' says Bianca.

'Thanks,' I say.

The stairwell winds up the centre of the building, lit by a huge skylight. The rooms and studios are arranged around the landings, and lit by walls of windows. The further up the building you go, the more London spreads out before you.

The print rooms on the second floor overlook the King's Road and St Stephen's, and are filled with printing presses for wood cut, lino cut and etching.

There are baths for soaking paper and lines to dry it on. There are racks for newly printed prints and acid baths for placing the etching plates. There are shelves with tins of ink, and a long wooden desk under the windows.

Round the corner, where the screen-printing press stands, the windows look over treetops towards the Fulham Road, and two girls stand at big basins in black plastic aprons, hosing ink out of the screen-printing mesh. The jet of water shoots out of the hose and turns red and yellow before coiling into the drain.

We look round Photography and the dark room, with the red light, and white baths of chemicals that flavour the air.

'I can't take any more!' says Bianca. 'I can't remember all these processes!'

Rob laughs. 'You don't have to, don't worry. It's just if you want to use this stuff, you have to have a vague idea.'

On the third floor we meet Steve, the head of film. He has long greasy hair that he smooths back from his forehead every now and then, slowly, with his whole hand, while looking sideways.

Bianca mimics his gesture and we get the giggles. He wears a jacket made of leather.

A tall girl with a scarf around her head strides out of a studio, saying, 'Who has stolen the red heads?' Steve tells us proudly that this girl is in the third year and has just been commissioned to make her *second* short film for Channel Four, and that red heads are spotlights.

There is a buzzing sound in the video rooms, and we watch a video of someone's hand putting pig's guts in a bucket, that goes round and round on a loop. Cecile pulls a disgusted face. Steve says, 'It makes a strong statement.'

In the editing suite Steve shows us how to use the projector and splice the film, the video equipment and where the spotlights are kept.

'I'm worn out!' says Bianca, as we come out on to the landing. 'I have to lie down,' and she lies down on the floor and closes her eyes.

We walk round the figurative studios, divided by a maze of white-painted partitions.

I walk past paintings of fossils and shells, screaming people and grey empty landscapes. The studios smell of oil paint, turpentine and white spirit. There is a quietness here.

In the life room the model is taking a break, wrapped in a blue curtain and drinking coffee from a plastic cup. She sits on the edge of the mattress, her pink toes stroking each other. The students are standing around and looking at each other's work. They turn to look at us with dazed expressions.

The technician's workshop is on the top floor. It smells of wood, and we meet Geoff, the technician, in a brown coat with a pencil behind his ear. He has a friendly open face and nods at each of us in turn and explains how to cut the stretchers, saw the angles, and nail them with corrugated nails, how to stretch the canvas over the stretchers, and melt the rabbit-skin glue to prepare the size. The ballerina asks him if you can make size without using animal products.

Sinéad, from Ulster, flicks her eyes up to the ceiling.

There are woodshavings on the floor and the circular saw makes a whirring sound as he shows us how to slice through the plank without cutting your hand off.

On the landing we meet Terry, the abstract tutor, who has bloodshot eyes.

'I've heard he has a drink problem,' whispers Sinéad, with a snort.

'This way,' he says.

Through the windows on the abstract floor, you can see all the way past the bend in the river to Westminster and the far-away blue buildings on the horizon.

The rooms are also lit from skylights in the roof, and I think that even this building, with all its light pouring in, began as a drawing; and before that it was a thought. And I'm glad the architect put so much light into his thought.

And I like wandering through the studio spaces full of abstract forms and sketchbooks bursting with ideas, stacked up on the floor or leaning against each other along makeshift shelves.

Sometimes the canvases are huge and fill a whole wall; cadmium-red singing on grey, with cobalt violet and sienna.

Sometimes they are small; collages made of feathers and corrugated cardboard and grey paint the colour of the sky and pigeons.

I sneak a look into a sketchbook and see pages of colour variations, like looking at different musical chords made visible and singing on the page.

Students begin to go downstairs for tea.

But when everyone leaves, the studios are not empty. The ideas are everywhere. They make the air hum. And I stand in the darkening space and see the twilight falling all the way to Westminster.

3

I take the silver lift down to the ground floor and feel a blast of cold wind from the open front door as I walk into the canteen. Through the wall made of glass, the big tree and the Henry Moore sculpture in the courtyard are turning blue. People are reflected in the glass.

I stand in the queue behind a tall young man in a tartan shirt that has dots of white paint spattered over it in an arc, that match up with the splashes on his trousers.

He has long black hair tied with an elastic band, blue-black like a crow. He turns his head. He smiles at me then frowns a funny frown and peers unexpectedly towards my eyebrows.

I have a spot on my forehead.

'It's about to pop!' he says, nodding at it.

'I know!' I say, laughing at his rudeness. We don't say anything else.

I get my mug of tea served from a big silver teapot by a lady in a white bath-cap.

'There you are, duck,' she says.

Bianca turns and waves at me. I sit down with her and Rob.

They are examining a list of options: etching, lithography, photography, animation, life drawing, painting: media and supports, sculpture: plaster/clay.

I look across to see where the dark-haired man went.

'Who's *that?*' says Bianca, looking round and seeing him too. He is leaning against a table, talking to someone. I like his easy way of moving.

'Oh, I know him. That's Zeb, he's a friend of Mick's. They did foundation together,' says Rob.

'Call him over, call him over,' says Bianca, tugging on Rob's sleeve.

'Hi, Zeb!' she calls out, but he doesn't hear.

Suzanne comes through the door. She starts talking to Zeb.

'That's his girlfriend!' says Rob.

'Oh, that is Suzanne's boyfriend!' says Bianca, looking disappointed.

The head of painting strolls into the canteen. He is a small man with hair that grows like moss. He stands with his feet apart and his hands on his hips inside his jacket, and surveys. He strides over and addresses us, and the tables nearby. 'Welcome to you, first years!' How are you settling in?' he says.

'When can we see your paintings, please?' says Bianca loudly.

I like the bell sound in her voice.

'Well! There are some in the library on slide, and quite a few catalogues of the shows I've had,' he says rather smugly, then takes a breath in to announce something else.

'No! the real ones! Can we see the real ones?'

His lips press together, slightly annoyed at the interruption, but he puts an easygoing face on things. 'One day I'm sure we can arrange a trip to my studio. Now then!' he rubs his hands together.

'When?'

He ignores her, and speaks up. 'I'd like you all to come to the lecture theatre in half an hour so we, the tutors, can introduce ourselves to you.' He bows a little, pointing his hands at himself.

'And you,' his hands go out to the side, 'can meet us! And then we can learn a *little* bit about what we expect from each other. Thanks very much!' He puts his palms up in the air and nods. 'See you later!' he says, and twirls round so his jacket twirls too.

'Creep,' says Bianca.

The next time I see Zeb is in the corridor when I've got lost on the abstract floor looking for film and photography, because we are doing animation. He is carrying a roll of chicken wire and some ping-pong balls. The balls are dropping and bouncing.

I start chasing them and pick one up; the other one drops down the stairwell and we both look over and can hear its musical bounce echoing as it falls through the floors.

'Well done!' he says, nodding at my eyebrow, and I just laugh.

And when I've finished drawing a hundred and seventy-two pictures of a small man doing a dance so his hips wiggle, and his arms wave, for one and a half seconds of film, I help him move the rest of his stuff down to his new work space. We talk about living in London, and the microbiology of the Thames.

Zeb is in the second year. He was put on the abstract floor until his paintings began to grow a dimension and they moved him down to sculpture. When he began to project film on to them they moved him back up to film. Then the pieces began to move so they put him next to the technician's office. Now they make sounds as well as moving, so they've put him on the mezzanine which used to be a storeroom.

'They don't know which box to put you in!' I say.

'I know,' he says.

4

The weeks begin to follow a routine.

On Tuesdays we have a class with Geoff. He teaches us how to make our own pastels with sieved earth and rice water, and lamp black pigment, by baking chicken bones in a biscuit tin until they are burnt; and how to size canvas and make primer with titanium white and rabbit-skin glue.

Wednesday life drawing class with Karl is compulsory for the first term. Thursday evenings is art history. Long lectures in the chilly lecture theatre, with Andrew Mackinley-Davis, who uses words like 'polemic', 'dialectic' and 'post-postmodern'. We come out of the lectures with glazed eyes.

On Friday afternoon it's 'museums and galleries'. We can choose what. It even includes an afternoon watching films if you want, at the NFT or ICA, as long as it's in a cinema with initials.

The rest of the time we spend in the studio, or drawing outside.

I'm sitting on the windowsill above the radiator, looking out the window at the far-away tower blocks on the horizon. They look blue.

'What do you vote, then?' I say.

'Museum of London,' says Rob.

'Sounds drab!' says Bianca, taking the coffee pot off the heat.

'Why not the V and A?'

'I don't want to look at *decorative* art,' says Rob.

'*Decorative art*,' mimics Bianca over the coffee pot.

Bianca has been moved up to the abstract floor, and it has become our habit to gather in her new space and drink real coffee that she percolates in her silver coffee pot on the ring she melts the wax on.

And after drawing in the cold wind all day, or struggling with a painting that won't work, or an afternoon stretching canvases till your thumbs are sore, it is a relief to gather in Bianca's space and sit on the windowsill above the radiators, looking out over the trees, and watch the weather changing in the sky.

'Tom says we should definitely go to the Hayward.'

'Who cares!'

'Paul says we should start with the National Gallery.'

'Which one's Paul?'

'Oh, I loathe them!' says Bianca.

'Tom's all right.'

'Who's got your goat now?' says Rob, crossing her legs and leaning against the wall.

'No one has my goat,' says Bianca indignantly. 'I have my own goat!'

'I don't like the small one, he's venomous,' says Cecile.

'Is that Paul?'

'What did he say to you?'

'That my work was twee.'

'That's very nice of him.'

'He's a bloody moron.'

'Have you seen *his* pictures?'

'No, what are they like?'

'Vertical stripes, that's all, vertical stripes of varying thickness.'

'You got to be careful what they tell you, they don't bloody know.'

'You know what Zeb calls them?'

'What?'

'Art officials!'

Bianca lies down on the battered chaise longue. She pulled it out of a skip. She wants it to lend some elegance to her painting space. It is faded orange-pink, worn through at the end, where the horsehair stuffing is coming out.

She puts her forearm over her eyes.

'Art officials,' she murmurs. 'Oh, I get it!' and laughs.

'You get tired easily,' says Roberta, sipping her coffee.

'It's because I have an illness,' says Bianca, still with her eyes closed.

'What illness?'

'Hepatitis.'

'Hepatitis?'

'Yes. Hepatitis D. I am very fashionable!' says Bianca languidly.

Rob finishes her coffee and gets up.

'Well, I'm going to the Museum of London. If you want to come, I'll meet you in our space.'

I follow her downstairs. We have been moved to a lovely space next to a big window. We've divided it with a butter muslin curtain that catches the light in its folds and glows white.

We pack our materials.

'I don't think Bianca will come, do you?'

But she is already at the studio door.

'I am coming!' she says. 'I have three sketchbooks, some charcoal, some coloured paper if we want to do collage.' She opens her bag. 'A box of oil pastels, three Conté sticks, some watercolours . . .'

'Hang on, hang on, Bianca, we're going to look at the museum.'

'I know, but I can't not take my things. Here, will you take some water?' She turns to me.

In the end we walk down the road with three canvas bags, two rolls of paper, seven sketchbooks and a vast assortment of media.

We take the bus along King's Road past the glittering shops, and the twiggy branches of the overhanging trees hit the window in the top deck so that we duck. We get off at Sloane Square and dive into the choking air of the Underground that shunts us to St Paul's, where we explode out of the darkness into the sunlight. We walk past St Botolph's, where there is a little garden and a fountain squeezed between the glass and concrete of the city like a slip of London from another time. We ride up an escalator in a glass tube and travel down a concrete walkway across a tangle of thundering roads and reach the Museum of London.

Bianca wants to go to the rooms that show Roman London. She's proud of her ancestors, and takes it personally when we call them invaders. Roberta and I wander into the Stone Age, where the sound of macaque monkeys squealing is played on a tape, and trilling birds, to mimic the sounds when London was a tropical jungle.

Rob unrolls her paper on the floor and begins a huge drawing in brown chalk of cave bears and rivers and crouching people, animal-headed women and large-leaved plants, and I have to walk away from her throbbing images in case I get pulled into her world, because me, I'm still looking for mine.

And underneath it all, under the shining glass and the old bones and the sounds of mammoths, and clay pots, behind the light-up displays and the touch-and-sniff, the lists of plants, the wall charts of climate change from the Palaeolithic to the Mesolithic, and the glass cases of rounded stones they brought to the river from Cornwall and Cumbria, Scotland and Ireland, maybe it's there, waiting for me to find it.

Rob has her paper spread out on the floor, sitting happily with her long dark curls falling on the page, her legs out at right angles, leaning over the drawing, with schoolchildren walking around her, stopping to glance at the mysterious animals and ancient landscape that flow out of her chalk and commenting to each other and whispering, two little boys in red V-neck jerseys pointing at the women with their breasts exposed, and giggling, until the teacher, with her clipboard, ushers them forward into the Bronze Age.

I look at the pots from 4000 BC marked with fingernails, and wonder, whose fingernail was it? who were you? and what did you think? It says here you thought the Thames was a deity and that's why you came from every end of the islands and beyond to throw your special stones into the water. When Pall Mall was a field of marigolds and mugwort, when artemisia was flowering in Mayfair and the ice had receded like a miracle, and the grass seeds had been blown on the warm wind, and the birch trees grew and the oak forests, and the red deer followed, and then along the river and through the trees you came and gathered round the hearth fires at night, that sent sparks upwards, the air filled with the smell of aromatic herbs and wet earth; and dawn, by the huge river, the reed warblers echoing off the water. A time of plenty, it says. I just like thinking of them all, sitting around in the woods, where Piccadilly is now, fashioning fine flint blades and listening to the birds.

I sigh. I don't like my little drawings of imaginary people sitting next to a river, dressed in skins.

I wander along the corridor following the timeline of Celts, Romans, Saxons, Danes and through a doorway into Londinium 47–550 AD.

Bianca is sitting by a replica of the Temple of Mithras, found beside the buried River Walbrook, listening to tape recordings of Roman soldiers shouting at each other in Latin.

In the large dark room the glass cases glow yellow and light up the faces of people as they wander through, like sleepwalkers, led by their headphones that are speaking them back through time.

We come out of the Museum and pass London Wall.

'Roman! says Bianca with triumph, and Rob looks cross.

Through the tall buildings of the city we can see the dome of St Paul's.

We step out into Ludgate Hill, and smartly dressed people are spilling out of doorways, rushing down the pavement and across the road and queuing at every sandwich shop. It is the city at lunchtime. We walk through the crowds and stand at a bus stop.

The big red bus opens sliding doors; we climb up the stairs and swerve down towards the glinting river.

5

I didn't know it when she said it, but it means something when Bianca says she'll ask around. She puts the word out into her enormous network of Italians, Venezuelans, Chileans and Portuguese, and within days you have a new sofa, a part-time job, a removal van, a free TV, or a new place to live.

The bedsit I move to is no palace, but even though the skylight is stuck open and the washing machine is broken and the kitchen as small as a cupboard, I prefer it to the double glazing, the blotchy linoleum, the striplighting and smell of institutions that I thought would gobble me up like that insect that lays its eggs in a frog and eats it from the inside.

I thought that would happen to me. I'd be sucked out somehow.

But thanks to Bianca, I have my own place now.

And every morning I cycle through the rowan trees, past the pyramids of cauliflowers and oranges, the stalls of red and brown handbags and different-coloured dresses, and climb up the stairs to the studio where Roberta paints her mysterious paintings.

I'm envious of Rob's paintings.

Downstairs in the basement, Cecile is painting huge flowers. Upstairs, Bianca is making work from glinting metallic paper, gold leaf and melted beeswax mixed with pigment; beautiful collages that glint in the light and glow in the half-light.

And I am painting London.

It is autumn and the city is lit by yellow trees. I walk around the streets, looking at paintings that haven't been painted yet, and I draw on the corner of streets at night, and by the river in the day, and from cafés high up above the road so I can see the distance is blue. And I take the drawings back to the studio and tape them on the wall to paint from. I paint Sloane Square from Peter Jones with a circle of trees and a red bus going up Sloane Street, and I draw Cambridge Circus from the Fruit of the Loom pub and paint the turquoise lamp-posts and orange brick buildings and a sky cut in half by the clouds.

In London the clouds have a habit of cutting the sky in half, so the sun shines from beneath and lights the buildings up yellow so they glow against the grey sky, and even the tower blocks look beautiful, lilac and grey with glowing pink windows reflecting the sunset shining against the dark evening sky.

And I learn about near, far and middle distance, and tone from dark to light, through all the in-betweens, and complementary colours that glow and shine together.

I look for them in the city streets and I see the sun shining through red leaves, next to green, and glistening on the wet grass.

I see a large yellow sun between dark lilac clouds, so it looks like a big eye with rays of lemon-yellow eyelashes.

I see an orange globe flashing at a zebra crossing when the sky is turning blue.

And Bianca calls it the yellow season except for the ash trees, their leaves flame-red, the tips purple so they glow from within like embers. I paint the dark street with brown madder, magenta and translucent Indian yellow painted over white, so it glows. The streetlight shining in the darkness, illuminating the trees.

I must have been invisible when I was doing the drawings for it, because a man raced past me with a bag in his hand. Not long after came a plump man, puffing, and then a lady with her hat askew, wheezing and clip-clopping on unsuitable heels. If they'd asked me I would have told them where he ran. But I didn't think to tell them, I was just watching the night.

And I paint the river. The beautiful river.

I go down to the river in the dark, and see the green lights reflected in the water, just after sunset when the sky is streaked with pink and the starlings gather and fly under and over the bridge with their startling precision.

I paint the river from Westminster Bridge, looking over St Paul's; from Albert Bridge when the leaves are turning, streaked with pink light at dusk; from Battersea Bridge, looking down towards the park and the serene gold Buddha.

I even persuade Rob to get up before sunrise to paint the dawn, and we sit on the police pier at Blackfriars and paint the sun rising over Tower Bridge. A grey green before dawn light that slowly turns to pink and lights the water, and then the streaks of yellow begin beyond the blue distant buildings, and we paint with watercolours, one, two, three pictures in as many minutes because the colours change so fast and the sky turns pink then yellow as the sun rises and shines down the river in a ribbon of light.

But Rob doesn't need the river, or the park, or the houses with the lights coming on, she doesn't need the street lights turning from pink to yellow or the turquoise shadows or the purple London night, or finding a place high enough to paint the bend in the river, or see the distance is blue. She doesn't even need the colours. She can make them in simple black and white, drawings and paintings endlessly pouring out of her, like dreams. Landscapes with paths and trees, and a man with a crown who holds his penis erect, and women who squat and give birth to other women, and horses, and people who she knows but has never seen; she knows how to make an unseen world into pictures and I want to know too.

6

'Will you come and help or just keep watch?' Rob says.

'Keep watch, why?'

'Well, they might not allow it.'

'You're only going to collect some earth.'

She shrugs. 'Well, you're not allowed to do lots of things that are perfectly reasonable.'

Ever since we went to the museum she's been obsessed with these ideas she won't talk about, only now they have to be made with mud, not just any mud, though, river mud. That's why we end up going to Battersea Park just before the gates close so that the twilight is beginning to fall and all the blackbirds and robins and song thrushes and blue tits in the park are singing their separate songs together in a big dusk chorus, and climb over the fence by the weeping willow with a trowel and a spade and four plastic bags, and dig up the mud from the river where it is low. But it's not the Thames, it's 'Tamesa', Rob says, which means 'the dark one', and she says a prayer to the river which embarrasses me slightly before we dig, which goes, 'Oh dark water, I am your daughter', but I am rather glad of the rhyme, and we spade the mud into the bags until they are full and ridiculously heavy, so we have to spade some of it out again, then realize that we can't climb up the walls that we've jumped down from, and

we have to call one of the joggers to get the park attend-
ant who we've tried so hard to avoid, so that he can fetch
a ladder from the gardens in the quadrangle where they
grow the bedding plants and get us out.

He says, 'What the hell are you doing down there?'

'Collecting mud for my painting,' says Rob.

'But she won't tell you the details,' I say. 'She's not telling any of us.'

'Oh, so you're the helper.'

'I am,' I say, as I climb back over the fence.

'Well, good luck to you. If you run outa mud just let
me know.'

'Thank you, we appreciate it,' says Rob, picking up the
bags.

'Tell us when the art exhibition's on so I can see what
you're up to,' he says, following us down the path.

'Certainly will,' says Rob.

'You sure you can manage with all them bags of mud?'

'Yes, we're fine, thanks,' says Rob, and we trudge out
the gates, the night turning blue, and the green lights
rippling over the dark water.

Zeb says that around every river is an invisible river. It
extends all around, down and to the side for 500 feet,
and it's full of micro-organisms, and the health of the
river depends on the health of the invisible river. And
I suppose that around every city is an invisible city also.

29

7

We walk into the dark courtyard, and through the glass wall we see Bianca and Cecile having tea in the lit-up canteen.

'They look like they're in an Edward Hopper painting,' says Rob.

Bianca sees us, and waves us in to join them.

We sit down in the canteen with the bags of mud.

'Where have you been?' says Bianca.

'Oh, don't ask!' says Rob.

'All right, I won't!' says Bianca, and turns back to Cecile. 'So anyway, what happened? She's telling me about the portrait commission. That awful woman's husband, and the photo of her smiling, with all her teeth showing?'

'Oh,' Cecile groans. 'He came to collect it, and said I'd made her look like a horse! I had to go to her gilt house with chintz everything and paint her lips again, this time closed, so the horse didn't show!'

'Oh my God, the horse!' Bianca squeals in a high-pitched voice.

'She wants a portrait that makes her look ten years younger!' says Cecile, who is so poised and demure-looking it is surprising when she swears. 'And fuck him! I changed it three times and he didn't offer me a penny more!'

Zeb walks past our table with his empty tray, and Bianca catches his arm.

'When are you going to show us your sculptures, Mister Zebedee?'

'When do you want to see them?' he says.

'Anytime!'

'Come on up, then!'

So we all troop up to the mezzanine, in a row, with Bianca making faces at us.

There are skylights in his space but no windows and the sink faces a wall. It is a big low sink with taps underneath it in the pipes. His space is crammed with bits of television sets, plugs and wires, old radios, their inner wiring exposed. There are projectors and canvases and cameras, some half taken apart. There are hammers and screws and rolls of steel wire, and copper tubing, and then there are his sculptures, which light up and tinkle. Strange otherworldly beings that have a logic of their own. Zeb's logic. Some ping rubber bands, some project light through bottles of different coloured water which quivers on the wall in a slow rotation.

'Wow! they are so fantastic,' says Bianca, touching them with her thin fingers, and looking them up and down.

Zeb stands in the corner, his hands in his back pockets and his head leaning over to one side.

He likes artists called Tinguely and Twombly and scientists who propose eleven dimensions.

He says he's seen his sculptures when he travels in dreams to other planets, but his don't work as well as those did.

'You like putting things together?' says Bianca, examining the constructions.

'And taking things apart,' he says, laughing.

'I wish you'd take apart my washing machine!' I say.

'I'll come and have a look if you like,' he says.

I didn't expect him to say that.

'That would be great!' I say.

Bianca looks at me out the side of her eyes. I glare at her. Bianca likes making up stories, even if she knows they aren't true.

'Well, I could come on Saturday morning,' he says, crouching down and looking through a box of tools.

'Thanks,' I say.

8

'Well, how late are you?'
  'Six weeks.'
  'Since it should have come, or since your last one?'
  'Since my last one.'
  'But that's not long, it's only two weeks.'
  'I'm never late.'
  Rob looks down at the bags of mud, and puts her hands
on her head.
  'I suppose I better take them home.'
  'What are you going to do?'
  'Bake it, then sieve it.'
  'What?'
  'The earth. Make it into pigment!'
  She looks at me and realizes, and we both laugh.
  She shakes her head.
  'Oh, it'll be all right,' she says.
  I nod. 'Course it will.'
  'I'll have a baby, I mean, why not?'
  'You'd be a great mum, Rob.'
  'Just didn't expect it quite so soon.'
  'You might not be, though. It's only two weeks.'

9

On Saturday morning I am sitting in my kitchen, and the doorbell rings.

I run down the stairs to let Zeb in.

'D'you want a cup of tea?' I say, showing him into the kitchen.

'No no,' he says. 'I'll get on with it,' and he has soon pulled the machine out from the wall and begun to undo it. I leave him to his deconstruction and sit next door, hearing all the little noises and clinks and thuds of the washing machine being taken apart. When I look through the curtain of plastic strips the washing machine is all over the floor, lined up in little rows, all the cogs and tubes and washers.

He looks up.

'I'm working out how it works,' he says.

'Don't you know?' I say.

'Well, no, I've never taken a washing machine apart before,' he says, moving the pieces slowly along the floor. His tall body is folded, and he is crouching on one knee. There is something graceful about his movements.

'Don't worry,' he says, looking up and smiling at me. 'It'll work fine!' and within an hour it is chugging away.

I watch him unfolding himself, standing up and stretching. He has to lay his hands flat on the ceiling.

'It's all right, isn't it, your little pad.'

'Yes, I like it. Look, you can see the river,' and I show him through the gap in the houses, and the rain pouring in slants.

'And you've got the market,' he says, pointing behind his head.

'Yes, I'm going there in a minute.'

'Well, I hope you've got your canoe!' he says, and I laugh.

'Look, Zeb, can I give you some money for this?'

'No-oh!' he says in a cascade of notes. 'It was fun!'

'Fun?' I say, thinking of my panic at all things mechanical.

'Yes, some people do crosswords,' he says, patting me on the shoulder affectionately. 'Anyway, it was my pleasure. Right! I'm on my way!'

'You're going to get soaked!'

'I will survive!' he sings as he walks down the stairs, and shouts 'See you!' when he slams the front door.

So I give him the magic shells instead. I leave them in his space wrapped up in a small drawing of a washing machine.

They open under water. I bought them in Chinatown when I was drawing pictures of Cambridge Circus.

I'd been lured down Gerard Street by the glowing lanterns and coloured paper decorations in the windows of the little shops, and out of the icy wind that was biting my face with cold rain, and making my fingers numb.

The lady in the shop couldn't speak English but she nodded at me and smiled and spoke Chinese and made delicate movements with her fingers and managed that way to explain what the little shells contained. I took them home and put one in a glass of water and waited. Nothing happened.

But next morning, I looked up and saw the shell had opened; the pink and yellow and blue paper flowers had unfurled, along with green fronds, and there in the glass was a miniature underwater garden.

10

Rob is preparing big pieces of paper seven feet tall, painting them with a wallpaper brush and PVA to coat the surface, and the smell of baked earth fills the studio, sweet and soft. Rob took the earth home, and baked it in her oven, while she waited for the line to turn blue. By the time she'd sieved the earth to a fine raw umber powder, and ruined the sieve, it was definitely dark blue. She said Mick was over the moon.

She is going to mix the earth, baked and sieved, with cold-pressed linseed oil.

'So you're sure?' I said.

'Yes,' she said.

'Well, well, well,' I said smiling, and I could tell by her face that she was glad too.

'But I want to keep it quiet for a bit,' she says, her eyes looking upwards to the ceiling, and I nod.

Behind the muslin curtain, on my table next to the window, I have a piece of smooth wood for mixing colours.

I notice a matchbox sitting there. I pick it up and push it open. A little yellow jack jumps out attached to a spring. It startles me and makes me smile. It must be from Zeb.

I make it ping out of the box a few times.

Then I leave it on the windowsill and pull a canvas out from under the table and get to work.

I rub the white surface of the canvas with rose doré, a translucent pink pigment made with gold. It is a delicate pigment; if you mix it with even the tiniest amount of another colour it disappears into it.

The colour prefers not to be mixed but to be laid over a white ground so the white shines through it and lights up its delicate pinky orange hue.

The surface is ready. It is a colour field.

I squeeze the tubes of oil paint on to the palette, one by one.

I love the colours and their secret singing.

Aureolin, a gentle golden yellow that is soft and hums, and high-pitched lemon yellow, sharp and startling, then the low velvet tone of alizarin crimson, and the seductive cobalt blue. It fills me with longing, if cobalt blue was a man I'd run away with him. He calls with a longing to far away. Blue is a calling-away colour and its sound is a sound so beautiful it makes you want to leave the earth. Not red though, red pipes up, especially cadmium scarlet. 'Do-do-doooo,' it says like a trumpet, it runs in your blood the same sound, 'yes, this is life!' It gets hot and passionate. If you put it in a painting it jumps forward, 'I am here!' it says, 'right here, ME!' and I love red for that. Then the beautiful violets, half red, half blue. Cobalt violet, singing in the range next to pink, but with more majesty, more mystery, and ultramarine violet, gentle, tender, like the shadows in twilight, but deep, with dignity and a hidden depth, like someone who walks among people but knows they are really a seraph.

Then translucent golden green that is like the sun shining through leaves, cinnabar green, spring leaves unfurling in the new light, chrome green, heavy like a green stone washed by the waves.

I couldn't work in the studios with music blaring because the ideas can't gather in the silence, and besides, you can't hear the colours.

I mix them on the palette.

The rose doré ground is ready. Orange pink. It is a small canvas, a foot square, but big enough for a world. I put some cinnabar green, some rose pink mixed with white, some royal blue. The colours sing together on the surface and already there is a space and a distance, a place for something to arrive.

I love the feeling in the studio, of the presence of the reality that we call into our pictures. It fills the empty space with invisible threads of light that touch that other realm. The ideas hang in the air, becoming more real with imagining, more robust and less wispy, until they are so real that they come and sit on the end of the paintbrush and get mixed in with the colours and appear on the canvas unexpectedly. An idea you might have had months ago will suddenly appear fully formed and look at you from the primed surface. The threads gather in the corners and on the ceiling like spiders' webs, but they aren't musty, they have a singing presence. You can feel them. They are halfway in, half out, between realities.

Roberta makes a quietness around her when she works. It is deep and palpable. I can feel it on the surface of my skin. She breathes and concentrates and the concentration makes a deep feeling that draws you into it; without her the ideas fly about untethered, with her in the room everything gathers and is brought down. We fall into deep concentration together, like a stone falling to the bottom of the sea, down and down, to the forest of coral, the flashes and flits of colour, the rippling underwater light.

I tell Rob her baby must be influencing us from his underwater world; half in and half out of this reality, his spirit still resident in the place where anything is possible. I think he must dart about among the ideas, spinning them around like toys.

11

'What happened? What happened?' says Bianca eagerly, when I walk into her space.

'What d'you mean, what happened?'

'On Saturday with Zeb!'

'He fixed my washing machine!'

'Nothing happened?'

'No. Nothing *happened*, Bianca'

'If you were Italian something would happen,' she says, looking dejected.

'Look, he's a friend. I like him,'

'Ah, how dull!' she says, waving me away.

I laugh and sit down on the windowsill, but I don't tell her about the jack-in-a-box.

There is a smell of resin. She is using egg yolk mixed with pigment. There are brown bags of pure cobalt blue, and ultramarine. The colours jump out at you when you open the bags.

The eggshells quiver as she walks across the floor, to place her pictures on the nails to look at them.

Her work has become more sturdy, on wood instead of paper.

As her collages have become more robust it seems she is getting fatter.

'Have you put on weight, Bianca?'

'Do you think so?' She turns round delighted. 'Have I? I hope so. I want a nice fat bottom.'

I love the smell of wax, it's like churches, and Bianca's paintings glint and glow like icons.

She goes out on Sunday mornings in Brixton with her dustpan to sweep up the hundreds of little green-tinted cubes of coloured glass from windscreens that have been smashed the night before, to use in her work.

'Are you religious, Bianca?'

'Don't be ridiculous! I want to sell my pictures to rich women in fur coats who wear too much perfume! They like things that glint!'

'You only pretend to be a cynic!' I say.

Cecile comes in with Rob, who has a big library book under her arm.

'Time for coffee!' says Bianca.

Cecile sits down next to me on the windowsill and Rob sits on the chaise longue, while Bianca unscrews the silver coffee pot and heaps in the coffee.

'Look!' says Roberta, opening the book and smoothing the photograph with her hand. 'They're amazing, don't you think they're just amazing!'

Bianca shrugs. 'You aren't interested in anything after 2000 BC.'

Roberta closes the library book of megalithic stones and puts her hands on her hips even though she's sitting down.

'Our history didn't start with ROME, you know!'

I start laughing. 'You two! Honestly!'

'All history books start with Rome!' says Roberta, turning to me. 'You should know, your dad's a historian.'

'Really, is he?' says Cecile, turning to me.

'Yes.' I nod, and think of the stacks of dusty books and the typewriter with its red and black ribbon, and the rubber bands he used to give me, that he kept in a box, lots of different-coloured rubber bands.

'There is a whole *history* of art!' says Bianca.

'Here we go! The Italian Renaissance!' says Rob.

'All over the world!' says Bianca, gesturing the whole of the world. 'You can't just ignore it!'

'I can do what I like!'

'There's a standing stone in London, did you know?' says Cecile, but Rob isn't listening.

'For you the only art is Italian art!'

'Actually, the period I like is Byzantium.'

She has postcards of the golden mosaics in Ravenna on the wall.

'Where is it?' I ask Cecile.

'It's opposite Cannon Street Tube station, under the Bank of China.

It used to be as tall as two grown men,' says Cecile, 'and it's been there for thousands of years. It's supposed to keep London safe. I'll lend you the book.'

'Thanks.'

'Maybe your dad knows about it. Did he tell you any stories about London?' she asks.

'Yes, he did, he told me stories all the time when I was little.'

I look out the window at the huge sky.

I remember a dragon dancing on a floating stage, and men pulling oars through water lilies in time to flutes. I remember the pigeons falling out of the sky with their wings on fire. I saw the city in the flames with the wind blowing outside after the twilight had turned the sea pink. I looked into the orange flames and saw it burning, and after that it was always there. I looked for it even if the story was from another time.

'All I'm saying is, open your mind. You only see one thing.'

'Well, same to you, Empress Theodora!'

'You can like whatever period you like!'

'And so can I!'

Roberta opens her book and turns the pages slowly. The coffee pot begins to hiss.

Cecile gestures with her eyes about the other two, and smiles.

'Has he published a book?' she says.

I look at the bottom of my empty cup.

'He hasn't finished it.'

And I remember the pages stuck together and the blurred writing where the whisky had spilt and the words had run into each other.

'Well, I'm sure he will,' she says kindly.

He's on his own now. On his own in that house. Alone with the wind blowing against the windows. And I don't want to think about my dad all alone in that house by the sea with the wind blowing against the windows.

'Can we change the subject now, please?' says Cecile.

'Of course!' says Bianca, who will have an argument about anything and forget it.

I look at Rob sitting under a brooding cloud of silence, and catch her eye.

'I'm in a bad mood,' she says.

'We don't mind,' says Bianca.

'I'm not in a bad mood actually, I'm pregnant!'

Bianca and Cecile open their mouths at the same time.

'How lovely!' says Cecile.

'Porca Madonna!' says Bianca.

'What are you going to do?'

Rob shrugs. 'I'm going to have a baby!'

'Wow!' says Cecile.

'Oh well,' says Bianca.

'It's not coming till the summer, I've got plenty of time.'

'How exciting!' says Cecile.

'Plenty of time!' says Bianca, shaking her head.

'What's the vote for this afternoon, then?' I say, before another argument starts.

'Giacometti,' says Roberta.

Bianca is walking about, pouring the coffee into our cups.

'See!' says Rob, holding out her cup. 'I like him and he's Italian!'

'Wow, a baby!' murmurs Cecile.

'Where's it on?'

'The Serpentine.'

'Let's walk,' says Cecile, looking out the window. 'It's a beautiful day.'

12

We walk down to the Fulham Road, Bianca and Rob
behind. We have to persuade Bianca out of the second-hand
clothes shop in South Kensington and drag her past the V
and A up Exhibition Road, but none of us can walk past the
Royal Academy Shop and we walk under the ornate stone
gate and up the stairs. Bianca and I buy sketchbooks. Rob
is wearing a big coat with holes in the pockets. The paint
stand is hidden behind the palette knives. She buys a tube
of titanium white, but when we come out into the street she
produces handfuls of stolen tubes from the coat lining.

'You are a criminal!' shouts Bianca.

'Shut up, Bianca!' says Rob.

'O wow, Rob, carmine! £25 a tube.'

'You're terrible, you're terrible,' I say as I look with joy
at the colours.

'Wait, look!' She hands me another tube.

'Oh, far out! Cobalt violet!' A colour as expensive as
a jewel.

Rob and I have a locker where we keep our materials.
Although we have our own, we also share. It gives us a
chance to try new colours.

These tubes are for both of us.

'We've got umber, ultramarine, and here, look!
Cadmium green.'

'Everyone does it!' says Rob.

'That is not a good rationale!' says Bianca.

'Yeah, like you're so squeaky clean!'

We walk into Kensington Gardens and the sunlight shines on the grass, the air is clear and the shadows are long because the sun is low.

We walk along under the tall plane trees, past the big dark Albert Memorial, to the Serpentine Gallery.

The tall thin sculptures make us quiet. We walk around them in silence. There is a room where the monumental figures are tiny.

'He spent ten years making small maquettes before he made them big!' Rob whispers, reading from the board. 'Ten years!'

'That's some gestation!' I say, smiling at her.

She laughs, and rubs her belly. 'Blimey, imagine having to carry it around for ten years!'

We walk out into the sunlight. The air is cold, but there is warmth in the light.

We walk under the trees and Rob takes her big coat off and we sit on it under a chestnut tree. She sits with her back to the huge trunk with her legs jutting out among the roots. I lean sideways and get out my sketchbook.

Bianca is doing qigong exercises. Cecile is copying her poses.

They both make an arc over their head with their arms, and stretch one leg out to the side, and bend the other. They move the arc from side to side, bending first one leg, then the other.

Their long shadows look like Giacometti figures slowly dancing. I am drawing them with pink chalk.

'This is called the rainbow!' Bianca calls out. I nod, looking up at them and down at my page. Kensington Gardens stretches behind them all the way to the Round Pond. People are walking along the paths in the grass from the Albert Memorial down to the Serpentine.

I close my book, now they are doing 'moving hands like clouds'.

They come over and lay themselves down on their coats. Cecile looks at my drawings.

'So why d'you think he wanted them so long and thin?' says Bianca, twirling a piece of grass.

'Maybe it's a pared-down thing, pared down to the core,' says Rob.

'It's the inner self, isn't it?' says Cecile in her cracked naked voice. 'The one everyone tries to hide.'

A dog leaps through the grass and sends a murder of crows flying up into the air, cawing. The dog is a poodle with ears that bounce, it is young and puppy-like. It bounces towards us and leaps on to Bianca and begins to lick her face.

'Get off, you horrible animal! Get off me, I loathe you! You are revolting!' She pushes it away and then kicks it. It yelps and its owner comes running after, calling, 'Fidelio, Fidelio.'

'Fucking Fidelio!' says Bianca, wiping her face with her sleeve.

We are laughing.

A large black crow swoops down and walks up and down before us. I open my sketchbook and paint with black ink, filling the whole page with the crow's head and shining beak.

It is hard to draw him as beautiful as he is. I follow the line of his head and his wings.

The crow caws. I paint his black eye. He walks slowly round in circles on the grass. His wings shine white in the sunlight.

13

When I walk my bike back home from college the sun has gone but the sky is still light; everything retains its colour, the grass is green, the pillar boxes still red, but the street lights have come on and glow in the gloaming. There is a tweet tweet beginning for the twilight chorus and the tall trees are black against the sky. The horizon is pale yellow, and shining pale blue, and the houses light up their coloured windows, and it is neither day nor night, and the dusk is alive with the colours of both.

Then Zeb is walking beside me. We are both surprised.

'Hey, how's the washing machine going?' he says.

'Singing a duet with the fridge,' I say, laughing. 'The sculpture going OK?' I ask.

'Yes, fine. How's the painting? You getting into it?'

'Sort of, bits and pieces.'

'That's good, bits and pieces is good.'

We pass by a garden behind railings. There is a gap in the railings covered by red and white striped tape. We walk past in silence. I've always wanted to sneak into one of those gardens in London squares. The kind that are locked, and look green and enticing.

'I've always wanted to sneak into one of those gardens,' he says. 'They look so enticing.'

'That's just what I was thinking!' I say, astonished. 'You spoke my thought!'

'Come on, let's!' he says.

'Oh, shall we? Someone might see!'

I chain up my bike and we look up and down the street.

'Go on,' he says, 'no one's coming, now!' and I dive under the tape into the rhododendrons. He follows. We are both giggling like naughty children.

'This is ridiculous!' I say in a loud whisper.

We climb through the rhododendrons and into a garden full of trees and low bushes and, in the centre, a lawn of grass, gently sloping to a fountain that is silent.

The trees have a presence that fill the garden.

By the fountain are three yew trees, and surrounding them are tall beech trees, and it is quiet, except for a crow calling from the corner of the square in a tree whose naked branches are reaching into the sky.

We make out a face in the foliage of the yew tree.

'Can you see it? Look there, see?'

'Oh, that's the nose, yes, I can.'

And we lie under the yew tree and look at the face in the dark branches and it looks and looks at us with intense eyes.

The crow caws again from a corner of the garden, we can see its black shape against the darkening sky, and Zeb says that crows see in two dimensions, and that's why they walk along like that, looking from one eye then the other, clocking two realities at once.

And I say it must be the great-great-grandson of the crows that have always lived in London, and imagine all the things they have seen if you could go back in time.

I begin to feel cold.

'I better go,' I say, standing up.

'Yes,' he says, 'me too.'

We sneak back through the rhododendrons under the striped tape.

He smiles and I notice he has asymmetrical dimples.

We go in different directions then, and as I bicycle through the night streets, the lit-up shops flashing past, I remember that he has one eye that looks at you with laughing in it, and the other one looks right into you.

Two-dimensional eyes.

I put my key in the lock and go through the green door; there are chips in the paint. Underneath, you can see it was once a mustard door, and before that it was pale blue. The stairs are narrow and the carpet is worn where the feet have walked. I walk up three flights, and let myself into my little flat.

I take my coat off and leave it on the bed, and go through into the kitchen.

The kitchen is very small, with enough room for a fold-out table and one chair.

I sit down in the dark and listen to the fridge. It has a language of its own, a repertoire of sounds that it chugs and hums and trembles through with dramatic pauses night and day. There are strips of plastic between the kitchen and the bedsittingroom which I have tied together and fastened to one side, so the doorway looks as if it has a hairstyle. I get up and put the kettle on. I make myself a cup of tea, put the light on, and take out my sketchbook. I look at the crow. I take out the drawings and put them next to each other.

I look through the window, up at the sky. There are pigeons flying in a flock over the buildings. The roofs are lit up by the moon's blue light. The street is in shadow or lit by yellow street lights. The pigeons are flying in a circle through the blue and yellow light.

The pigeons descend in a cascade and land on a roof.

And I look at the blue-black crow with a black eye and through the eye I see twin hills, I see the stillness and a wide river reflecting the sky. I see marshes and small islands and fires being lit and glowing in the dusk. I hear the sound of marsh birds and the zither-zing of swans in flight. I'll go down to the river and walk by the pale pink globes that light up the evening, and tomorrow I'll bike through the city to Cannon Street, and visit the London stone.

14

I cycle along the street, feeling wide open, colours splashing over me like waves in the sea. Clashing colours, honking noises, people with their different feelings trailing behind as they rush up the street. The air is cold but clear. The wind has blown the last of the leaves off the trees and turned autumn into winter. I ride along Knightsbridge and set out recklessly round Hyde Park Corner, sticking my hand out in front of buses and taxis, but I get pulled into the wrong stream and find myself sailing past Piccadilly and round the corner into Grosvenor Place. Sometimes you have to go with the flow on a bike in London or you might get squashed under the wheels. I dismount and take my bike down the steps into a tunnel that has colourful graffiti and someone playing the guitar.

Far away in my mind I think of dad and wonder if he's out walking along the cliffs in the wind.

I push my bike along the echoing corridor and into Green Park. I walk under the naked trees. I bike across the park to St James's Park, until I am told 'you're not allowed to bicycle in here', by a man in a maroon jacket, and I walk slowly round the lake and stop on the bridge to look at the water.

Has he built a fire in the study? Or is he wearing his thick blue jersey under his tweed jacket so his arms bulge?

I get out my sketchbook to draw the trees and the water and the tiny buildings in the distance that are just dashes and dots on the page. There is a stillness here after the traffic frenzy. It is a blue cold winter feeling.

Is he all right, d'you think?

I put my sketchbook away and then I remember the stone that has stood in the centre of the city for more than two thousand years.

It must have stood in stillness once. It has seen the cars pass, and before that the carriages, and before that the litters and the chariots. It has watched the people come and go, the Saxons, the Danes and before that the Romans and before that the Celts.

I walk over the bridge, and out a gateway down Horse Guards Parade to King Charles Street.

The stone was here before Charles walked under the ceiling painted with cherubs on his way to the block, before Elizabeth's dancing courtiers and dresses sewn with pearls, before Henry's madness and Eleanor's gentle hand.

I find myself in Whitehall and think I'd better look at the map.

I like wandering about the streets, it's like slipping in and out of different periods in history.

At last I come out on to Victoria Embankment and the Thames, bringing its blue river light, breathing its fresh river breath into the clogged city air. I ride on the pavement alongside the water, under Hungerford Bridge and past Cleopatra's Needle.

After Blackfriars I get tangled in a web of alleys and lanes; White Lion Hill and Knightrider Court. The air is dirty and sweat is pouring down my skin.

The stone was here before Alfred, the king with the

wisdom of an elf, before Canute told the waves to go back, before Arthur and Uther and Merlin's chilling prophecy, before Caesar and Boudicca, before Hengist and Horsa, before Estrildis and Brutus Greenshield.

I come to Walbrook where the buried river runs and at last, the Bank of China.

But when I squat down on the pavement opposite Cannon Street Underground station, and peer behind the bars and into the alcove, I see a small piece of whitish stone. It is shabby and the glass is covered with a layer of grime from the wind of passing traffic, and maybe there is nothing remarkable in this sorry piece of limestone, that has stood the test of time but that is all, and I walk away disappointed.

But when I navigate my bike through the jam on Ludgate Hill, and ride on the pavement along the Embankment so I can look at the river, when I chain my bike and walk across the footbridge to the Hayward Gallery on the South Bank so I can watch the water slipping under my feet, something in me stirs.

And as I reach the other side I know I can't walk up the steps to the gallery because something is rising through me like water bubbling up from an underground spring, and I see gold light behind my eyes.

And when I walk under the bridge and along the river, watching it glint and ripple, I feel a wide-open hope spread through me, that makes me stand still just to breathe the feeling of it.

And when I go back to college I draw pictures of the paintings I will paint; the forest and the beautiful river, the swans as big as horses and red wolves who roamed Cheapside when the Thames was a deity.

*   *   *

56

And I don't know if it is the spirit with his dark beauty trapped in the un-reverenced stone, or Zeb, who touches the edges of my dreams, and makes me wake up with a longing that is so intense, so deep, it feeds me with its mystery even while the emptiness of it could swallow me whole.

15

'Those bastard tutors!' says Bianca. 'It makes me bloody furious!'

'Pretentious! What about his stupid pictures!'

'Listen, he hasn't had a show for twenty years!' says Rob.

'Well, that tells you something!' I say.

Cecile had a crit this morning, and came up for coffee with red eyes. She doesn't tell you much but her eyes filled with tears when Rob asked her about it. She shook her head and swallowed and gave a little laugh, but the tears fell out anyway.

The tutors didn't think much of her big flowers.

'He just likes sticking the boot into other people's work.'

'It doesn't matter now,' says Cecile.

We are sitting outside in the quadrangle under the big tree. The day is mild and clear.

'Well, it does!' Rob says. 'They should allow us to take a friend in, to speak up for us,'

'That's a good idea.'

'So what exactly happens?' I ask.

'You have to take all your pictures into the assessment room along with all the sketchbooks', says Bianca, 'and the tutors . . .'

'. . . who are *all* men!' interrupts Rob, 'put the work all over the floor, line it up on tables, and against the walls, riffle through your sketchbooks, and then proceed to take the work apart, ask you the point of it, and tell you you're doing it wrong!'

'And when you're thoroughly devastated,' says Cecile, 'they pack you off with a set of instructions about how it *should* be done, how it *ought* to look, and what you're *really* trying to achieve.'

'Is it their habit to tear everyone apart?' I ask nervously. Cecile shrugs.

'Did they devastate you?' I ask Rob.

'I just told them I'm painting the "inner visions of my pregnancy",' she says in a wafty voice that makes us laugh, 'and they couldn't get me out the room quick enough!'

'Yes, tell them it's something menstrual,' says Bianca, 'that'll terrify them!'

'What do you do?' I ask Bianca.

'Oh, my English is really not very good, could you repeat the question?' she says, mimicking herself.

'What if you don't know what you're doing?'

'Exactly.'

'If only some of them didn't know what they were doing they'd be more sympathetic.'

The door to Sculpture opens across the quadrangle and Zeb and Suzanne come out arguing.

They both stop talking and she sits down with her arms folded. He squats down by her, then unfolds himself, his long legs make an upside-down W. I cannot hear what they are saying to each other but I can see that she is raising her eyes to heaven and hitting the air with the back of her hand. He is leaning sideways, reasoning with her.

He holds her forearm. She blinks her eyes, her lips press together and she looks away.

Zeb raises both his hands in a question.

'Those two are always arguing,' says Roberta.

'What do they argue about?' says Cecile.

'Oh, she wants him to behave when he meets her flash friends. Be different to what he is,' says Rob.

'Is that what Mick says?'

'What flash friends?

'TV people. She wants to work in TV.'

'Why's she doing sculpture?

'How should I know? She's got herself some job doing a commercial in Barbados.'

'Is Zeb going?'

'Doubt it.'

'It's probably very passionate,' says Bianca, 'very sexy to be so bad tempered.'

'Is it?' I say.

'And very addictive,' says Bianca.

'How d'you know?'

'I know all about boyfriends, I've had oh so many boyfriends,' says Bianca, lying down on the slab and looking up at the big plane tree, and stretching her hands out as if she wants to touch it. 'All about boyfriends, all about addiction.'

She draws the twiggy branches with her fingers up in the air, opening one eye and closing the other. Wherever she lounges she looks elegant. She wears a shirt from Guatemala with bright pink and green and blue squares and stripes, embroidered with red thread, and a pair of linen culottes with braces, both slung over one shoulder. No one else could wear the eccentric clothes Bianca wears.

'What were you addicted to?'

'Heroina! Now I have hepatitis as my protector. Without it I would go out and score right now!'

'Would you really?' says Roberta, rubbing her belly.

'Of course!'

I notice Zeb and Suzanne have stood up and she is gesticulating this way and that, shaking her head about so her long hair quivers.

I can hear the sound of her crossness from here but not the words.

'Everybody is addicted to something.' Bianca carries on tracing the twigs.

'Don't think I am,' says Roberta.

'Your baby! And your painting, and when it comes they will conflict!' says Bianca, who often makes pronouncements with great authority.

Roberta shrugs and smiles.

'What about me?' I ask. 'What d'you think I'm addicted to?'

'You are addicted to the pain of unrequited love!'

I put my hand up to my mouth. I want to say, 'We're friends, it's not like that!' but my mouth stays open behind my hand and I don't say anything.

'However, as we can see, he has his own addiction.' Bianca waves towards the arguing couple.

Roberta laughs.' Don't be silly, they're just friends.' She nods at me and Zeb.

'Hmm-hmm-hmm,' sings Bianca with her eyes closed.

The door to the sculpture department slams and Suzanne has stormed off in a huff.

'I didn't say they didn't love each other,' Bianca says with her eyes still closed.

'Yes, I think they do,' says Roberta, looking at the door. But Bianca didn't mean them.

I watch her as she lies there, the twig shadows trembling on her face. Sometimes she has to lie very still and be quiet. Her illness makes her suddenly tired.

'Does it make you tired being pregnant?' Cecile asks Rob.

'Nope!' says Rob.

'Are you looking forward to it?'

Roberta shrugs. 'Think so.'

'I loathe babies, they are so disgusting!' says Bianca.

'How can you say that!' says Cecile.

'No really!' Bianca says, getting up on her elbow. 'I was in a restaurant. A woman took out her tit and began to feed her baby, milk everywhere, all over the baby's face, all over the tit! Porca miseria! I stopped eating! I couldn't eat! It was too disgusting.' She lies back down and closes her eyes. 'They should hide them away! Roberta, when you have your baby, hide it! Put it away in a cupboard or something!'

I look at Rob to see if she's offended but she gives me a laughing exasperated look.

'Lucky your mother didn't think like that, Bianca!' she says.

'She did! She was a totally unnatural mother! Why do you think I am so fucked up! She telephones me with her anxiety: "Bianca, what are you going to do about this? What are you going to do about that?" When I leave the telephone I'm a nervous wreck! Listen, she could win a PRIZE for anxiety! She worries about EVERY THING! She's thinner than me!'

16

'FIRST-YEAR CRITICAL ASSESSMENTS' it says on the door.

I don't like waiting out here with all my work, I don't want to spread it all around the room and have them riffle through my sketchbooks asking the reasons for things and entering my private world as though they have special privileges. I have left the new drawings upstairs, in case the ideas get frightened off by the scrutiny.

Sinéad comes out the door and makes a face at me. Her eyes slide diagonally down to stare at the floor, as if to say 'You have no idea how horrible that was!'

Tutors follow her out with stretchers and stacks of sketchbooks, and pile them outside the room.

Inside, three of the tutors stand with their arms folded, talking to each other by the window. The door swings back and forth as the other two bring work through, back and forth, till all her work is outside the door.

There are five altogether. Terry, who's always drunk, Paul, the head of painting, Sergei, who made Cecile cry, Tom, who has a streak of kindness in him, and one with an orange beard who speaks to you as if he suspects you of something. I glimpse them all as the door swings back and forth.

'Would you like to bring your work through?'

I follow them in with a pile of sketchbooks. It is a big square empty room with splashes of paint on the floor and windows down one side. There are some grey tables near the wall and a stack of red chairs. They put the sketchbooks on the grey tables and the rest of the paintings round the room, propped up, or scattered on the floor.

There is the painting of Cambridge Circus, with turquoise lamp-posts and orange buildings, with a black and white sky and wet pavements. There is the purple sky and yellow light the night the robber ran past. There is the river in the dawn, and the river at dusk, and a portrait of Roberta painted with a carmine background. There are sketches of Sloane Square made with black ink, and watercolours of dawn from the police pier.

They flick through the sketchbooks and breathe in, slightly bored, as they look. They stand around looking at the pictures.

I am so glad I didn't bring my new drawings. The sketchbook is hidden upstairs.

Except one has slipped through.

Sergei picks it up and looks at it.

'Keep away from this kind of thing, you're better at drawing what you see,' he says, holding it in front of him with a finger and thumb for me and the others to see.

It is a blue figure with the head and wings of a swan.

Paul turns the corners of his mouth down and moves his head from side to side, assessing.

'I don't mind it.'

The red-haired man with the beard doesn't say anything but looks at me suspiciously. He flicks through a sketchbook.

Then he says, 'What are you trying to achieve here?'

'You mean at art school?'

'No, on the planet. Yes! At art school!'

'Umm . . . to learn to paint.'

'But what for?'

I wish I was Italian or pregnant, I'm sure it would make it easier to answer these questions.

'How do you justify being an artist?'

'I don't know.'

'I mean this is very nice . . . soufflé! but what about MEAT AND POTATOES! I'd like to see some MEAT AND POTATOES in your work instead of this . . . soufflé!'

I'm confused by the soufflé.

'Why don't you make more LARGE sketches?'

'She needs to make bigger paintings.'

'Yes, use less colour'

'And bigger brushes. Make a breakthrough!'

Paul nods. 'Yes, you need to make a breakthrough. This is all very well, but it's . . . very *pretty*.'

'Yes, you need to think outside the box.'

'As it is, you could even call it . . . illustrative.'

'Maybe go into monochrome. Try a seven-foot canvas!'

'Paint with a wallpaper brush. Expand your ideas!'

'Stay away from this imaginary . . . stuff,' says Sergei, nodding and putting the offensive drawing back in the pile.

I leave the assessment room in a state of shock, and carry my canvases and sketchbooks up the stairs.

'What was it like?'

Bianca is standing over the red ring with the coffee in her hand. 'I have just made a pot for you.'

Roberta is sitting on the sofa with her hands wrapped round a mug.

'Yes, how did it go?'

Cecile is on the mattress. She looks up.

I sit down next to Roberta. I just shake my head and can't find words. 'Oh, something about meat and potatoes.'

'What?'

'And soufflé. Oh, I'm just glad that's over, I don't know what I'm going to do next term, though.'

'Why?'

'Well, when they expect to see a seven-foot canvas in monochrome painted with a wallpaper brush!'

'Is that what they want?'

'Why do they always want everything to be enormous?'

'What do you want to paint?' asks Cecile.

'Small paintings, with more colour, from my imagination.'

She nods. 'Well, you do that then.'

I take my coffee from Bianca. 'Just as long as I don't end up with that bloody Sergei as my tutor next term.'

17

The next day when I go upstairs, Bianca is packing up her studio.

'Will this still be your space after Christmas?'

'Yes, thank God!'

'Oh, I'm glad. Me and Rob are keeping ours.'

'Are you going home for Christmas?' asks Bianca.

'Don't want to much,' I say.

'No? Not to see your mother and father? The family?'

'My mum's dead, Bianca.'

'What happened to her?'

'She died.'

'Yes. But how?'

'She drowned.'

'What happened?'

'No one knows really, she went swimming.'

'How old were you?'

'Five.'

'Can you remember?'

'No. I can't remember a thing about it.'

'Nothing?'

'The funeral, vaguely.'

'You blanked out the rest?'

I shrug. 'I suppose so. But I don't remember her very well, anyway, she wasn't around much.'

'What about your father? Did he remarry?'

'Nope.'

'Why do you say it like that?'

'Because I wish he had.'

'Do you?' says Bianca. 'A stepmother?'

'Someone to bloody look after him!'

'Is he old?'

'No, but he drinks too much.'

'Oh.'

'I think he's been holding it together for me . . .'

'. . . and now you've left, there's a big hole. Well, you have to live your life.'

'I just don't feel like . . . I mean, I feel I should . . .'

'Take care of him? Of course. In Italy you would. There was an old lady in Rome that looked after her father until she died. She was seventy-nine, and the father was still alive. He'd worn her out! Her whole life devoted to him.'

'Yes. I suppose they do that in Italy. Anyway, my dad's not a tyrant.'

'But he drinks too much.'

'Yes.'

'That's not easy.'

'No, it's a bloody nightmare.'

I sigh and look out the window.

'I don't know what to do.'

'Natale con i suoi, pasqua con chi vuoi!'

'What does that mean?'

'It means *I* should be going home for Christmas instead of staying here.'

'Are your family making a fuss?'

'You are telling me.'

I like it when Bianca uses phrases like that. It makes me smile.

'What are you going to do?'

'Stay here!' And her hands go out either side, palm upwards, as if to say 'obviously!'

'Oh, but Bianca!' I shake my head and look out the window. 'Am I supposed to go back there to look after him? Am I? Because mum's gone? Because he doesn't have a wife? Because he's all alone? Well, I don't want to!' I say, hitting the table. 'I don't want to sit in that house with him making clinking noises in the Weetabix cupboard, when it's bloody breakfast time, and slurring his words by lunch, and sitting slumped in that armchair next to the fire by teatime, and then making some big song and dance of opening a bottle of wine at exactly six o'clock as though that's the first drink he's had, and starting all over again. And there he is in that bloody armchair, his eyes all bleary, having revolting sentimental conversations about "Oh darling, do you love me?" when all I want to say is "No, I don't, you self-indulgent bastard. How dare you ask me that!" But that's not what I'm supposed to say, is it. I'm supposed to go home for Christmas and be a good daughter.'

'Who says you're supposed to? Just out of interest.' says Bianca, not in the least perturbed by my outburst.

'Everyone.'

'Everyone like who?'

'Magda probably.'

'Who is Magda?'

'Just a neighbour,' I say, and I look out the window for a moment, because she isn't just a neighbour. And I remember the smell of the woodstove and the steam rising off the wet clothes in the kitchen when we came back from the cowshed, and holding on to her trousers when we walked through the forest of cows.

'A neighbour?'

'No. More than that. She used to look after me a lot when I was small.'

'So he has someone nearby?'

'Well, they argued. They don't talk now.'

'That's up to him,' says Bianca, lifting up her hands. 'But you think you should go home?'

'Yes.'

'Because?'

'Because I feel so bloody sorry for him!' And then I put my head into my hands and cry great monster sobs, and Bianca doesn't say 'there there,' or put her arms round me and try to make me stop, she just lets me cry.

'He didn't use to be like this, you know, Bianca, he didn't, even after mum died. He was strong and big and lovely, and noble. Now he's, oh, he's ... he CRIES! He cries all drunk and sentimental and I want to hit him. That makes me horrible, doesn't it?'

'No.'

'I don't want to go home for Christmas.'

'Then don't.'

So I don't.

18

I sit on the radiator and look out on London in January. It looks naked and drab. The clouds are grey and weigh down the sky.

'Stop moping! I can't stand you moping, if you mope you must go downstairs!' says Bianca.

'I'm not moping! Wasn't it nice, our studio?'

'There was no light!' says Bianca.

No. The studio didn't have much light, that was the only thing; just a little frosted-glass window that opened about six inches, because it was on a metal hinge that squeaked when you opened it, so it only let in the sawdust-smelling air, and the sound of the saws, and the men shouting at each other as they stacked the wood on the lorries. But I got used to the darkness in a way. I had to make the colours glow.

'You see! You are being nostalgic. I can't stand it.'

'I'm not, it's just January, and I've got bloody Sergei as a tutor.'

'Well, you have lots of work to show him! You used that studio twice as much as I did.'

The idea of showing Sergei the new paintings fills me with horror.

'They might put some life into him!' says Bianca, smiling.

I laugh. Bianca's name for Sergei is 'the zombie'.

'What he needs is a few minutes in the corridor! *"AMEN! Praise be the Lord!"* '

We both laugh. Next door to the studio we borrowed over the holiday the Church of the Cherubim and Seraphim also had their premises, and we could hear them doing exorcisms in the corridor. Bianca and I would listen with our eyes wide open and hands over our mouths, as the strange wobbly voice cried out: 'Don't marry her! she is a baaaad person!'

'Praise be the Lord!'

'She will take your money!'

'Amen!'

'Find another woman!'

'Praise be the Lord!'

They had about five thousand candles burning every time they did a ceremony, and wore long white robes and pork-pie hats like bath-caps. The children wore the same in miniature and sang songs which rocked the studio.

We liked them being next door with all their incense and songs, speaking in tongues and spirit voices, and one day a big woman came to the door and asked me what I did, and I showed her my paintings, and she said in a beautiful low Nigerian voice, 'Ah! Your pictures are full of spirits.' I must have looked alarmed because she said, 'Good spirits, good spirits' and we both laughed.

I was thrilled she liked them.

'It just feels weird being back in an institution, that's all. No freedom.'

'Yes, with a technician upstairs to cut your stretch-ers,' says Bianca, 'and a shop in the canteen you can get everything half-price. Freedom is not free! It's expensive! We didn't pay for the studio, don't forget.'

We'd borrowed it from Bianca's cousin's ex-boyfriend, who went back to Italy for Christmas. It was behind the timber-merchant in Acre Lane so the air smelt of wood.

'Well, we made some money! I liked those jobs!' I say.

Through Bianca's network we'd found a studio *and* part-time work.

That's how we ended up spending a dark afternoon on a sunny day in a dungeon under the Coliseum, burning our fingers glue-gunning pearls on to Elizabethan dresses that the chorus complained about because their voices got lost in the ruffs.

The next time, it was a tiny room up in a tower, stitching hooks and eyes on to pink-embroidered pale green tutus with lots of netting. That was at Covent Garden. I had to explain to Bianca that someone was playing a joke on the receptionist when her high voice came over the tannoy, 'Could Mike Hunt come to reception, please.'

'Oh God, you are so romantic! Life as an artist out there is tough! TOUGH! It's not all pale green tutus!'

I laugh. 'No, I know that. But at least there's no Sergei.'

'Ha!' she says, pointing at me with a wagging finger. 'I know exactly what is wrong with you!'

I blush and look out the window.

Suzanne is making a sculpture in the courtyard down below. She has a welding mask on and her overalls undone and tied round her waist, so she is standing in the cold in her vest with her brown arms exposed. The sparks are flying.

She is back from Barbados.

'It's so vulgar to have a tan in January!' says Bianca, looking over my shoulder.

I can't help laughing at Bianca sometimes.

Of course I wish I hadn't told her, but I had to tell someone, and it's obvious I can't tell Rob.

It happened in a moment in the canteen, and it's annoying that Bianca was right all along.

'Hey! What about you and Geoff?' she says.

'Oh, Bianca, please. Just forget it.'

But one moment can change everything. One moment in the canteen.

I could hear the saucers being laid out in fours, then the cups being unstacked and placed in the saucer, and the tinkle of the little spoon; clink clop tinkle, clink clop tinkle, and Zeb was telling me about white: titanium white is a blue white, but it can turn yellow if you get the cheap kind; zinc white is a purple white, it has a metallic tinge; lead is yellow white; and I picked up the teaspoon to look at the white sugar crystals and the teaspoon flipped over and the sugar went on the table. I leaned over to wipe up the sugar and I looked at him.

I looked into his eyes.

And the moment opened like a flower and stood still. And I saw what a lie time is, because it all stands still. And eternity is right there.

For ever, I've known you for ever.

So I looked away. And now I can't stand next to him, or come into the room or pass him in the canteen without blushing or blurting out some rubbish, and we used to be friends, and it was easy. And anyway, Suzanne is Zeb's girlfriend.

19

Maybe I should tell him! I stand up quickly, woken by the idea and the terror of it. Quick! before I lose my nerve.

'See you later!' I say

'I didn't mean it, you can stay and mope!' says Bianca, following me to the door.

'No, it's OK, it's not that. I'll see you later.'

I run down the stairs to the mezzanine with my heart beating. The door to his studio is open.

Zeb is standing with his back to me. He is reaching up to a high place on his peculiar tinkling sculpture that looks as though it's come from another world. It lights up with coloured light, it twirls things and it tinkles. The sleeves of his dark blue paint-spattered shirt are rolled up above his elbows so his upper arms show. I can see his shoulders under his shirt and the curve of his biceps. He screws something high up above his head, so his arms reach up and make a diamond. His long fingers twiddle something and the structure shivers and tinkles. His head is tilted a little. I follow his black hair falling down his long back and his dark blue shirt is only half tucked in, and his long legs in jeans; one leg straight with the weight on it, the other sometimes a little off the floor like a dancer, as he reaches upwards.

On Wednesdays Karl sometimes makes us do drawings for three or four seconds and the model changes her pose.

I could do a drawing now with diluted ink: his beautiful shape, and the shirt half tucked in, that I want to put my hand inside, want to travel up the spine, under his shirt all the way to the back of his neck, touching the curves of his body, the smooth skin. I want to touch him. I want to touch him.

I run back up to the studio, clatter clatter up the glossy stairs.

I stand in the studio, breathing. I put my hands on my cheeks and look out the window at the white sky.

'Rob, let's go to the RA.'

'It's not Friday,' she says from behind the muslin curtain.

'Let's go anyway. We can draw.'

'But it's a collection. I don't like collections, I prefer one artist at a time.'

'Oh, but Rob,' I say, going through the muslin, to stand in her space, 'they've got the dancers, we might not see them again, and the Red Room, and Cézanne, and Kandinsky. Let's go. Come on.'

She puts down her paintbrush.

'Oh all right,' she says.

We get off the bus and walk along Piccadilly.

Pigeons are cooing and bowing, in sunlit corners of the pavement, making gentle burbling sounds as they circle one another, then flutter together on high-up ledges as though they are cliffs, with a sea of people below them, to-ing and fro-ing in tides.

We walk into the Royal Academy across the courtyard and up the wide steps.

When we enter the tall rooms, we separate. I walk slowly and look at Cézanne's pale blue mountain, hot light and cool green trees breathing the air, and Monet's pond, the light slipping over the ripples on the surface of reflected trees. I see how he paints a poppy field with cobalt violet and salmon pink, so it looks like sunlit red poppies growing as far as the eye can see, and how he paints the stalks of grass that glow in the shadow under a haystack, which is made of colours you can't describe, only they are the colours of hay in shadow: pink-grey, blue-grey, green-grey, yellow-grey, if you look close.

The red dancers blaze in the centre of the next room; bigger than life-size, moving all the time since they were painted, the red bodies vibrant against the blue, and singing with the green.

The dancers turn pink in a blue studio, and a pink chair stands in front, the white dashes on the blue cushion pulling the chair into the foreground.

I move through the big doors and see Chagall flying his wife like a kite in a purple dress, over green houses and a pale pink church, and friendly Kandinsky celebrating in rainbows and spillikins.

And then I find the one I like the best and need the most. It is a lonely curved path, in winter, with spindly black trees. But the snow, how he sees the snow! It is pink and yellow and many different pale blues reflecting the sky. The mountains are covered in blue fingerprints. The picture glows in constant twilight.

I look and look at it, till Rob pulls me by the sleeve and says, 'It's time to go,' and we walk out into the Piccadilly evening.

20

'What have you done, Bianca?' I walk into her studio space and it's orange.

She is lying on the chaise longue with one leg up, the other down and a piece of Paisley-pattern material over her eyes.

'I am suffering!'

'What's wrong?'

She sits up and takes the material away from her eyes.

'Oh, no, I can't bear it!' And puts the material back and lies down.

'What is it?'

'Oh, it's PMT. Why else does anyone paint their space orange!'

'You can repaint it! I quite like it.'

'No! No! Don't mention it! Don't look at it! I don't even want to imagine you looking at it!'

I look out over the city and into the far distance. I am restless too. Every dot of air has Zeb in it.

And I've got a tutorial with Sergei in one hour.

'Oh, you are in one of your far-away moods, go away! I can't bear you when you're like that!' she says.

I sit down on the end of the chaise longue.

'I can't work today.'

'But listen!' she says, sitting up, the Paisley pattern flying. 'I have a plan for you!'

She starts busily piling up pieces of wood.

'Oh, not me and Geoff!' I sigh and go over to the window

'Oh, yes, yes, yes, I have all these stretchers that need their ends cutting.'

I look into the courtyard, the sparks are flying from the welding gun.

There's Suzanne. I mean, it's not surprising, is it? Standing out there with her overalls half undone, the arms tied round her waist, with her long blonde curls tied up in a fetching cascade, welding that *thing*.

I passed by it with Rob and tried to get her to criticize it with me.

'I mean, look at it, what is that?'

'Well, she's just experimenting.'

'Yeah, but come on, it's pointless!'

'Well, it's quite a skill, welding.'

'Oh please. She just does it because she looks good in the gear. The welding mask, stripped down to the waist. You know, to weld a bloody pointless monstrosity that just gets bigger and bigger and tips over if you so much as touch it, loads of skill in that! Yeah, right!'

But Rob just looked at me then, and I thought I ought to shut up.

'Are you listening to me?' says Bianca, close to my ear.

She looks out the window at the welding.

'Ah! Like her sculpture, she is a spider!'

'No, I don't want a date with Geoff,' I say, walking away from the window.

'He really likes you and you like him, he's patient, you admire patience!' she says with a scoff.

It's true that he is patient. He bends over the ruler and cuts the wood to the right millimetre, when all the panic-stricken third-years are lining up to get their frames cut in time.

'Listen,' says Bianca, slowly putting the stretchers into my hands and talking in a kind of sing-song way. 'Just listen to me. You aren't going on a date, you are asking him to Silvia's party. Say it after me: "Would you like to come to Silvia's party?" See? Easy peezy lemon squeezy.'

I laugh. The phrase sounds funny in her Italian mouth.

'Up the stairs . . . up one floor,' she says as she steers my shoulders from behind out the door of the studio.

'Look, I've got a tutorial with Sergei!'

'There's time!' she says.

I walk upstairs and into the workshop with my pile of wood. The sky shines through slanted skylights. The room smells of wood. There is a circular saw in the table, and freshly planed wood shavings on the floor. Geoff is leaning over the ruler marking a notch with his pencil, which he puts back behind his ear. He looks up and smiles. He has short brown hair but the fringe goes in his eyes.

'You want to cut those corners?'

'Yes,' I say.

'What d'you want to do? Knock them together with corrugated nails?'

'Yep, that's what I'll be doing.' I nod.

'OK, here, use this vice.' And he sets up the saw so I can saw them through at the right angle.

I set to sawing away at the wood and think, what on earth am I doing this for? And can't think how I ended up cutting all these stretchers for Bianca. Then I remember a vague plan about Silvia's party and I look up at Geoff and watch him as he bends over the measuring and his hair falls in his eyes. He turns his lips inside as he measures. He looks up and catches me looking at him and smiles.

He looks down again and says from behind his hair: 'There's something really good happening this Saturday, want to come?'

'I . . . oh, what's that?' I say, trying to remember if that was the way round the plan was meant to go.

'Have you heard of Billy Graham?'

'Oh . . . yeah . . . the preacher,' I say, my heart sinking.

'He's a really wonderful speaker, he knows what life's about and he fills you with this kind of warmth . . .'

But I'm picking up my wood, saying 'Thanks so much for . . . you know . . .' trying to walk backwards out the door with a handful of planks.

I clamber down the stairs and into Bianca's space.

'What happened?' she says, 'Did you ask him out?'

'Of course he's a patient carpenter!' I say, throwing the stretchers on the floor, 'he thinks he's bloody Jesus!'

21

'Line them up so I can see them!'

Sergei is in my space. He is leaning against my table
with his legs sticking out and his arms crossed. His
glasses are on the end of his nose and the sneer is on
his mouth, curling back his lips to reveal brown teeth.
Eyes like nails look at things with a cold sharp pricking
look.

I feel as if I am lining up my pictures so they can be
shot.

I turn them to face him, some I hang on the nails and
the others are lined up on the floor against the wall.

They have tender colours. None of them are finished.

He takes his glasses off and puts the end of the arm
in his mouth, eyeing along the row and sniffing out, as
though he's laughing at something.

They are my new pictures, explorations into another
world that is hidden.

Sergei is shaking his head

'What are you trying to do with these, what is that?'

He points to a painting of two figures.

Phthalo turquoise, and alizarin crimson mixed with
cadmium red, create a dancing vibrance, and as I tried to
make the colours sing together, a winged man appeared
in the paint and spoke to the figure sitting next to the

river. It whispered in her ear and it stood on its toes, as one leg reached behind, its wings outstretched as though it had just landed. She listens.

Sometimes the images come by themselves.

I wanted the two colours to sing.

'What is that supposed to be?'

'It's not supposed to be anything. I wanted to make the colours harmonize, and the figures came along.'

'You're really better painting what you can see instead of this mumbo-jumbo. You're going way off track here, who are you trying to be?'

I wasn't supposed to answer that question.

He shakes his head. 'There's far too much colour in it anyway.'

'Well, I'm just experimenting.'

'Just experimenting! You've got no tone in it! It's all one tone. Don't you know anything about tone? You have to work out what it is exactly that you're trying to achieve, and then follow a plan to achieve it. You're all over the place. It's a mess! And what's that?'

He points to the painting with the blue figure.

She has a body made of water. She feels everything. She stands on the bridge with the water flowing beneath her and it is telling her its history in visions that flow through her like memories.

'That's a figure made of water.'

'Another cliché,' he says under his breath, 'angels and bloody mermaids. This isn't the eighteenth century, you know, things have moved on! Don't you look at what is going on around you?'

'I want to paint my own things,' I say, too quietly for my liking, suddenly transformed into a too-small person with this ugly smelly pale-skinned man with eyes like nails, and words like hammers.

'You don't know *what* you want.'

There is a tall painting at the end, standing upright. It is the largest and only just begun. I want to paint the spirit in the stone. The London stone. The first time I imagined him he was flying above the blue river over Albert Bridge and Battersea Bridge, and down to Blackfriars past Lambeth Palace and the Houses of Parliament. He flies over Tower Bridge to the Tower of London and his finger is pointing. He is making the sky orange and the air pulse and throb.

'What is this, an attempt at Chagall?'

'I was trying to paint the spirit in the London stone.'

'Ah, so we've gone from the eighteenth century to what, the New Age? Is this a New Age fad?'

'No,' I say, offended on behalf of the ancient spirit. 'No, that stone has been there since before the Romans! It was probably erected by the druids.'

'Druids!' He puts his forehead in his hands and shakes his head. 'Oh God give me strength!'

He looks up and his face is suddenly yellow, the rims of his eyes are red. He opens his mouth and I see his brown teeth.

'Are you an idiot?' he blares at me.

'What's wrong with that?' I say.

'What world are you living in? Airy fairy land? Escaping into some world of your own!' He bangs the table to give emphasis to his words. 'Live in the real world!'

He sighs and looks down. 'Here you are, tra-la-la-ing through your degree, painting fairies and fauns. I'm just trying to bring you into the real world,' he says in another tone.

'But is there any point,' he says under his breath, standing up and brushing his coat and walking out of my space without a backward glance.

I stare at the table he's been leaning against.

Roberta pokes her head through the curtain.

'Wasn't too bad, was it?' she says.

'Are you joking?'

I look at her with my mouth open, and all my joints go limp.

She laughs.

'Come on,' she says, putting her arm round my shoulder and guiding me out of the studio. 'Don't worry about the zombie! He hasn't painted a picture in twenty years!'

'I know. That's what makes him lethal!'

22

'I think you should wear this one!' says Bianca, putting a red velvet dress over the side of the bath.

She flicks through the dresses in the wardrobe.

I'm sitting in the armchair between the chipped stained-glass window and the communal dressing table, which has a row of twenty lipsticks under the mirror. One of Silvia's copper-coloured bras is lying in the doorway.

'Or this one?' She holds up a green Indian dress with gold thread and sequins around the neck.

I shake my head.

She looks at it with her head tilted.

'No? OK,' and puts it back. Clip clip through the hangers.

'Here is one of Silvia's.' She holds it up. It is a communal wardrobe for the overflow of clothes. The dress is gold, ruched, 1940s-looking.

I shrug. 'I'll try it.'

I pull off my T-shirt and pull the gold dress on.

'Take off your trousers!' shrieks Bianca. She gets up and pulls the dress down and zips it up, then steps back and looks at me sideways.

Silvia steps in the doorway and picks up her bra.

'What do you think?'

I find it touching the way Bianca speaks to her Italian flatmates in English if I am there.

'Yes, you look very nice, I like it, I like it,' she says. and crouches a little, to see in the mirror and put dark purple lipstick on her lips.

She doesn't seem to mind that it's her dress. Silvia has long dark auburn hair, and a curvy body.

'Well, I think you should try the red one,' says Bianca

I feel constricted by the structure in the seams, and breathe out with relief when she undoes the zip.

The girls Bianca lives with do textiles at Goldsmiths, and the flat is hung with velvet curtains printed with spirals, and quilted spreads sewn with appliquéd animals are thrown over the sofa and chairs. A piece of pink silk is tied around the shade, which tints the light in the sitting room.

I walk in, wearing the red dress. Bianca nods, and points her finger at me.

'This one! Yes, this one! What do you think?' She turns to Silvia.

A huge cauldron of minestrone is bubbling on the stove in the kitchen. Silvia stands in the yellow-lit doorway, holding a huge chunk of Parmesan cheese wrapped in silver foil.

'Yes, I like too,' says Silvia.

'Now shoes,' and Bianca gets up, takes my hand and leads me into the corridor, where there is a long row of shoes.

'Try these!' She calls through to Carlotta, 'Porti quelle rosse sta notte?'

'No.'

'Allora, try these.'

I slip my feet into shoes that are far too high.

Bianca kneels back on her heels and looks me up and down with satisfaction.

'Ha! ha! now you can steal him!'

'Are you sure this is the best way in, Bianca?'

We have climbed in the end of the garden, which is more of a waste land, two gardens knocked together behind houses that are mostly squats. I am walking in the dark on high-heeled shoes, through piles of rubble and old tyres and a forest of sycamore saplings, my heels sinking into the mud.

Bianca is giggling. 'Maybe not!'

As we near the party we hear the dooff dooff dooff of reggae beats thumping under the grass. A bonfire is crackling and sending sparks into the air. Some home-made torches have been stuck in the ground and light up flickering patches of the garden, and smell of paraffin. The sky above the sparks is a clear indigo night and the red moon looks strangely afflicted. There is a dark bite in the bottom corner. The moon is being swallowed.

Many people are piling out of doorways on to the grass, and the smell of chicken and rice and minestrone flavours the air. Silvia has brought the cauldron of soup, and bowls of food are spread out on a table that has been hauled outside, along with bottles and glasses and paper cups. Inside, the people are thick, bodies are sweaty and pulsing together with the music.

The thumping rhythms fill the air and the drums pulsate in the ground and the bass pounds in our ears.

There is the smell of marijuana mixing with the chicken.

I feel suddenly nervous and the air has become strange. The moon is half swallowed by the black shape. The flickering torches leave their imprint on my eyes so my vision is dotted with purple and blue flashes over the dark garden. Bianca is surrounded by people. They chatter away like geese in Italian and Spanish. She has a big piece of Parmesan in her hands, wrapped in silver foil, which she is undoing and grating into the huge pot of minestrone. I can smell the cheese from here through the clouds of aromatic marijuana that two tall men with long dreadlocks are smoking with their backs to the bonfire. The flames fly up behind them, making them into black silhouettes.

The moon has been swallowed. It feels cold without loss of temperature and quiet although the music still plays. A glimmering, eerie feeling.

Zeb walks up the steps from the basement. He must have slid through the bodies. He stands still, looking. He can't see into the dark.

He could be an Apache, with his long dark hair. But I think he's a Crow man.

He sees me and nods. He walks towards me and the quiet intensifies. Time stops passing. His eyes look at me out of the dark and I can see the fire reflected in them. He stands over me like a tree.

He opens his mouth, but doesn't say anything.

'Look at the moon,' I say. 'It's just been swallowed.'

Everything feels wrong. Disjointed. Jangling.

My voice doesn't seem to synchronise with my mouth. I speak, and hear it echoing.

A thin sliver of red moon appears out the other side.

He looks up at the moon and back at me.

His eyes are strange.

Bianca is suddenly there beside us. 'Zeh-Beh-Deeee!' she calls up at him, holding his hand and reaching up to kiss his cheek. She winks at me.

'Look, you must have some wine! Where is your cup?'

'I'll get some,' says Zeb, going over to the trestle table.

I watch his back walking away and stooping over the table.

'Here! I have a bottle!' she calls to a knot of people next to the tree, and walks over to them, holding her bottle up in the air.

I look across at Zeb but now Suzanne is at the table too and she is talking. She wears a yellow dress and it shows off her tan from Barbados.

'Blondes should never wear yellow!' says Bianca, coming back with her bottle. 'It clashes with their hair! I will break up the fight.'

She walks across to the table, and smiles to one and then the other. Suzanne doesn't smile. Zeb glances over at me and hands Bianca a cup. She comes back.

'Here you are.' She pours it as she walks towards me.

'Thanks.'

I take my wine under the tree where Rob and Mick are lying on his coat with their backs leaning against the trunk, gobbling chicken and rice from paper plates.

'How are you?'

'Did you see the eclipse?'

'We're not going to stay that late but you can get a lift back with us if you like.'

I nod and wander round the garden to look at the shadows and the purple flashes. I can see Zeb and Suzanne having an argument in silhouette in front of the bonfire. I'm sick of him and his love life.

I wander past them into the seething mass of bodies in the basement. Silvia is dancing with her boyfriend. He is a muscular black man in a white T-shirt, he has a bald head and it shines. Silvia gyrates her hips slowly, looking at him all the time. Her hips move but her head stays in the same place.

I close my eyes and dance. The music fills the darkness, pulses through me in colours, and sweat runs over the surface of my skin.

The music becomes slow and people are pressing up against one another. I slide through the writhing bodies to the doorway and the garden. On the edge of the crowd Zeb and Suzanne are dancing. She has her arms in a circle round his neck.

Bianca is at the top of the stairs. She nods over at them and shrugs.

I walk past the embers of the bonfire. The torches are spent and the garden is dark. Rob and Mick are cuddled up under the tree. Mick has big arms and he squeezes her to him.

'Are you ready to go?'

I nod.

'Come on, then.'

We drive up Acre Lane, past two people fighting, with a crowd shouting around them. I feel dark, closed in by the buildings, and deep down within me is a crying sound. We drive round a corner to Clapham Common and the sky is purple with orange clouds.

The trees are dark against the sky. We flew the kite here. Zeb brought fishing line and attached it to the string, it just kept going higher and higher, until it was a tiny speck. When the fishing line ran out he let it go, and Bianca said, 'I didn't realize your intention was liberation!' and we all laughed.

Suzanne wasn't there. She wasn't there for the whole Christmas holiday, when we'd met up in the Portuguese café and had crispy custard cakes and fish-balls with the Italians every Sunday.

I have to put Zeb out of my mind. Not feel these feelings. Fold them up, put them away somewhere, then take them out and paint them secretly.

We drive past Battersea Park gates and I look into the dark trees, and then out on to the bridge. I love the river at night, reflecting the coloured lights. We cross the river and I feel the water flowing beneath us. Rob and Mick are talking to each other, but I can't hear. There is a crying sound. Far away. It is the sound of the moon. It hangs over the river, eclipsed. But there is another moon; to find it I have to follow the sound to within my own world. I know it. I have painted it. There is a forest there. It is still. Sometimes the moon disguises itself and looks at me with intense eyes. When I find it, and paint it, the crying will stop.

We drive along past the barges with glimmering lights outside, and up Edith Grove. Litter is being blown about the street by the wind, and a huddle of men in dirty clothes sit drinking on a traffic island lit by yellow light. They are calling out, their arms flailing, and I don't know if they are sad or singing. The city has a peculiar atmosphere, as though it has slipped through time to another century, or the veil between time is thin and other centuries are showing through. Zeb knows about those things.

We drive up and along the streets and stop outside the peeling porch of my house. A drunk man is curled up outside my door.

'Oh dear!' says Rob. 'You've got an alkie on your doorstep.'

'D'you want me to help you shift him?' says Mick, as he pulls the handbrake.

Something hits my chest. I breathe in quickly.

'Oh my God!'

Roberta looks at me.

The breath is knocked out my body.

'It's dad!'

Part Two

1

'We'll help you get him up the stairs,' says Rob, making a decisive move that wakes me from my shock.

He is a dead weight when Mick and I try to lift him, and smells of sour alcohol. He mumbles and groans as we lift him. I open the door and he falls on to the mat. My one room, with a small kitchen at the back, is too small for his presence. It fills the air with his weight. I open the windows. I have a sofa and a bed, a table and a chair. In my kitchen there is a small table covered in formica with bananas and apples on the shiny white surface.

Rob has made tea.

We have laid dad on the sofa and he has fallen to the side and now his head is on the arm so his face is pulled sideways and his mouth is open.

Mick is standing up, looking out the kitchen window, through the gap between the houses where you can see the dark river under the purple sky.

I look at Rob, bewildered.

'He didn't say he was coming.'

'Is he always like this?'

'You mean drunk?'

She shrugs with one shoulder.

'Yes, I mean, it's been getting worse.' I sigh. 'He's all

alone in the house now and . . . Oh, I don't know, I don't know.'

I get up and look round the door at him lying squint and uncomfortable on the sofa. The sour alcohol smell fills the room. I don't want him to be there.

'I don't want him here, I don't want this.'

'Well, he's here,' says Rob, 'and he'll sober up.'

'And then what? What's he come here for?'

'To be with you, I expect.'

'I don't want him here. I can't look after him.'

There's such a horrible combination of disgust and tenderness and anger and panic in me that I begin to tremble and I put my shaking hand on the door lintel to steady myself.

'Sit down,' says Rob. 'Just sit down a minute and drink your tea.'

And I think of Bianca still at the party and Zeb dancing with Suzanne. Then I look over at the sink and start thinking odd things, like Mick's back pocket is torn and maybe he should sew it up and will Rob do it, and then I imagine her sitting under the light, sewing up his pocket.

The surrealness of the night continues. The apples, pears and bananas are too bright, divided by their bamboo squares. The flat feels overcrowded with energies that do not belong here.

'You must go home,' I say, looking up. Even Rob looks strange. Her lips are purple.

I blink my eyes. 'God, I feel as if I've taken acid or something. D'you think someone spiked the drinks?'

She looks at me. 'No, I don't think it's that.'

I shrug.

She gets up and Mick turns round. He puts his arm round her.

'You'll just have to send him home when he wakes up.'

'I can't imagine him, I mean, getting on the train, oh well.' I give a half smile. 'I'll be OK. Off you go.'

They close the door. My flat is too full. His presence is heavy.

I sit on my bed and look at him. My eyes are too wide. Something in me is trembling.

'Dad? Dad?'

He moans.

'Dad?' I lean across to shake him. His head falls off the arm. I move to catch him, and tug him back on to the sofa.

'What are you doing here, dad?' I know he won't answer. 'What d'you expect me to do?'

He suddenly opens his eyes and clutches my hand with both of his.

'I'm frightened, Eve. I'm frightened of dying.'

'But, dad, you're not going to die.'

He holds my hand so tight that it hurts. And squeezes his eyes shut, but his mouth is open, his teeth clenched together in a look of acute pain.

'Oh, dad!'

I sit back on the bed.

He suddenly, violently, rolls off on to the floor and lies on the mat between the bed and the sofa. From the acrid smell and a trickling sound I realize that he is pissing on the floor.

'Oh, for fuck's sake, dad!'

I get a bucket of water and a cloth.

'For God's sake, dad!'

I pull off his trousers. I wrap him up in a towel, and ease the mat from underneath him. I mop up the piss and take the mat between my thumb and finger and rinse it in the sink. Then I shove it out the window, weighted down by a packet of washing powder and a pan filled with cutlery.

When I go back through to mop the floorboards he is lying in a foetal position with the towel wrapped round him. He looks like a big tiny baby.

I take the blanket off my bed and throw it over him.

'For goodness sake, dad!'

I lie under my duvet and look at the yellow window on the ceiling. I don't want to close the curtain, so the yellow streetlight shines into the room making the shadows brown and the light lurid.

I can feel a presence in the room that isn't just dad. As though he has brought something else with him. I'm afraid it will get into me when I'm asleep. I lie with my eyes wide open. A blue window is flicked around the room by the headlights of a passing car.

2

All morning, at college, I've been listening for sounds: someone clattering along the corridor, bumping against the thin partitions, slumping down somewhere. Like he might turn up any moment in my painting space and piss on the floor, then fall over and lie with his chin resting on his breastbone, and his legs splayed out at right angles.

I am scared he's going to come in to the college and show me up! That's what they used to say at school: 'Oh, my dad, did you see what he was wearing? He really shows me up!' That's when you're thirteen, it's all right to be ashamed of your parents, afraid they'll make you conspicuous, make you ashamed of them. That horrible feeling squirming inside your belly that makes your toes curl. They really do. They curl sideways so you stand on the outer edges of your feet. It makes you hold your breath but the cringing is the worst part. Everything seems to turn inside out; all the intestines and the stomach. You clench it but it does it anyway.

Rob puts her head through the curtain.

'D'you want that?' she says, handing me a cup. 'I don't want it.'

'Why not? It's still hot!' I say, taking the coffee.

'Dunno, it's making me queasy,' says Rob, sitting on the stool and getting out her tobacco to roll a cigarette.

'So what about your dad? Where did you leave him?' She licks the paper closed and puts the fag in her mouth.

'Should you be doing that?'

'Listen, I'm down to three a day so shut up.'

'OK, OK.'

'Well?'

'He was still sleeping when I left this morning,' I say, looking out the window.

'So he's usually like that?'

'Mostly, I suppose.'

'What's he doing here?'

'I have no idea.'

'Maybe he wants to come and stay with you.'

'Oh my God.'

'You'll have to kick him out, it's your life.'

'Rob!'

'Well, you have to be like that, alcoholics are hard work!'

'Is that what my dad is?'

'Obviously.'

'Oh Rob, I just hope he doesn't come in here drunk!'

'Why should he?' says Rob.

'To see me, I suppose.'

'Well, he might find a friend!' Rob laughs and gives me a nudge.

I know she means Terry and I laugh half-heartedly.

Rob picks up her bag. 'I'm going down the Housing Benefit,' she says along with a puff of smoke and stomps off with the fag in her mouth.

There is a feeling of drama in my body. A trembling that I cannot quieten. I feel shocked. Something in me is shaky and unsteady. And all my ideas, which usually congregate in a humming throng of colours, are scattered about in a disconnected distance from each other.

There is an emptiness around me where the ideas usually are, and all I see is the dream that I woke from with sweat on my face, trying to cry out that it wasn't my dream.

I'd been pulled down a tunnel with wet walls. The ragged people had despair in their faces. My dad was there and they were clutching at him. There were broken bottles among the filth. The dark river in the tunnel was full of rubbish. They saw me, and began coming towards me.

'Let's get her,' one said.

I tried to run on the slippery stones, and woke up shouting, 'This isn't my dream!'

I want to paint the dream to get their pale bony faces outside of me and on to the canvas. I can still feel their groping fingers and smell the stench of the river.

I mix the colours on the palette: chrome green, raw umber, Naples yellow.

I paint their greenish faces on the canvas, in dark filthy clothes.

The painting has grown ugly. I don't like looking at it. The colours have turned to sludge. Sometimes all you can do is make a mess. When I try drawing with charcoal and spill the turps over the drawing so the charcoal smudges I decide it's time to stop for lunch.

I walk into the clatter of the canteen, and the smell of beans and chips. The dinner ladies stand behind the chrome counter chatting to one another, holding long silver spoons. I buy my sandwich and coffee. The wall down the side of the canteen is made of glass so that when you come into college at lunchtime you walk past a row of chewing faces. Suzanne is sitting with her friends next to the glass window. They are talking loudly together and laughing. I sit down in the corner by the wall. Suzanne has her chair tilted back. They are looking out the window.

'What the hell's he doing?' one says.

Then they are all quiet, their faces sideways.

'Oops, no! Didn't make it!'

I look, but cannot see what they are looking at.

'Someone should tell Stan or there'll be a whole crowd of them here in a minute.'

'Oh-oh steady! Nope! Down again!' and they all laugh.

'Oh God, I think he's puked!'

'Here's Stan!' They all look out the window and are silent for a minute.

My arms and fingers have gone limp so I have to put down my sandwich. I know who they are looking at out in the courtyard.

Stan, the caretaker, has white hair and black eyebrows and a name so unpronounceable he's called Stan.

'What's he saying?'

'Asking him something.'

He's a bear from an Eastern European country with huge hands, and even before I see him walk back across the courtyard and through the glass door I know he will be coming to find me.

He walks through the double doors of the canteen. He looks about the room and sees me. He motions to me with his finger, just quickly; a little twiddle in the air.

I get up from the table and leave my coffee and sandwich. I follow Stan out the door.

The eyes in the glass wall follow me. I feel as if my body has turned into thousands of little slithery balls that all slide up against one another and slither.

Slimey slithery sliding balls. I am glad big Stan is with me. I want to hold his hand.

He puts his big body between me and the wall of eyes as he bends to talk to dad, who is slumped down next to the Henry Moore sculpture with his legs splayed out at right angles and his chin resting on his breastbone.

'Here is your daughter.'

Dad looks up. Tries to sit straight.

'Evie, there you are! Evie.'

'Oh dad!'

'Oh there you are, Evie. Evie, there you are.'

I try and lift him and Stan helps and together we hoist him up to sit on the edge of the wall.

'Dad, let's go home'

I try and hitch him up by putting his arm round my shoulders. He stands and staggers. He's a dead weight. Stan hitches him up the other side.

'Home later, now bench,' says Stan, and we stagger with him to the bench on the other side of the road.

I look up at Stan, who nods to me and walks back over the road. I sit with dad on the bench out of sight of the wall of eyes.

'Evie, oh Evie.' He holds on to my shoulder.

'Dad, for God's sake, what are you doing here?'

He is sitting bent over, feeling the raised blotches on his forehead. The drink has poisoned his blood.

'I wasn't like this,' he says pointing at the pavement.

He looks up at me with watery eyes. 'Evie, I wasn't always like this!'

'I know, dad, I know.'

'I wasn't . . .' and he tries to stand and falls back down. He tries again to pull himself upwards but he crumples down with a wobbling movement, puts his head in his hands and sobs out a dark painful cry.

I sit on the bench with him, not knowing what to do.

Zeb comes through the door, and walks quickly across the courtyard and over the road to us. I can see Suzanne in the darkness behind the glass door with her hands on her hips. He comes over to the bench.

'It's my dad,' I say out of awkwardness.

'Had a few too many? Done it myself,' he says.

Dad looks up at him and growls.

Zeb wants me to feel better, but there are too many feelings in me with him there as well, and I can't bear his presence.

'Can I get you something, Eve? Some coffee?'

'Go away,' I say, my voice cracked, 'please just go away.'

'OK,' he says, and goes back over the road.

Then I feel I've been sawn in two, but not across like the woman in the box. Lengthwise, like a fish when they pull the guts out.

3

The stairwell of the house my bedsit is in always smells of damp. The carpet in the hall is thin and worn and olive green. Under a chipped mirror is a table where the post piles up and every day I flick through it to see if there is anything there for me. But there isn't.

How did we get back? Somehow. After I'd left him to sleep under my coat, after plastic cups of black coffee from the machine outside the lift, after hauling him up, weighted down by his heavy arm and steering him along the King's Road and clambering and nearly falling into the bus, and pushing him out at the stop, when he fell against the wall and banged his head, and all the people going home with shopping or coming back from work didn't really pay attention to us at all, we finally climbed the stairs, and this morning I'd left him lying on the sofa, still sleeping.

Not all of the strip of olive green carpet is nailed down to the yellowed wooden stairs. You have to be careful the carpet doesn't slide underneath you. The landlord doesn't like to fix things. Dad had slid on the stair carpet when the three of us were trying to haul him up the stairs.

I wonder if he is sober, and I roll the piece of paper in my pocket as I walk up the dark stairs.

When Bianca saw the painting of the nightmare, and heard about dad, she had marched me up to Miss Pym's office and looked through the telephone directory to find out the time and the place of a meeting for alcoholics nearby. I have the piece of paper rolled up in my pocket to give to dad.

'Darling,' she said, 'he is an addict like me!'

There's a skylight at the top of the stairs. The glass is crusted with something brown and translucent, but I prefer the dingy light to the bare light bulb that hangs down on a long wire and reminds me of a horror film.

I put my key in the lock and open the door.

Dad is sitting on the sofa. He is dressed and everything is neat, his hair combed to the side. He stands up. He is sober.

'Evie,' he says.

'Hello, dad. I'm going to make some tea.'

I throw my canvas bag on the bed and go through to the kitchen. I feel awkward and so does he. I put the kettle on.

'Listen, dad,' I say, unfolding the piece of paper.

He stands in the doorway of the kitchen.

'Darling, there's a letter for you,' he says.

'Where is it?' I say, looking round the door.

He is putting his shaky hands in one pocket then another.

'Oh, I must have put it down somewhere,' he says glancing up at me apologetically and looking about him. 'Where *did* I put it?'

'Oh dad, couldn't you have just left it downstairs?' I say impatiently. 'That's where I always collect my post.'

'Sorry, darling,' he says, looking about the room, 'so sorry, I know I had it.'

I sigh and go back into the kitchen. I light the gas and put the kettle down on the stove, and then I see that on the table next to the biscuit tin, standing against the empty teapot, is the letter. It is from him.

I take it out of the white envelope and unfold it. I read the letter, in his beautiful handwriting. It is a gentle letter. It tells me how sorry he is for being this way. That he loves me, that I am a good person, that he is ashamed. The letter makes me cry, because I feel so sorry for him. Cry for his shame, for the way he makes himself loathe himself. He is a good noble person, and that noble nature is horrified by the drunk. I know that he is, and so am I. When you love one and see it being destroyed by the other, what can you do? All you can do is go into the next room where he's standing with his head bowed and pull his big arms round you and cry into his jacket, and say, 'But I love you, dad, don't worry about any of that, so what, it doesn't matter, dad, it doesn't matter.'

And he strokes my hair and whispers into it about how sorry he is.

'I know,' I say. 'It doesn't matter.'

'But, darling, it does.'

And he's right. It does. It does matter. It tears you apart, that's why it matters. And forgiveness has nothing to do with it, because it still tears you apart.

The kettle whistles and I make the tea and blow my nose on his big handkerchief and we sit squashed together round the kitchen table, and I unfold the crumpled piece of paper with the address and the time, and he takes it and nods. 'Yes, darling', he says, 'tomorrow.' And I squeeze his hand and nod at him. 'Yes, dad, please.'

4

'How's it going?' says Rob, coming into the studio with a
new roll of paper.

'Oh, it's OK.'

I tell her about the letter, and the meeting. 'It's at the
church, practically opposite.'

'That would be good.'

'Oh, it would be such a relief.'

Rob puts down her shopping and goes to fetch tea, and
I go back to my work.

I have been painting a strange picture all morning, I
know it is horrible but I have to paint it; a girl with many
slithery arms and legs like an octopus walking past a wall
of eyes. I am painting the feeling I had. It has many tentacles and the face of a frightened child.

I smell him before I even hear him but he is already
in my painting space. He is looking over my shoulder,
breathing down my neck. I am startled and look round
with a jerky breath.

'Oh my God, Sergei! You scared me, please don't do
that.'

'I am walking round the studios, it's my job.'

'Well, you could knock on the wall or something.'

He ignores me

'What is this? Art therapy?'

'I don't know what you call it, if you want to call it that,' I say, confused, wanting to hide it away.

'This isn't an art therapy course.'

I don't answer.

'Surrealism is one thing but there has to be a reason for it. It comes from the imagination, but it isn't *self-indulgence.*'

'I'm painting what I feel,' I interrupt him.

'What you feel!' His eyes look at the ceiling and he nods with his usual sneer.

But last night dad left me his letter; the sad beautiful letter from the man he once was, and Sergei's quivering wet lip, his cold eyes looking at me with their closed blue gaze, repel me.

'Fuck off, Sergei!' I say in a tired voice and I turn away from him.

'I beg your pardon?'

'You heard,' I say, turning back to face him, and raising my voice. 'And I'll tell you why! I'm fed up! Fed up of you coming into my space and criticizing everything I do, fed up of your useless advice. So just go away!'

He pats the air with his yellow hands as though smoothing it down.

'There is no need to become over-emotional.'

I just stare at him. He swallows like a lizard, with unblinking eyes, and turns to leave, saying 'Women!' under his breath.

'Far out!' says Rob, putting her head round the curtain. 'It's about time someone told that old bully!' She is laughing.

I take the tea from her and shrug. 'Oh Rob, to be honest I don't care about Sergei. I just hope dad goes to the meeting. I just hope he goes.'

5

But he didn't go. He looked at me with bleary eyes, lifting his eyebrows and blinking slowly, unable to shape the words 'Sorry, darling'. He was slumped in the chair, an empty vodka bottle at his feet when I got back from college.

'But dad, you said you would!'

It was no good talking about it because he just made gestures to the window, his eyes looking lost then returning to mine, his head shaking slightly, and trying again to shape the words, until his eyes looked at nothing and he didn't even try to speak. And I kicked the door with tears in my eyes.

'Oh dad, for fuck's sake!'

And in the morning, with his hands trembling, he made tea, and he was present in his eyes, and once again he said, 'Yes, I will today, I promise.' But when I came back he hadn't gone anywhere except the off-licence and his watery eyes looked at me sadly and he put his hands up in a helpless gesture, until finally one morning I took the kettle from his shaking hands, when he was trying to fill it under the tap, and I pushed past him to light the blue flame, and said, 'Dad, just GO! I don't care where!' And when I came back the flat was empty.

That was three nights ago, and I don't know where he went.

I didn't mean it, dad, and now I don't know where you are. You didn't take your keys. You're somewhere on the street, and where did you sleep last night?

I open the front door, half expecting to find him on the doorstep. The sky has a threatening look. It's going to rain.

I walk past the church and look through the railings to see if he's asleep on one of the benches.

I run across the road to take the short cut down the alley. There aren't many cars yet; I woke up so early that the market is only just being set up. A man in an apron, and a fag in his mouth, is joining two poles together. 'It's gonna piss down in a minute!' he says, jerking his head at the sky.

I walk by the skeleton of the market, the bare metal stalls with no awnings; boxes piled on the pavement and bits of wrapping blowing about on the road.

I thought he'd go to the address on the slip of paper. I thought it would all be solved. He'd find out what to do. Find people to help him.

And I imagine him curled up on a damp piece of cardboard.

A black and white dog comes up to me and sniffs me and goes trotting off down the street.

Roberta came with me to the police station, but that didn't do much good.

The sergeant said, 'Do you know how many people there are in this city, young lady?' in a tired voice. His colleague must have taken pity on me because he pushed him aside and said, 'How long has he been missing, love?' and took out some forms. I said three days. He gave a little smile and didn't look at the sergeant, who was pushing his chin back into his chin and nodding with his lips.

'That's no time at all!' he said, patting my hand. 'He'll be back, don't you worry,' but he wrote down the details anyway.

Rob was waiting outside on a low wall, smoking one of her three roll-ups of the day.

'Well?'

I shrugged. 'They say he's not officially missing after three days.'

I walk along by the closed shops and people are unlocking the roll-up metal sheets with loud grating sounds. Suddenly the sky darkens and the light turns greenish. It starts to pelt.

I keep remembering the night before I left home in Cornwall; and dad looking up the stairs with those eyes.

I run for shelter and stand under the awning of the Turkish cake shop.

That 'you're leaving me' look that he'd tried to hide.

I stick my hands in my pockets and look at the rain falling outside the awning. The road shines and trembles with busy drops.

But I'd seen it in his shoulders too. His jacket had that weighed-down look, even when he took it off and hung it on the back of the chair there was that round weighed-down look on it, and when I picked it up once, to try it on, the jacket weighed my shoulders down too, so it looked as if I carried something, and it made it hard to breathe, and I took it off quickly and felt frightened.

Now the rain comes in sheets, slanting and bouncing off the pavement. I feel the wind of it on my ankles.

Where is he going to go in this rain?

I'd been upstairs packing up my paintbrushes in an old dishcloth, sorting out the tubes of paint, when I heard him on the stairs.

'Would you like a cup of tea?' he said.

It was a little white room that looked over the moor and the blue hills. I liked looking on to the land. I used to set my easel up and paint out the window, watching the light change the colour of the hills from deep green to glowing orange when the sun shone. Then I painted out of the window that faced the sea; the Mount in the far distance changing colour every day, sometimes obscured by the mist, sometimes dazzling yellow, lit up by the sun, sometimes like a mysterious green isle.

The sea changed all the time; rippled like a snake-skin on a cold grey day, with a sky dark and brooding; then pale blue that glowed so gently it made your heart limp; then in the morning when the sun rose and the sky was flushed and rosy the sea would turn pink. The whole bay between the distant Lizard and Land's End would be pink. I loved painting the bay. I loved watching the sea.

I still loved it, but he didn't. He hated the sea now.

The drops drip from the awning to a slower rhythm. The air is filled with raindrops, water slants all landing on the pavement so it is a sheet of bouncing drops, making puddles in the dips, and rivers in the gutter, the traffic whooshing through it.

He'd looked up the stairs with the tea in his hand and said, 'We've been all right together, you and I, haven't we, Evie?' and I looked down the stairs and his face was at the bottom looking up, with my shadow falling over it.

'Haven't we, Evie?'

'Yes, dad, of course we have.'

He'd nodded 'I'm so glad,' he said. 'Something good came out of it.'

I'd followed him downstairs.

'Dad, you'll be all right, won't you?'

I knew he'd say, 'Yes, be off with you, get on with your packing, you've a train to catch tomorrow.'

But he didn't.

He looked at me and he breathed hard with his mouth open, and closed his eyes for a few minutes with a frown on his forehead.

'Dad? What is it?'

'Oh, it's all right, Evie,' he'd said.

'Will you be all right, dad?'

He'd looked away, out the window, and said, 'Oh, there's a storm coming in.'

He wouldn't be.

I'd known he wouldn't be and so had he. He couldn't lie about it and it was stupid to ask him to. But he also didn't want me not to go.

He just didn't have enough to live for on his own.

A slender boy walks through the rain, smiling, with his hands out, doing a strutting bouncy walk. It lessens. Only a few drops come through the air now.

I walk out along the wet streets.

That white breathing face.

The gaping mouth, looking out of the window at the grey sea.

When I reach the turning to college I meet Rob coming the other way, pushing her bike.

'Any news?' she says.

I shrug, and shake my head.

'Come on,' she says, putting her hand on my shoulder. 'Let's get a tea and sit by the river a bit.'

We go to the newsagent that sells takeaway tea, along with newspapers in every language, and boxes of exotic vegetables.

'It's all right, Eve, he'll turn up,' she says, as we walk down the street towards Albert Bridge, past a man lying on a bench, his coat tied up with string, and I double-check to see if it's dad. His face is old and grey. He has white bristles. He is asleep on a rolled-up sleeping bag.

We cross the beeping road and lean over the wall to look into the olive-green water. On the other side are the calm trees of Battersea Park.

'It said in the letter he didn't want to burden me. What does that mean?'

She shrugs and blows on her tea, then sips it in little slurps.

I watch the river water slipping over itself. It runs fast and full after the rain.

'He's not going to throw himself over the bridge or something. He won't do that will he, Rob?'

'No, I'm sure he won't.'

We sit down on the bench held up by Egyptian figures with the faces of people and the wings of birds. Grimy daffodils tremble in the traffic wind. The sky is low and heavy. We sit in silence for a long time until our tea is finished.

'Think it's going to rain again, Rob.'

'Listen, things work out in the end,' she says, and squeezes my arm, as we get up from the bench and leave the river behind.

As we walk fast in the spitting rain along Oakley Street, Rob tries to tell me not to worry, and dad has to live his own life. I just nod, and stick my hands in my pockets, while all the time planning the places I will go and look: the railway stations and Underground stations where there are waiting rooms; tunnels and passages where there is shelter and warmth.

Then suddenly, as we reach the King's Road, a car drives through a puddle, just missing Rob, and I see blue glass smashing into small splinters and pink water splashing on a wall, and then an almighty crash, and I wonder why I am seeing Zeb's sculpture splintering to pieces in my mind.

'Can't you just leave him to it?' says Rob, after we've got back to the studio and hung up our coats and unpacked our bags.

'How d'you know I'm not going to?'

I am sitting at my small table and Rob is taping a huge piece of paper to the wall.

'Because you've got the *A to Z* out, and you're planning where to look,' says Rob, who must have eyes in the back of her head.

I shake my head at her intuition, and put the book away.

'Well?' she says, standing in the doorway, holding the muslin curtain aside. 'Why not? Why can't you let him go, and find his own way? It's his life.'

'I don't know,' I say, undoing the cloth full of tubes of paint.

The reason is too deep for me to reach, yet I know that part of me is inextricably linked with his dark journey, and it fills me with dread.

'He's a grown man, Eve,' she says, and lets go the curtain.

I look at her figure moving about behind the see-through muslin that absorbs the light from the white sky. Rob's huge pictures of women painted out of river mud glow from the walls. They are seven feet tall and smell of baked earth.

'Anyway, how d'you know he's on the street, there are places he can go,' she says with her back to me, as she sizes the huge piece of paper with long strokes.

'I just know,' I say, looking down at the colours I am mixing. Cadmium yellow, cobalt green and blue, lamp black. I have left out any form of red so nothing can go brown.

The cobalt blues and greens are making gentle combinations that calm me. The picture is by the river. The road is green because of the light.

Why can't I just leave him to it? I say to the green painting.

'Better that he's gone!' says Rob matter-of-factly as she bends to size the base of the paper.

I look at her as she kneels and swishes the size with a wallpaper brush, then look down at my colours. Lamp black has got in with the cadmium yellow and turned it a rotting green. The colour of the slime in the river when the water is low, I think to myself, and from deep down in my imagination comes an image; the slime they find the bodies in when they are pale and cold, and I shake my head to dispel it.

6

I wait among a crowd of people outside a lift. We push together as it arrives with a ping, and troop through the silver doors. We squash inside, breathing each other's breath, and with a clanking grinding sound we lurch upwards, trembling beneath the arhythmic flicker of a zinc-white striplight.

The cool air of the night hits my face. I walk beside a looming building and through tall trees. I am glad to be out in the air.

I've been looking in bus and train terminals, in Underground tunnels, under bridges, on park benches.

I've been to Paddington to look in the alcoves of the echoing station, to bleak and windy King's Cross and the nooks and crannies of St Pancras, looking at the grimy faces to see if I can see dad's. I've been along brown tunnels lit by yellow light, up escalators and down tiled stairwells, going to as many places as I can with my one-day travelcard.

I walk under the bridge. The streetlights reflect off the river and throw glimmering shadows on to the underside of the steel girders and gently stroke the dignified faces of the bearded refugees with trembling water light as they sit, pale and proud, on their makeshift cardboard beds, each bowing slightly when I look at him. They have lost their home and their possessions but they have their souls still with them. They do not belong among the people who crowded my nightmare when I woke and knew I had followed dad into his dream. The place his soul had slipped. I walk up the dark stone stairs.

I stand on the bridge and look into the black water and see the green lights reflected in rippling lines until they crash and splinter apart, broken into by the wake of a night-time police boat. At the same time a siren makes a frantic eee-aw eee-aw along the road and a blue light flits between the trees and fades away. He must be somewhere in this huge pulsing noisy city; lying on a piece of cardboard or a bench along the river, under a bridge or up a dark dirty alley where the restaurants put their rubbish, out of the cold wind. It is blowing in my face from the river, and the black water flows under my feet.

I have a feeling in me, clogged and heavy like red mud, and it has a sound, a moaning sound.

I don't know if it belongs to me or dad, and I walk into the middle of the bridge where the traffic is loud. I lean over the edge and make the long red moaning sound into the wind, and the feeling uncoils and flows out my mouth and is carried away by the river; and the sound has memories in it. They dig into me and pull up more memories from the mud. They flow through me and unfurl in the windy air; and I remember being held in his arms next to the fire, in the warm green room, and walking with him along the cliffs, he shielding his eyes to look at the far-away islands, and along the shore, the sun shining on the belly of the waves so it seemed they were lit from within. I remember the bonfire in the woods at night when all the trees came in close, and we baked potatoes, and I remember him walking with his big stick in the long grass, me collecting things to show him, snail-shells, twigs and feathers. And I remember his eyes at night, 'Bless you, darling!' 'But I didn't sneeze, dad,' and the light from his eyes when he smiled. And I remember him walking by the graveyard on the anniversary, and not even looking over the wall.

I walk back across the bridge and away from the river and the indigo night.

Poor dad. He couldn't bear the pain of losing her.

I duck beneath the scaffolding and walk between striped poles past the skips. I peer into the dark brown shadows of a tall doorway at the bodies swaddled in sleeping bags that are tied with string. Dad doesn't have a sleeping bag. The yellow streetlights bounce up and turn the sky orange.

I walk across Trafalgar Square past the huge lions, and climb on to a bus that zooms along the Haymarket and drives so fast round Piccadilly Circus that a woman falls over and shouts 'We all want to get home, love, but have a heart' at the driver, and I sit on the lower deck and look out at dark and bright Piccadilly flashing past, too tired to shield my screwed-up eyes and see if I can spot dad in a dark doorway.

I remember picking petals out of the grass when the wreaths had tumbled over each other in the wind as though they were racing. The men chased them, their hair blowing sideways, and the women held their black hats on to their heads so they wouldn't be blown down the oblong hole that was surrounded by planks of wood holding down tarpaulin; you could only just see the red mud cut clean and plummeting down into the dark. Dad threw a handful of earth in and handed me some earth to throw in, and I threw but it landed on the tarpaulin. I thought it was a kind of game. And above our heads the sky was moving, and through the salty blowing air I could smell the earth.

After dad let go my hand, and I looked up and saw his face contorted and felt a tear-drop on my face that had been blown on to my cheek from his eye, so I knew that he was crying, the wind blew a crowd of dark clouds over the cemetery and it began to rain sideways so even the people under the umbrellas got soaked down one side. And I got pulled next to someone's legs, but dad stood in the rain with his hair being plastered down straggly over his eyebrows, his mouth open and his teeth showing, but not his tears, and the raindrops splashed on the planks of wood and poured into the oblong dark and made a drumming sound, and the piles of earth on either side began to move in red muddy rivulets down the grey flag-stoned path. And someone put a mackintosh round my shoulders, but dad stood on his own, getting wet to the bone.

The driver speeds so fast around Hyde Park Corner that we all lean sideways and hold on to the poles. He doesn't even stop at the bus stop at the top of Knightsbridge, and cross shouting voices are left behind in the night as we career along the road, while frantic people pull the cord, ringing the bell to stop him so they can get off.

I climb off the bus and walk along my road, and up the stairs to my bedsit. I take off my clothes and get into bed without putting the lights on. I don't want to remember any more.

I lie in bed, listening to the girl upstairs practising the violin and hitting the wrong notes. But the musical notes in the wide black night are beautiful and comforting, coming from her body movements I can see in my mind's eye, and her longing and her hope. The big wide night, lit by a pale half moon, embraces the sound and me in bed, and her longing, and the nearby river, and the street-lights and the person clipping along the street outside. It is holding it all, and the sound of the violin accompanies it, colouring the night with its warm sound, and gives the night a heart.

7

Today the studio is cold. Rob hasn't arrived yet and I miss her presence.

I am mixing the colours on my palette but they are making horrible combinations. I put down the palette knife, and look out the window at the trees and the grey buildings.

Sometimes I am afraid of the white canvas, afraid of what can happen on the smooth sized ground, the mistake that can turn all the colours to mud. It's always the same mess. It must wait somewhere for its chance; and then it slips down the brush and on to the surface. It gets itself in all the colours and gobbles them up with its deadness. It gobbles up the clear bright colours and regurgitates them so they are ugly next to each other. It turns it all to mud, but not the mud we scooped out of the river that has been baked in the oven so it fills the studio air with a warm sweet smell, not that kind of mud; and I look through the muslin curtain at Rob's paintings and wish she would arrive.

At coffee time the door opens and Rob and Cecile and Bianca all come through the door, talking at once.

Rob plonks her bag down.

'Eve, you forgot Karl's class.'

'Oh, it's Wednesday!' I say, putting my hand up to my forehead.

'We were doing three-second poses,' says Bianca, mimicking the poses and changing them every second to show me.

'It's all right,' says Cecile, 'he didn't take the register.'

'That's the second time, Eve,' says Rob.

Bianca comes through the curtain to look at my picture.

'Oh Evie, your paintings are getting uglier and uglier.'

'I know,' I say. 'It's awful!'

'Well, it isn't just about making pretty pictures!' says Rob through the curtain.

'It's because you have a worry,' says Bianca.

'I think it's interesting', says Cecile, leaning over to look.

'Interesting is always an insult,' says Bianca, laughing. 'What happened to all your beautiful colours?'

'Are we going up to the abstract floor for coffee?' says Cecile.

'Well, I'm not staying here for Rob's instant!' says Bianca, making a face.

'Are you all right?' says Cecile as we follow the other two out of the door.

'I suppose,' I say.

'You think everything should be beautiful,' says Rob to Bianca as we walk up the stairs.

'Well, who wants something ugly on the wall?'

'You aren't really, are you?' says Cecile to me.

'No,' I say, shaking my head. 'I suppose not.'

'Then you should only express nice things, should you?' says Rob.

'No! Look at Goya. I'm not saying that!' says Bianca.

'Sounds like it.'

'But why paint in those ugly colours? Eve has a sense of colour!'

'You have to paint what you feel sometimes.'

We walk into Bianca's space, filled with light from the huge windows, and glinting gold and crimson.

It is a dark and light day, with sunlight through rain, and lit-up buildings against black clouds. The racing raindrops have rainbows in them. Bianca's collages catch the light and also the dark, reflecting the weather that shines and glints and glowers over the city.

'Not everything can be pink and gold!' says Rob, with disdain in the 'p' of 'pink'.

'Well, not everyone wants *mud* on their walls!' says Bianca.

Cecile makes an exasperated face at me.

'Who cares what they want on their walls!' says Rob. 'What about Francis Bacon, he's not pretty.'

'I didn't say that anything had to be pretty! That's what you said.'

The conversation continues and includes Frida Kahlo and Brueghel and though I want to join in, something in me is listening to a far-away sound, as though dad has taken part of me away with him.

Bianca goes to fill the coffee pot for another cup and returns with her face animated and a little flushed.

'Oh my God, I just heard some gossip on the landing.'

'What?' we all say, looking round.

'It's not good. Not good at all.'

'Well, tell us!' says Rob impatiently.

'She smashed his sculpture!'

'Whose?'

'Zeb's.'

'When?'

'Who did?'

'Suzanne, of course.'

'How could she?'

'Poor Zeb.' I turn to the huge window looking out over London.

I'd seen it in the puddle when the car tyre split the water to smithereens.

'Why, though?'

'Were they having an argument?'

'He's split up from her, that's what I think.'

I look across the buildings at the far-away distance as they talk about who heard it from who, and who said what, and I think of Zeb walking down the road, looking forlorn.

Rob stands up, rubs her back and says that whatever's happening in anybody's love life it's time she got back to work. Cecile nods, and Bianca gets out a sheaf of gold leaf and sits down. But I don't want to go back downstairs to my mess of a picture. I just want to sit up here above London and watch Bianca glueing gold leaf to a piece of wood. When she leans close to it the outbreath from her nose makes the gold leaf flutter.

'Why don't you go and see him?' says Bianca, after the other two have gone downstairs.

'Who?'

'You know who! He likes you, you like each other. You told him to go away, remember.'

'I can't, right now. I just can't.'

'I know your father is missing, Eve. I know that it's hard for you, but . . .'

'I just can't deal with all the feelings. I feel stretched taut like a drum with too much in me. One more feeling and it would all split apart.'

'What would split apart?'

'Whatever it is that's holding me together! I'm just somewhere horrible at the moment.'

'And Zeb isn't?'

'Well, he's not in the horrible place my dad's in.'

Bianca looks up at me. 'And I don't think you should be either!'

The sun comes out and floods the studio through the raindrops, and the gold glitters and flutters to the floor as Bianca stands up and says, 'I know! I'm going to take you somewhere!' And begins to pack up her sketchbook and collage materials. 'He's the patron saint of Londoners!' she says, pulling on her coat, 'and we are Londoners!'

'Bianca, what are you talking about?'

'Come on, downstairs! Get your stuff! I'm taking you on a pilgrimage!'

'But you're not religious.'

'No, but I am superstitious,' says Bianca. 'And I think you are losing it.'

'Losing what?'

She just looks at me.

'D'you think so?' I say.

'It's in the eyes!' she says, pointing at me with two index fingers.

So I let myself be led downstairs to get my coat and sketchbook and out the door into the sunlight and the rain.

8

On the top deck of the bus Bianca gets out her guidebook and translates from Italian about Rahere who went to Italy and saw a vision of a six-winged animal with lion's feet who took him up to the top of a mountain to meet St Bartholomew who told him to build a church in Smithfield, because it was a holy place.

'The meat market? Really?' I say.

We climb out the bus and walk down Smithfield, past men in blue and white striped aprons, carrying dead pigs and cows from refrigerated lorries down metal ramps and through the gates of the meat market.

We walk away from the road and the iron smell of blood down Rising Sun Court and come upon a grey church and a grass garden dappled with sunlight from an overhanging tree, hidden behind buildings, with a feeling of stillness. We walk into the garden. The quietness encloses us. From the branches a dove calls roo-coo, roo-coo.

Sometimes you walk through an invisible curtain that divides one atmosphere from another. It is a gentle thing, but within the gentleness is something that could completely rearrange you. Your whole being might turn into dots and become part of the air.

The garden feels separated from time.

Bianca and I go down the steps into the church, which envelops us in flickering darkness and the smell of frankincense.

And I feel as if we have fallen beneath ordinary reality where the air is thicker.

We walk past a statue of Bartholomew carrying his own skin.

'Poor thing, is that what happened to him?'

I light a candle for dad.

Bianca is turning the pages of an enormous red leather book with gilt-edged pages.

'Rahere built it in 1123 with the help of children and beggars,' she whispers, and the whispering fills the air with 's's' that linger and echo, as she tells me stories from the Book of the Foundations.

'So many people were healed that he's only going to tell us about the ones he's seen with his own eyes! the writer says,' she whispers.

'Maybe he can heal your hepatitis,' I say.

'Oh no,' she says, 'if I didn't have hepatitis I'd go and score heroin straight away. It is my protector!'

While Bianca sits at the back of the church in a tall wooden pew, making collages with metallic sweetie wrappers nailed smooth, I wander up the dark corridors and wonder what it was like being alive then, shuffling up the aisle with your legs in a basket, pushing yourself along on sticks, so you could get to the altar among the songs and the glimmering candles and be healed by a saint you can't see. And far away I hear a church bell and I feel the reverberation of the sound in my cells.

We sit outside the church for a while. The rain has stopped. The little garden glistens. Bianca has bits of coloured paper all over the bench. I draw a picture of St Bartholomew by a wide blue river and a church built by children from the time when people were healed by invisible hope.

A wind blows through the plane tree and Bianca's pieces of paper flutter. She chases them across the grass.

Then the bells start ringing, dong-dong ding-ding-dong, in different rhythms. Once they must have rung all over the city, telling about times to pray, and the hermits who guarded the gates of the city and the holy wells, with their long matted hair and ragged clothes, would have closed their eyes.

We walk away from the sound, out of the old gateway and past St Bartholomew's Hospital and into the city streets to catch the bus home.

9

It is Saturday, and the college is closed. I bike along the river with my paintbox, a jar of water and a tube of white. I chain up my bike in Victoria Gardens and walk between the plane trees that eat up the traffic fumes and keep London clean, and up the steps to Lambeth Bridge. The dark clouds have gone and the river shines with light.

I stand on the bridge, looking towards Westminster, and paint the curve in the river. I follow the wall with my paintbrush all the way up to Westminster Bridge, which is distant from me, but little on the page. I follow the arches with the tip of the brush, making sure they are small enough, and behind the bridge, the dome of St Paul's, a curve and a dash of blue. My brush follows the line of the water's surface. I put in the trees in Victoria Gardens, then a frenzied tumult of dashes and spires, and among them a circle; the face of Big Ben.

The brush follows my eye. I paint the surface of the water. Little dashes far away, ripples nearby; a small boat in the far distance, a large passenger barge on the bottom of the page.

I wait for the paint to dry and look into the river and watch the water slipping over itself, brown and deep. Down there among the stones, something is lodged. I see dark orange rust spots behind the silty water, and the rippled blue surface that reflects the sky.

The sun slips out and the Houses of Parliament light up, all spiky.

I turn the page and draw with my pen.

A barge moves over the water and under Westminster Bridge. A yellow lorry crosses over the bridge at the same time, and an aeroplane moves slowly across the sky and disappears behind a blue and grey striped tower block. I keep up with my pen. They describe the near, the far and the middle distance, and help me make the small page into a big space.

Tied-up boats slide gently over the up-and-down of the water in the ribbon of reflected sun, sending tiny ripples and dots of light over the surface. Then the clouds come from behind me and little spots of rain begin to smudge the ink.

The castellations of Lambeth Palace begin to drip downwards into the trees.

The bridge vibrates with the weight of a bus.

I walk towards the café on the river, opposite Lambeth Palace, in the rain. It sits over the water and the windows look down the river to Westminster.

The window-pane is covered in raindrops. I can see Westminster Bridge in the misty distance.

I draw the frowning sea serpents coiled around the globes of light, and the green lions holding circles in their mouths along the curved wall.

I turn the page. I am learning the scene. I draw quickly in black ink, the spiky towers, the distant bridge, the curve of the water, the lions and dolphins in squiggles and the pavement under the trees, with the castellations of the palace behind. On the bench is a man. I am making him up. He is hunched on the bench. The trees are holding the sky in twiggy branches.

I turn the page. I draw just the man on the bench, I can see the trees and the bench and I copy the shapes, but I am making up the man. He is surrounded by dark shapes. They are crying out somehow.

I turn the page. I can't go there.

I take out my paintbox. I think I am painting the olive-green water, and the verdigris lion, but the paint coagulates on the page and there is the figure stooped over on the bench, surrounded by other figures. I draw them in the paint. They are the people of his despair. I'd felt their presence in the flat and entered their city in my dreams. Their eyes were hollow, their mouths chewing nothing, fingering me with greedy hunger, and I'd fled from them along a dark underground tunnel, knee-deep in water, and woke myself trying to scream.

I close the book and don't care if the pages get stuck together. I am comforted by the sounds of the coffee machine and the smell of coffee, and the man in a knitted yellow hat that keeps his hair in a bundle. I look out the window. The other side of the river is more and more hidden by white mist; the spiky Westminster towers poking up in ghostly silhouette, Big Ben's face still visible, but the river beyond the bridge is obscured behind white, and raindrops rush down and make the surface of the river shiver with hundreds of droplets.

When the rain stops I walk out into the white day. The air is clear, washed clean of dust, and the wet pavements reflect the sky. I feel heavy. As if weighed down by a memory that is living in my chest. I stand still. It is living under my breath. If I stop and close my eyes and stop breathing maybe I will see it. It is far away.

Then I see his crumpled face.

When the wind had come along with the rain, and the black sky had broken and lashed his hair, his face crumpled into a strange shape; while everyone stood under the umbrellas, he stood by the gaping hole with streams of water running into it, and clenched his hands together instead of holding mine.

I walk along by the benches that are placed up on little plinths so you can see the water.

A smartly dressed man in a hat and a brown raincoat, with a crease in his pinstriped trousers, lays a newspaper on the wet bench and sits down on it. He looks like he belongs in a 1950s film when everything was dark red and pale green.

I wonder if the gold and silver statue people will be standing still beyond Hungerford Bridge or maybe they're worried the rain will wash them clean.

I look into the water. It is swollen with the rain.

I am remembering the cold church with the wind outside and an old lady saying 'Poor child' as if I wasn't there, while I touched the face of a mermaid carved into a chair. I looked round at her while my hand felt the contours, to tell her that I knew she meant me, because my mother was dead, but she looked away, and I looked back at the mermaid who had strange eyes.

I breathe in the river wind. The mist is lifting. I copy the smart man and climb up the steps and put my sketchbook down on the rain-spattered bench.

Big Ben booms out his dong that colours the air. I take

my book from under me and draw his portrait. He started life as a drawing, and before that he was just an idea in Pugin's mind. He is difficult to draw. It is easier to draw quickly.

But suddenly I put my sketchbook down and leave it on the bench to go down the steps and lean over the side and look into the flowing water.

I had new goggles. I wanted to swim in the seaweed forest, deep down where the waving fronds grew high, and the sun made shivering underwater ripples on the sea floor.

I saw it floating upside down with its mouth open; it slowly bounced towards me and touched me, a dead dogfish, with white stuff, omelette-like, coming out of its mouth. I screamed all the breath out of my body, and heard the scream fill the water. I fought my way back to the surface, heavy without air, and spluttered into the above-water daylight, coughing out the water I'd gulped instead of breath, until I was hauled out, laid flat on the rock, and she'd blown breath into my body through my mouth, until the gurgling water in my lungs spewed out of my mouth in a long stream.

The sun comes out from behind the clouds and lights up the river.

The water glitters and I close my eyes and feel rippling light on my eyelids.

But I am still seeing memories.

I remember Mrs Tregenza held me against her white apron, and I didn't like it because it smelt of fish, and I didn't like her fishy hands, that sliced the long silver mackerel bellies so the red guts tumbled out in bloody coils, fingering their way through my curls.

'He'll be back in a minute, darling, don't cry,' and she'd jigged me up and down against the scaly oily apron until I'd seen dad outside and run into the drizzle to be with him. His hands had made tense starfish and clenched together in a jerky rhythm but in time with each other, I couldn't hold those hands, while Bob was murmuring to him and making my dad's face go strange. And the pavement was slippy and the sea came into my Wellingtons, as I hurried after him between the boxes of fish with their red eyes staring. They didn't frighten me. It was the rhythmic pulse of the starfish hands.

I open my eyes. The sun has gone again and the water is brownish green. I turn back to the bench and sit down next to my sketchbook. I open it and draw a little girl underwater, swimming next to a dead dogfish.

Then I remember it. The image that was conjured in the slant of light, by the words that came through from the kitchen along with the cooking smell: 'They've found the body by Lamorna, the eyes wide open,' and I'd imagined my mother wrapped in seaweed, the kind like hair, her eyes staring, with a frill of egg-white floating from her mouth.

It must have all happened within a few days.

I nearly drowned and then she did.

I bicycle slowly back. The memory has opened a shaking space within me. I bike past Millbank and the wide stairs of the Tate, through Pimlico and the red houses of Chelsea, and by the silver river all the way home.

I climb the stairs and lie down in bed although it's not even time for the streetlights to come on, and lie looking at the ceiling until my eyes close on their own.

10

I wake up with a start. It is dark outside. I can still hear dad's voice calling to me out of my dream. It is so real I think it's in the room. There is a car alarm going off in the street. I switch on the light. It's only 11:30. I get up, put my clothes on without thinking, and pick up my keys. Surely if I follow the feeling I will find him.

I go down the stairs and out into the street. There is a wind blowing. The sky is dark blue, with stars. I walk down the dark streets, looking up the alleys and along the King's Road, lit up with coloured light, people coming out the pub in crowds. I pass three men, their arms round each other's shoulders, singing 'Here we go here we go' and laughing.

'All right, love?'

'Hello, lady of the night.'

I walk up to Sloane Square. Two figures are lolling in the centre of the square, under the trees. I feel like I've walked into one of my paintings. One of the men gets up and falls over.

I walk up Sloane Avenue towards Knightsbridge. The wind is blowing through the leaves. A police car whizzes past me, its siren blaring, the blue lights flashing. I feel the wind of it, it drives so close to the pavement.

The sky has gone brown with orange clouds. I walk along Knightsbridge beneath the tall buildings, imagining

I am following his footsteps, sure I'm being led to him, if I just follow my feet.

Under the hotel in Knightsbridge some old men are sitting by the big-leaved plants, and chatting to the door-man in his top hat and gold buttons, but dad is not with them. I trudge on up to Hyde Park Corner. I keep think-ing I'll just go on a bit further. I'll find him if I carry on.

By the time I've walked up Green Park and Piccadilly to the Circus I feel as if my body doesn't fit together. People sit around the fountain under Eros, dressed in ragged clothes, with lurid faces which change colour in ripples under the advertising lights. The lights make rhythmic circles and zigzags and wave patterns and flash out Coca-Cola and Fuji film.

Cars are zooming, more sirens flash past, and the sounds begin to echo.

Maybe I will find him if I carry on down the Haymarket, maybe he's sitting on the steps of the National Gallery or among the lions made out of melted-down guns. That's the sort of thing Zeb tells you; and the cross on St Paul's weighs the same as seven cars, and reality is 80 per cent invisible.

Someone by the fountain is screaming. Two men are fighting on the pavement. I see the man's head wobble as it is pounded by the other man's big fist. I run away from them, down a dark street, past whistling scaffolding pipes. A man gets up from the bench on a ledge, and bursts into tears.

A night bus slides past and opens its doors. I recognise the number and clamber in. I sit down and close my eyes.

140

11

'You look fucking terrible!' Rob says as she comes through the muslin curtain into my space.

'I feel it, Rob!' I say, sitting down on the stool.

'No, really, shit! You look bad. You're a state! Your eyes have got rings under them. Look at yourself!' she says, getting up and fetching the mirror she uses to paint self-portraits.

'Oh don't, Rob, I don't want to look.'

'Listen! He's missing, he'll turn up, you can't spend your nights and days tramping the streets!'

'Yeah, but what if he turns up dead, Rob? What if he turns up in the river, or frozen to death on a piece of cardboard?'

'It's spring, it's getting warmer.'

'It was freezing last night! And that wind.'

'Yes, and you were out in it, listen to me! It's not your responsibility! Are you listening? He's NOT your responsibility.'

'That's just words, Rob. What if your dad was out in the street? Probably drunk in a gutter?'

'I think you should go and see Safi.'

'Who's Safi?'

'The college counsellor.'

'Oh and she'll help me find him, will she? The police were fucking useless!'

She shakes her head at me, and puts the mirror down in my space.

'Look in the mirror,' she says as she goes through the curtain, 'and see Safi.'

I look at myself. My eyes are wide open and scared-looking, with dark rings. My face is shockingly pale with a yellow tinge, and I have a squint look.

I stand outside the red door. And look at the label. Mrs Safi Irfan.

'Oh, bugger this.'

I walk down the stairs halfway to the canteen, then turn around and go upstairs again, and stand outside the door. I breathe in and knock.

'Come in,' says a voice from within.

I open the door.

She sits behind a desk, and looks round to me.

'Come in, dear,' she says.

She has a soft Indian accent, her hair is grey at the roots and dyed dark chestnut. She has high cheekbones and dark eyes.

'Sit down, do you want to sit down?' she says, standing up. 'I can make you a cup of tea if you want to talk for a little bit.'

I want to walk out the door but I am touched by the pretty way the words sound in her mouth.

I sit down.

'Would you like a biscuit?'

All the consonants are softened, and there is a melody in the sentences.

I just nod to everything she asks, that way ending up with a biscuit, a cup of tea with two sugars, none of which I really want.

I would like to sit in here and listen to her saying ordinary things all day.

'My dear,' she says kindly, 'you are here to talk to me?'

'Well I . . . yes,' I say.

'What would you like to talk about?'

I look out the window at the white sky.

'It's my . . . well it's about my . . .' I swallow and look at her, and her look is so deep that it reaches into me where my tears are; the look says, 'It's all right, you know,' and the tears begin to silently pour out my eyes.

She sits nodding slightly until the tears stop.

'My dad,' I say in a whisper.

'Yes.' She nods. 'It is difficult for you.'

I feel as if she knows it all already.

She has seen him on my front steps, slumped against the railings, and us dragging him up the stairs. She knows that he pissed on the floor and I had to change his trousers, and about the beautiful letter he wrote.

'He said he was sorry, you see,' I say, and she nods. 'Sorry because of all of it, that he didn't want to be that way.'

She nods.

'And I remember . . .' I say, shaking my head slowly at her while the words are stuck, and the memories are in the air round her head, so I'm sure she sees them too, 'I remember how he was.'

She nods. She can see how he was; so noble and tall.

'He doesn't like what he's become, you see.'

She nods. 'And its hard for you, too,' she says, and something cracks in me and and I begin to sob.

'You see, he left because he's ashamed, I made him ashamed, that's the thing, and now he's out on the street

143

in the cold. On some park bench,' and the tears pour down my cheeks.

'My dear,' she says gently, 'you didn't make him ashamed.'

'I did!' and my voice has a screech in it, 'I did! I told him I didn't want him in my flat, that I couldn't put him up, I couldn't cope with him. TO GET OUT. To get out.'

'And what if I were to tell you that you did the right thing?' says Safi.

'The right thing' sounds beautiful in Safi's mouth. The trill of the 'r' is soft. It opens some kind of doorway in the air that reveals many possibilities. The doorway closes abruptly.

'But what if he DIES on the street? He might DIE!'

Safi stays perfectly still.

'That is his choice.'

The melody in her voice makes the word 'choice' end on a high note. And I hear that his choice comes from a place within him that I cannot reach.

'You cannot make that choice for him.'

I nod, she has made me see it.

'And you cannot protect him from it.'

I look at the many-armed deity Sellotaped to her diary. She turns the book round for me to look at, the colours are pink and green and gold.

I talk with Safi until the sky darkens and she switches on the light. I tell her about the far-away memories; the day mum went missing, and Bob telling dad, and her funeral, and dad crying in the rain. I tell her about nearly drowning and the dead dogfish, and my mum's kiss of life. I tell her about Magda and the farm, and escaping from dad's despair to come to London. When I stand up to leave she comes round the desk and takes my hand. Her eyes look into mine.

'You don't have to be in there with him,' she says. 'Despair is a lie. There is always hope.'

And I see the spirits of his despair whispering their lies, and I see hope as a bright place brimming with possibilities. Safi's words contain reality in them. They are not empty.

'Come and see me again. Ring me any time,' she says, giving me a telephone number, and I take it and thank her and walk upstairs to the abstract studios to see if Bianca is still working.

But the studio is empty and I look out over London as the streetlights come on, and sit among Bianca's pictures in the glinting dark.

12

I go and see Safi again and tell her things I've never said before.

I tell her about dad, and how he used to tell me stories on the green sofa while I looked into the flames, how we went walking together on the cliffs and the moors and fishing sometimes when he had the time. I tell her about finding all the empty bottles in one go and noticing the bleary look in his eyes, and the scared feeling as it happened more and more, and the horrible fear it turned into, watching him slowly fall apart.

Safi asks me about mum, and I remember how I longed for her when I was small, but never really knew her. She was on the stage, and I imagined it as a huge platform on stilts. She used to walk out of the station in high-heeled shoes and lean over to kiss me, and then she'd be gone again, waving out the window; and the longing in me that was attached to the train and the waving hand would stretch out long and thin as the train moved away, and after the train disappeared I would cry into dad's jersey.

I remember all the feelings because of Safi's eyes. She has eyes that overturn places in you, that turn over pages in your mind you haven't seen for years and look at them with you.

I tell Safi that I missed mum when she died but not like dad did. I felt dad's howling grief in the depths of me and saw it every day in his eyes. And when I got older her absence sang through our lives like a sad song you hear in the distance.

Safi says an absence can have a powerful presence in people's lives and I see a person-shaped emptiness behind dad, and feel its magnetic force, and realize that's why I had to get away.

'Your mother is not an absence, Eve,' says Safi, 'that is your father's pain. Your mother is a presence,' and I close my eyes and feel light feelings pass through me in whispers. And even if it's faint and far away, I can feel her presence, and I wish I could find dad so I could tell him that.

'But you must let him go,' says Safi, 'and set yourself free.'

And even though I don't understand, I can feel what Safi means, and I breathe in and look out the window at the sky, so it fills up my lungs with sky light.

And she asks if Magda is my aunt. I say no, she was a neighbour, but I used to call her auntie. 'Did she look after you?' And I remember the smell of the slurry in the farmyard and the sound of the cows breathing, and the warm kitchen with the wind outside and the coats steaming in front of the stove. 'Yes,' I say, 'she was like a mother to me.' Safi nods, and I tell her how I used to hold on to Magda's legs when my mother came back because they were safe legs. Safer than my mum's in her high heels, that wobbled and clipped and clopped. And besides, she might say, 'No don't, you'll ladder my stockings.' And I didn't like the nylon skin that could break into ladders if you touched it.

I tell her about the argument Magda had with dad. How I didn't even know what it was about, but I was a teenager and took my dad's side. She says, 'Why don't you ring her?' I say, 'She doesn't have a telephone.' 'Then write to her,' she says.

So I do.

13

I am sitting next to the window in my studio so the light shines on to the palette. The colours I am mixing are neutral and quiet.

I told Cecile I was tired of the ugly colours.

She said the ugly colours make the other colours look more beautiful, but I said I was tired of those colours of despair. She said, 'What colours are those?' and I said, 'Like Indian red mixed with Prussian blue,' and she mixed it to see what colour it made. She said she thought that was rage, maybe rage gone stagnant. I said, 'Yes, it could be that.'

We were sitting downstairs in her space after her tutorial, and she was fed up because of what the tutors had said. It was an insult, after all.

That space down on the ground floor isn't like the other studios; less cosy, people do huge pictures and there are ramps and pulleys and loud music, and I looked at her pale delicate face as she considered the colour she had mixed. She has naturally red lips and orange eyelashes, and was frowning slightly as she put her head on one side. Its true that her pictures are huge, and stretched above us in flower shapes and spirals so you could be looking at undergrowth or outer space; but I never feel that Cecile really belongs on the ground floor.

Then I mixed the scary green from cadmium yellow and lamp black, just to show her, and told her it was like the rotting seaweed at low tide, that when you walk through you have to keep your mouth shut because of the flies. 'But it could be despair, couldn't it? Wouldn't that black-green weigh you down? I mean it wasn't one to lift your spirits, was it?'

She said, 'No, you're right, you'd have to be careful of a colour like that, it might murder someone!'

I laughed and said, 'Especially if a bunch of tutors had just told it to "get a job painting window displays!"'

And we laughed at the idea of the colour having a tutorial.

'If anyone ought to paint window displays, it should be the head of painting and his endless vertical stripes,' said Cecile, and I nodded in agreement.

But even so, she looked at the green and said, 'I can imagine painting with that colour, it all depends what colours you put it next to.'

I said, 'I'm sure you're right but I'm not taking any chances. I'm going to make my paintings out of grey from now on.'

So I'm mixing neutral colours now; browns and greys and dirty whites. Colours that speak like stones and bricks, scaffolding pipes and cement. Unnoticeable colours. The blue-grey of the paving slabs after the rain, and mud stuck in the grip of tyres, the colours of rags and dirty string, and sacking and wet cardboard and paper blowing across the street, and the bone colours of discarded bus tickets pressed into the road by lots of feet.

These colours and their tiny shift towards blue, hint of purple, or tinge of pink, I like them. They comfort me.

14

'No, I'm not saying I don't like them,' says Bianca, balancing on one spindly leg of the chair and trying to do a pirouette holding on to the table edge. We are sitting in the canteen next to the glass window.

'It's just they're not those beautiful colours you used to use. I mean, people go through phases, don't they? This is your drab phase.'

I laugh.

Rob shakes her head.

'What?' says Bianca. 'It's my opinion. Come to the Rothko! That'll cure you!'

'Oh, let's go,' says Cecile. 'I really want to see those paintings.'

'The colours are fantastic!'

'Yes, and the real thing is completely different from the reproductions.'

'Yeah, some just don't, do they.'

'Don't what?'

'Reproduce.'

'Cézanne doesn't, either. You don't get what he looks like in the flesh, until you see him.'

'The flesh?'

'Stop being so annoying, you know what I mean. In the paint, then.'

Bianca's chair skids sideways and she ends up sliding down the glass wall, so Rob has to catch her and the chair and pull her straight, while Bianca is squealing and Roberta is laughing.

Suzanne walks into college arm in arm with a man with hair so short he looks bald, and sunglasses on the top of his head although it is not sunny.

'Is that her new boyfriend?' says Bianca, looking round.

They walk through the door into Sculpture on the other side of the quadrangle.

'Is it?' She turns to Rob.

'How should I know?'

'Because of Mick. They're friends, aren't they?'

Rob shrugs. 'Doesn't mean he tells me everything that's going on in his friend's ex-girlfriend's love life!'

'Have they really split up?'

'Who knows with those two!'

Bianca looks at me. But I look away at the grey paving stones. So what if I like drab colours.

Bianca puts her elbows on the table and cups her face in her hands. She slides across the table so she's looking up at me, her mouth stretched wide, and lifts her eyebrows up and down.

I laugh at her.

Rob and Cecile get up and take their plates away.

She slides back again and sits up and cricks her neck from side to side.

'I'm glad you're back,' she says. 'It's like you've been walking in the realm of the dead. I didn't like you being a zombie!'

'Is that what I seemed like?'

'Yes! You got lost.'

'Was I lost?'

'Yes, of course! Junkies do it! They go off. You look in their eyes and they're gone. I have done it myself!'

'Where did you go?'

'Oh, I don't know, into oblivion.'

'I wonder where I went.'

'Maybe your soul was out looking for your dad.'

'I'm glad it's back, then,' I say, looking out at the quadrangle through the glass, and the pigeons pecking under the statue.

'Listen, come back with me for the weekend. Come to Brixton. Get away from your little place and stay with us. You need some good food. You need some normal life. OK? Then you will be able to do the most normal thing in the world, and go and see,' and she inclines her head upwards to the mezzanine, 'that friend of yours.'

'Thanks, Bianca, I'd like to.'

'We can go for a walk, we can make a nice dinner,' she nods. 'It's a good plan.'

15

It is a grey London day. It looks like it might rain.

The air is damp. I am on the bike following Bianca's pink and green Guatemalan shirt. She gets off her bike at the embankment and we cross over the thundering road. We stop to look over the wall into the water reflecting the white sky.

'Let's bike through the park,' she says.

So we cross Albert Bridge by foot, just to see the river flowing under us, and lean out over the water and shout each other's names into the wind. It begins to spit and we hurry through the park gates and ride our bikes with our heads down against the drizzle, to the shelter by the fountains. We stand in the shelter to wait until the drizzle stops. There is a man in there. He has a low voice and his voice booms round the shelter when he says, 'It's wet, isn't it.'

Bianca says, 'You must be an opera singer.' He says that he is, and he's from New York and here to sing Mozart. Bianca says, 'Oh could you sing something for us, please.'

He booms out 'Don Giovanni,' and it makes the hairs on the back of my neck stand up and my mouth fall open, the sound is so big.

But Bianca glances at me, and says to him, 'Oh, not that, please' so he sings 'Moon River' and the sound reverberates around the shelter, and I look outside and the trees are glistening in the evening light, and the river turns into something sorrowful.

'Oh, it's beautiful!' says Bianca. 'It's heavenly.' And he laughs and his laugh also fills the shelter.

We cycle away when the rain stops and realize we didn't ask his name.

We ride between the glowing green playing fields and into the trees and bushes that line the lakeside paths, past the blue boathouse, and the café and the ducks on the rippling lake, and the peacocks and peahens who strut about behind wire mesh calling their plaintive call, and through the gates into the rush-hour traffic. Bianca winds her scarf round her nose so she looks like a bandit, and we dodge and weave between the cars following the 137 round the corner and up Queenstown Road. We dismount and push our bikes up the hill. Then Clapham Common spreads out before us large and flat, where we flew Zeb's kite. He attached it to a fishing line so it reeled out and out, and up into the sky, until it was a tiny speck and there was no more fishing line and Zeb let it go, so it floated off into space. It must be up there at the edge of the ozone by now. And we cycle along the tree-lined road and round the corner into Acre Lane. We pass the timber merchant where we had our studio and the air smells of newly sawn wood. Past the café where we had our bacon sandwiches and mugs of tea, past Reggae Records and the sari shop, and the Ritzy Cinema, where I automatically check the old men gathered on the steps drinking Special Brew, and into Bianca's road.

When we've chained our bikes to the banisters we walk up the stairs. On each landing there is a different-coloured strip of stained glass, and as I follow Bianca up the stairs the strip of coloured light passes over her, changing the colour of her clothes. Red, green, yellow, pink. When she stops at her front door and takes out her keys she has a strip of turquoise light across her face.

'Why did you tell him not to?' I ask.

'Not to what?'

'Sing that song.'

'Never mind why.'

'Why?'

'Because it's the father's ghost singing and I thought it would be bad luck.'

And I stand still, on the doorstep, while the strange feeling passes through me.

We have fennel tea made from what looks like dried grass stalks, from a flat black teapot that Bianca bought in the market. The tea smells of liquorice and tastes of aniseed, and Bianca tells me a story Silvia has written, about a woman whose body is a landscape: her breasts are hills, her thighs are valleys.

Later, Bianca's sitting room flickers with candlelight, and there is a smell of garlic and herbs. She is standing at the table with three grey squid on a newspaper, attempting to cut out the ink sack. The ink is spurting out onto the newspaper.

Giacomo has brought two pots of sturdy basil, and a jar of damson jam he made himself. There is Eduardo from Venezuela, and his wife Anna, and Cesar from Chile, who is cooking the tomatoes in the kitchen ready for the squid, and looks through the door every now and then, to join in the conversation, in his apron and holding a wooden spoon.

His wife Maria Ines is bringing the pudding.

'Here, help me,' says Bianca and hands me a knife, and I cut into the strange quivering flesh.

When Maria Ines arrives we cram round the table in the sitting room and everyone is talking a mixture of Italian and English about which shop sells fresh food, and what the food was like in Egypt, where Giacomo just went. The coloured velvets glow and flicker, and Eduardo touches my foot under the table, and I frown at him because he's sitting next to his wife Anna. We drink wine and eat, and the wine warms me along with the laughter and the red velvet curtains printed with spirals, and the coloured throws on the sofa, and the cushions glinting like gold in the candlelight.

Bianca gives me an embroidered nightdress and I sleep in her big bed, listening to the sirens outside and the crowds of people coming down the road shouting, after the pubs have closed.

In the morning we lie in bed and Bianca tells me another story Silvia has written, about a woman who has a fold-up forest that she unfolds around her when she feels like it.

We get out of bed to make coffee.

We pass Silvia's open door. She is lying diagonally across the bed with one arm flung above and her auburn hair cascading sideways.

She opens her eyes and looks at us.

'Allora?' says Bianca. 'Last night?'

Silvia stretches and smiles. 'I was dancing till three.' 'Make me a coffee!' she says, and folds back the covers, 'and come in with me.'

'Get in,' says Bianca. 'I'll bring it.'

A piece of lace covers the armchair and a copper-coloured bra is slung over the arm.

I climb into the bed next to her.

'Did you sleep well?' She has a kind of lisp.

I lie beside her. Her skin smells of milk. I ask her about the story. She says, 'I will read it to you.'

I close my eyes. I can smell the forest that she unfolds around her. The flowers exude a thick scent. I smell the forest floor in her hair: the leaf mould, the moss, and the tiny orange chanterelles with earth still clinging to their roots.

Bianca brings in the coffee.

There are animals in the forest too. I smell their fur and their nut-flavoured breath.

'Move over!' says Bianca, so I am squashed between them.

Siliva laughs. She has freckles on her face. Her lips are stained dark purple.

'Oh, but I like me,' she says, and lies back. Her arm behind her head slowly stretches up through her hair. 'Everybody likes me.'

Her long silky auburn hair exudes a fragrance.

She turns over and flings her arm round the dip between my ribs and my hip.

'You smell nice,' she says. She has a low soft velvet voice. She squeezes me and her hand moves over my breast.

'Oh, you have enormous breasts!' she says, laughing. 'How did you keep them hidden so long?'

I start laughing, her laugh is infectious.

'Did you know her breasts were so big, Bianca?'

'Yes, I have noticed!' says Bianca, sipping her coffee.

'Remember it took half an hour to get the gold dress off!' says Bianca, and starts to laugh, so she spurts coffee and has to put the cup down, and I am sandwiched between their giggling bodies.

'Shut up!' I say.

'No, listen!' she whispers, putting her finger up.

'What?'

The door opens down the corridor.

'It's Carlotta's boyfriend. Call out to him, Silvia! He's so English, let's pretend we've had a night of passion.'

'Oh Tony! Tony!' says Silvia in a low seductive voice.

Bianca and I listen. He passes the open door.

'Would you like to join us?' says Silvia.

He clears his throat like a caricature of an Englishman, and walks past the open door with a startled face, and Bianca puts her hands over her mouth as though she is ashamed, but Silvia is laughing, and the sun shines through the thick lace curtains and lights up our faces in intricate patterns.

16

The sun shone all weekend. But now the raindrops are dripping down the window of the studio. They even drip in shadows over the cotton duck I have stretched over the frames. Sometimes the sun comes through and lights up the drops in glinting colours then disappears again, and all the coloured lights go out.

I have knocked the frames together with corrugated nails and stretched the canvas till my thumbs are sore, and now I'm waiting for the soaked rabbit-skin glue to melt into gloopy liquid so I can size the surface.

We went with Silvia to her African dance class after we got up. Partly because Bianca had told me, and I wanted to witness, the cascade of love talk that hurtles towards Silvia from every corner when she walks along Railton Road.

'Oh please, darlin', talk to me. I want the whole street to see me talking to you.'

'Beautiful queen!'

'Oh sugar!'

'Woman sweet honey!'

Bianca and I stood at the back of the class in T-shirts and leggings, and watched the leopard-skin leotards and gyrating-in-time bodies moving in breathtaking synchrony with each other and the djembe players; while we jumped too soon, kicked a beat after, moved our hips in the wrong direction, and ended up getting the giggles because we couldn't keep time at all.

The studio is filled with the animal scent of the melting rabbit-skin glue. It gets up your nostrils and stays there for days so you think you smell it everywhere.

In the evening we went to the crypt in Lambeth to listen to jazz, and the drummer couldn't keep his eyes off Bianca. It was a dark little place under an old church and I wondered if it was old enough to have been there when William Blake lived in Lambeth. My ears were ringing because I stood too near the saxophone.

I stir the glue round and round. It is melting into a smooth honey-coloured liquid. The texture is just right. I take it off the heat and let it cool.

On Sunday morning we biked along Brixton High Street and up the road, past the paper factory to the Portuguese café in Stockwell. Bianca sang 'Sunday Morning' into the wind with her own words. Everyone who came to dinner was there, as well as Giacomo's boyfriend, and Mikhail, the refugee from Serbia. We sat outside in the courtyard and ate fishcakes and drank galão, and they talked about politics and the war; then Bianca told them about dad. I was embarrassed at first. In a minute, everyone was talking about my father. About alcoholics and people going missing, about where he could be, and who they might ask to help look for him, and when did you last see him? and what was he wearing and how old is he? and where did you look? and how are you feeling? and did you go to the police? no, they're never any help, and how long has he been drinking? and what! He has no wife, ah well, he drinks because he's lonely, and so you have no mother, poveretta! and the plates piled up and they ordered more coffee and custard pastries with burnt tops, and I told them about the dark tunnels, and the railway stations, and the benches looking over the river. And by the time the conversation moved to Giacomo's cousin who went missing in Mexico, to Mexican food, and Steve Hatt in Essex Road, the best fish shop in London, I felt as if everything I went through all alone and full of terror, had been somehow warmed by the light of their attention, been taken from a dank ashamed place and aired along with sunlight and coffee and turned into stories that people share on Sunday morning, and even though dad is still out there, missing, I feel less strange in the world, and less alone.

We walked round Brockwell Park after all that coffee, and ended up in the little garden among the lavender and green hedges, watching the blue tits sipping water out of the fountain.

It was all to make me normal, Bianca said, normal enough to do a normal thing like go downstairs to the mezzanine and knock on the door.

When I've sized the last canvas and they are standing in a row against the wall, stinking out the studio, I get up and look out the window at the sun trying to come out and decide it's time to go and see Zeb.

17

I walk downstairs into Zeb's space. He is sitting mending his sculpture.

The light is streaming in and shining through the bottles of coloured water so they shimmer and tremble on the wall in sunlit reflections. Each time he twiddles a screw the water light twirls and trembles on the wall.

He looks up.

And looks down again.

'Howsit going?' he says to the screwdriver.

'Fine,' I say to my fingers.

'Could you pass me that screw,' he says to the back wall. I look behind him and pass him the box, and one of us drops the box, so I say, 'Sorry' and we both bend to pick them up and bump heads, and both say, 'Sorry,' and I sit back down and he takes a screw and the rest lie scattered between us, twirling across the floor till they come to rest.

He screws the screw into the metal frame, biting his lip.

I breathe in and look at the door

'Looks like it'll be all right, then, the sculpture,' I say to the door.

'Mm-hmm,' he says, another screw in his mouth.

'Better go now,' I say, getting up and rolling across the screws.

'No, don't go yet,' he says. 'I'm nearly finished it.'

There is a tiny squeaking noise as he screws in the last screw.

'There! Look, it stands again,' and he wobbles it to show it's steady and all the glass tinkles, and the coloured light shivers on the wall.

'Yep,' I say. 'Looks good!' I nod. 'Steady, anyway.'

We both nod at the sculpture for a few minutes.

'D'you think . . .'

'D'you want . . .' we say together.

'What?'

'No, what were you going to say?'

'Just thought we could go and get a coffee.'

'Yeah.'

We clank downstairs but our awkwardness can't fit through the door of the canteen, and we stand in the hall looking out the window until the sunlight pulls us outside.

We cross the courtyard and sit on the bench on the other side of the road, out of sight of the wall of eyes. And I remember sitting here with dad. But now it's Zeb I'm sitting next to.

'Are you . . .'

'Is your . . .'

'What?'

'No, you.'

We look at each other.

'Honestly, what are we like,' he says.

I smile.

'Your dad?' he says gently.

'He's still missing,' I say and look at the tall building of the art school; the layers of glass and concrete, stretching up into the sky to catch as much light as it can.

'Somewhere,' I say, and lift my chin at London. 'Somewhere out there.'

A silence falls. With Bianca I can leave my worries for a while, but with Zeb I feel all the way down to the deep places.

'Are you still looking for him?' he says.

I glance up. His eyes are looking at me. His look says, 'It's all right, you can say what's true.'

I close my eyes. In the dark part of my mind I can see my dad's journey; by the river, down alleys, on benches, in tunnels. I can see the empty buildings, the littered paths along dark canals, the bridges by gasworks and steps that lead nowhere, and tears are in my closed eyes.

'Oh, Zeb, I can't find him.'

'No. I know you can't,' he says, putting his hand on my shoulder. 'I don't think you're meant to.'

'I never know about "meant" to.'

'I don't think he wants you to.'

'Find him?'

'Look for him, even. I don't think he wants to be found, do you?'

He looks at me and his eyes are so deep they reach into me. I look down at my hands and my voice comes out cracked.

'Oh, Zeb, I know everyone says so, and sometimes I think it's true.'

And suddenly the lovely time I had with Bianca breaks apart and something comes up from underneath. And I hear a voice crying, 'Help me, don't leave me to this. I'm ashamed of how much I need you.' It is calling into the dark to be found, to be found, to be found.

'My poor dad,' I say, and Zeb puts his arm round me.

'Oh Zeb, my poor dad,' and Zeb holds on to me and says, 'It's OK, it's OK.'

We sit on the bench and the breeze blows through the branches of the big plane tree. It blows through the weight that sits between us made of feelings about dad.

When the feeling eases I see the weight between us is not just dad. And when I ask Zeb about Suzanne, he draws his arm away from my shoulders, leans forward, presses his long fingers together, and breathes out slowly in a big sigh.

'I mean I've got my own things to sort out,' he says, looking off down the street at the cars zooming along the King's Road.

In my mind's eye I see a slender shard that must have leaped out of one of the bottles, and pierced him when the sculpture smashed. She'd meant it to, it was made of an intention, not of glass, and it has wounded him.

'The school is taking the second-years to Barcelona next week,' he says. 'Just for a few days.'

'Yes, I know,' I say. 'It'll be good.'

'There's a chance a couple of us could do an exchange.'

'Exchange?'

'With the art school in Barcelona.'

'Oh Zeb, are you going away?'

My voice is quiet because I don't want him to.

'It would just be for a couple of months next term,' he says. 'I think I need to get away for a bit.'

He turns back to me. 'Eve, I'm so glad you came to see me. Look, even if I go, I'll be back!'

I put my hand on his arm and nod, and his eyes look at me like sunlight.

18

'What did he say?' says Bianca. 'Did he talk about Suzanne?'

We're on the Tube going to the Rothko show, sitting in two twos. Rob is sitting at the other end of the carriage with Cecile. The Tube is full of bodies pressed together, breathing the same breath in and out.

'Not really,' I say, but we are going through a noisy juddering and she can't hear a thing anyway.

'What?' she shouts.

'I said not really.'

Two Japanese girls sit opposite us in orange and purple platform shoes. Bianca keeps looking at them.

The train slows down and Rob and Cecile are making signs at us from the other end of the carriage.

'We know! We know! We're not morons!' says Bianca.

We come out the station at Embankment and walk up the steps and across the footbridge beside the thundering trains. People are playing drums. Cecile is excited about the colours she is going to see.

We stand on the footbridge and a passenger barge passes underneath us and we look down the river to St Paul's.

'Let's get a move on,' says Rob.

Bianca slips her hand through my arm.

'You could have asked him to come and see the show. Ask him round to dinner at my house next week.'

'The second-years are going to Barcelona next week.'

'So he's going to Barcelona?'

'Yes,' I nod.

'And you don't care?'

I look at her but I can't say anything.

Cecile looks stricken when we pass a man in a wheelchair with no legs because everyone has given their change to the smiling djembe players.

She stops on the bridge, trying to find change in her handbag.

'Come ON!' says Rob.

Cecile finds a coin and slips it into his cup, looking relieved.

We walk across paving stones, up a concrete stairwell, through a glass door, and into the galleries of the Hayward.

In the beginning there are pictures of houses and landscapes. But then he sets the colours free; and the canvases emanate colours like notes of music that go right through you in harmonies of pink and red, yellow and blue, blue and crimson. They bathe us in coloured light. The combined colours sing together. As I walk through the galleries my whole body hears the colour harmonies as though it is a big ear. When I reach the last room I feel as if I've swallowed the colours and they are singing within me.

He paints the colours of sunlight and the colours of earth, and the in-between colours of twilight. And then he paints the dark.

In the last room the paintings are black; huge spaces of many-layered black.

They make me hold my breath. Oh my God, I know where he went, from all that light, to no light at all.

'They were the last paintings he did before he killed himself,' says Bianca, subdued. And we look and look at the colours of his despair.

'Poor Rothko,' says Bianca.

I nod but I am thinking about dad.

We gather outside the gallery, jumping and shivering to keep warm. Rob's going to Waterloo to take the Tube, she only lives by London Bridge, and Bianca says she'll walk down with her and get the 59 to Brixton. Cecile is meeting her husband at the Royal Festival Hall to hear a concert by a famous Japanese violinist.

'You all right?' she says, looking at me, concerned, her hair blowing about her in the wind.

'Course!' I say. But I feel overcome by an agony of leaving them.

'OK, see you then.'

I turn away, embarrassed by the intensity of my feeling, and wave at them without looking round, then almost run along the concrete walkways of the Hayward.

I just thought we would all walk across the footbridge together, by the thundering trains and see the river, in the dark, gliding beneath us towards St Paul's.

When I walk across the footbridge alone I feel desolate. I lean on the railing and look into the dark water. It looks like black oil. I can hear a far-away sound. It is beyond reach. I hear it with my ear that hears the colours. He is walking in the cold wet wind. He needs the cold and the wet to distract him from the scream within him.

Because the abyss has no edges.

He doesn't want to be alone with the moaning wind. There are others like him. I see them in the tunnels, their coats tied with string, and I speak into the dark river, 'It's not hopeless, dad, there's always hope. I love you, dad. Don't let it go black!'

But even when I've got home and cooked spaghetti and hung the washing on the squeaky pulley, and washed my hair in the basin, I can hear the voice of his despair, speaking in my blood.

19

And when I sleep it calls me in my dream.

It is an ugly light, the yellow light that lights up the black night and turns it brown. He is in the doorway of a filthy tunnel that smells of urine.

'This is where I belong,' he says. 'This is dark enough for me.'

'Help me!' he says to the dark bricks. 'Help me!' he cries out in a cracked voice, collapsing on to the wet pavement that reflects the lurid light.

It is not a cry but an animal that moans in him. The tunnel is still echoing his moan.

'I can't get free. I am trapped here, and I can't get free. Find me!' he cries, 'because I cannot find you. Find me!' he cries, in the voice of a child. 'I'm afraid!' And the night swoops around him, dripping, and he shuffles himself into the corner away from the water reflecting the yellow light. His feet are wet from the puddle, and he clutches his knees under his chin. Folded up, waiting, while he quivers and trembles from cold. He has reached a place of darkness. He has gone down a tunnel with wet walls and found the wind.

There is a feeling weighing down his shoulders and clenching his breath.

'Where is hope?' he cries out, but no sound comes out of his mouth because of the wind. First he hears it in his ears, like a roaring, and the roaring separates him from sound, and he is in a world of silence. The wind comes once more and he no longer feels the hard, the cold, the wet. It separates him from his senses and the world disappears. There is no smell of traffic wind that blew down the tunnel, or urine that stank from the walls. There is no lurid yellow light and no sound at all, except the wind receding into the distance. And he takes a long breath till all the air is gone.

Then, from far away, lying curled up like a baby, his hands between his legs, from above, looking down, he sees himself. 'Was that me?' he says, in a clear voice.

I wake up with a start and vaguely remember the dream.

'Dad?' I say to the bedroom. I want to go back to sleep to find him. I feel that he is free, like the sun breaking through cloud in rays of light, and something in me responds and shivers, shaking off its own darkness.

'Are you all right, dad?' I feel something light pass through my atoms in waves. It is strange.

20

'There was a bad frost last night!' says Bianca, pointing at the white camellias, their petals tipped with brown.

'It's confused all the flowers!' says Cecile.

Karl has sent us out to draw in the cemetery, the space under the trees. First we had to draw each other upside down in the studio, and Rob said, 'For fuck's sake, this is doing my head in!' and Bianca said, 'It's meant to.'

'Oh, why's that?'

'Because you don't need your head, you need your instinct!' said Bianca, mimicking Karl. That's when he sent us out to find a cemetery to make a space on the page.

'Why it has to be a cemetery, I don't know,' says Cecile. It was Bianca who chose Putney and we all clambered on to the number 11 and took it all the way to Putney Bridge.

The river is silver. The sky is pewter, and we go through the gates of the cemetery past the camellias and walk through the cemetery and between the yew trees that spread their branches over the gravestones and drop their needles over the graves. Crows fly about among the tall beech trees, cawing at each other and dancing from one branch to another. We sit down under the metallic sky.

For some reason I feel happy, touched by an inexplicable hope. Maybe dad is all right. Maybe, after all, dad is OK.

'It's gonna bloody rain,' says Rob.

'No, it won't, it won't,' says Bianca. 'Just sit like that. I want to draw a Madonna next to the tombstones.'

'Look, he just wants us to make a space, not a bloody icon!'

'No, but wait, like that! I like it, it's good, please, Rob.'

Rob huffs and puffs, and sits down on the bench and gives in with a shrug, and takes out her own sketchbook to draw the big yew tree, and the path emerging underneath it, and the church beyond it and the graveyard all around it, and I draw both of them; one sitting on a bench, one standing under the tree, looking up and down, intent on their drawings. We stay absorbed until Bianca closes her book, cricks her neck from side to side, and looks about her.

'What did you draw, Eve?' she says, coming under the birch trees to where I am standing in the flowerbed.

'I drew the two of you.'

'Oh, did you? Let me look!'

I open the page and show her the smudged charcoal figures and the trees and the black and white sky.

'Oh yes, I like it!'

'I don't think I better show mine to Rob,' says Bianca, laughing at the same time as speaking. She takes it out. 'It doesn't quite work,' she says, laughing again.

I look at the picture, at the short legs and big belly,

'Well, the proportions are a bit ...'

'I know, I know,' Bianca interrupts, 'but I wasn't measuring and you know I'm crap at drawing!'

'You always say that!'

Rob comes over, cautiously picking her way through the twigs.

'Time we were getting back,' says Bianca.

'No, wait! I want to see,' says Rob. 'Show me what you've done.'

But she doesn't like the picture.

'Never mind Madonna!' scowls Rob. 'Looks more like the hunchback of Notre bloody Dame.'

'Don't be offended!'

'I'm not offended!' says Rob, sounding more offended than usual.

We walk through the yew trees and between the stones to find Cecile, pale as a ghost, and chilled to the bone, who has been drawing bark.

'Trust you!' says Rob, looking at her drawings, while Cecile does a bouncing dance to keep warm.

We take the bus back in a hurry because Bianca has a tutorial with Terry.

21

'Why don't you just go and tell Miss Pym you want to change tutors?' says Rob when we're back in the studio.

'Can you? I mean, would she?' I say.

'Well, you can ask, can't you?' says Rob, mixing the sieved earth with an acrylic medium and setting to work on a new picture. 'Go on, she liked your blue painting, remember.'

Miss Pym likes turquoise. She always wears it, sometimes with white and black, sometimes with pink, but always there is turquoise, and when she passed our space one day and the blue painting was hanging on a nail, with the muslin curtain pulled back so I could see it from afar, she opened her arms wide at the blue river. 'Oh, I like that painting!' she said, and asked for the names of the colours. 'Phthalo turquoise and manganese blue, not cerulean, no, that's too opaque, but, yes, if I could afford it I'd try cobalt turquoise.'

I like Miss Pym. She has two selves. The top one is the efficient secretary that most people are quite scared of, including Paul, the head of painting. Everyone knows that Miss Pym runs the school. But the one she speaks under her breath is quite different; naughty and mischevious. To some she only shows her officious face, but the other one glimmers underneath. I like seeing it.

I knock on the door. She's sitting straight-backed at her desk with her arms leaning on either side of the open diary. She adjusts her spectacles.

'Yes, dear?'

She's in her efficient mood.

I clear my throat.

'Well, I was just enquiring if it was possible . . .'

'Yes, dear?' She looks up at me over her glasses.

'Can I change tutors?'

She looks down at the big diary and flicks to the back page. She puts it to one side and looks at her rota.

'Who do you have?'

'Sergei.'

She follows the names down.

'Yes, Sergei.' She is looking at the sheet.

'So . . .' she says, still looking at the rota. 'You don't like him . . .'

'Well,' I begin. 'It's just . . .'

'. . . either,' she says and gives a tiny laugh, then returns to her efficient look.

She purses her lips, following the list with her index finger.

'Andrew!' she says, and looks up and lifts her eyebrows up at me in a question.

'Fine!' I blurt. 'Absolutely! I mean is that it? Just that easy?' I say.

'Yes, dear . . . if I want it to be!' she says, breathing in, and looking at me. 'Now I've got work to do.'

So an hour later, when I'm called back, 'Hey, the secretary wants to see you!' I think it's because of Sergei, or maybe Andrew, and I wonder why she has arranged a chair for me sideways and placed the phone across her desk, so I can speak into it easily and not have to lean across, and I wonder why she hasn't got her efficient face, or even her mischevious face on, but instead a truly concerned look, and I ask, 'What is it?'

'The police, dear, they want to talk to you. they said you left them this number if there was any news.'

My heart starts to thump.

'Yes,' I say, and look out the window at the sky, breathing heavily and swallowing back my fear of the voice on the other end.

'We don't know,' the voice is saying, 'three older men. dead. may not be your father. identify. if possible. soon as possible.' May not be, may not be.

'It may not be,' I say to Miss Pym, handing the receiver over the desk, though the phone is near me.

'It may not be,' I say and smile weakly as I go out the door, then down the corridor to the studio where Rob is cleaning mud off her brushes.

'What is it?' she says, alarmed, and I wonder how she knows.

'It may not be,' I say, 'want me to identify . . .'

'I'll come with you,' she says, pulling her coat off the hook and throwing the rest of the brushes into the bucket so they plop into the water. I look at the surface of the water and the splashes on the floor

'Hadn't you better clean them? It'll ruin them, you know.'

So we slowly and carefully clean the brushes one by one.

When they are stacked together in the paint tin, Roberta says, 'All right then, are you ready?'

I must look scared because she says, 'It's all right, it's all right, I'll be with you,' and rubs my arm.

'Thank you, Rob, thank you.'

22

We are led into a room that smells of strange chemical smells like formaldehyde. There are white tiles on the wall, and silver edges. The floor is white, there is a trolley, and a white sheet covers a body. I know it is not my father from the shape under the sheet. It is too squat.

I am relieved, but there is another body under a sheet and she leads me towards the trolley. It was a cold night, cold that kills people.

Oh, dad. But it is not him; I can see from the belly that sticks up under the sheet, and the hair that is long and grey.

I turn away from the pale dead face, and then something strange happens: time slows down, it slows down so slowly that I can look carefully at every little crease and hair in the policewoman's face. I look at her mouth as it slowly forms the words, but I don't seem to be able to comprehend the meaning, because she slowly puts her hand in the small of my back to guide me, while her other hand gestures forwards, and opens the way.

I am filled with a strange sense of awe at the beauty of the world, and the humming sound of the air conditioning has many voices in it, singing in a low harmony, and when I look at the body under the white sheet on the third trolley, I know at once from the shape that it is dad.

I look at the white sheet, and in the long moment time seems to have wound down to a standstill, long enough for me to see clearly memories flowing past.

I see him holding up the crab, and bringing me my first yellow fishing net, I remember the rockpools like gardens of beautiful flowers, I remember the walks through the gorse when he held my hand, and lifted me up on his shoulders so that I saw, not only over the gorse that smelt of coconuts, but over the trees below, down over the rolling grass to the bay stretching out, with St Michael's Mount and the line of silver along the horizon. And tying ribbons to the twigs, and in his study that had a green light in the summer because of the plants that grew over the window and the sunlight shone through the leaves. And in winter with him in the big chair by the fire, and the orange flames that contained the mysterious city.

And then to my surprise part of me is clawing at the sheet, shouting, 'Dad, my dad!', wailing like an animal wails, tears pouring out my eyes, wrenching up from my belly, and I am collapsing forward on to the trolley, touching dad's cold body, and the policewoman is holding me, and pulling me away from the trolley, saying, 'It's all right,' and giving me something to hold, and I am sobbing over the body, and at the same time part of me is perfectly still in a gentle feeling, being held by my father's memory, not memory, his being, his invisible self. He is there, he is there, and it's all right. I can feel him, and at the very same time as this strange convulsion is racking my body, I am being held in the arms of my father's beautiful ghost; as though a door is open and two worlds are existing together that are quite different. And the world my father wraps me in has a singing light, and yet there is the hard floor reflecting the striplights and the metal tubes and the animal that is wailing a grief-stricken wail, but the two realities exist at once. And then the policewoman guides me into Roberta's arms, who is standing there. I want to tell her that it's all right, because she has tears in her eyes and strokes my hair. I want to say, 'It's all right, he's here! You can't believe how beautiful it is, how lovely it is to feel him here, and know he's all right, that he's with me. Can you hear the sound of the music in the air conditioning? Can you feel the ribbons of light that are flowing through this room? He's here, my father is here, and I can see memories,' but I can also see that the way I am behaving would make it hard for her to see that, because I am distraught.

Then another strange wave of reality comes. It is quiet; a kind of numbness. It is as though I can see it all, but I'm not really feeling it, and I am calm and it's different. I dry my eyes. I say, 'I'm all right, Rob, thank you for being here.' I turn to the policewoman and ask her what needs to be done, what is the procedure, I even use that word 'procedure', and she says 'this way,' and we all file out of the humming room, and along a corridor with yellowed peeling paint and through a door, and there is a table and file trays and plastic chairs and my mind is lucid but only for the black print on the forms. I remember every detail that I need to: postcodes and dates of birth, names and addresses and doctors. It's amazing. They all pop up in my mind, and

I am going through these strange motions with abso-
lute efficiency.

When it's all done Roberta says, 'I'll take you home,'
and she puts her arm round me and walks with me out
of the building.

Part Three

1

I am relieved after the clamour of Paddington, the echoing voices, the rushing people and flicking stations, to lean
my head against the cool window and surrender myself
to the rhythm of the train. I don't have to do anything
but sit here for six hours. I can just breathe and be held in
the rocking motion and let the jittering strangeness of the
last few days move through me. It is dark outside, and the
people around me look quivering and pallid in the electric light that reflects us in the windows. I close my eyes.

I think of Zeb in Barcelona, sitting at a café in a narrow
street with orange walls among a crowd of smiling people,
and think maybe he will forget all about me.

I walked up the stairs to his studio when I came back
with Rob from the police station. She said to stay with
her and Mick that night but I had to get my things. I don't
even know what things. I felt like my body was made
of lots of bits and pieces that didn't fit together. When I
walked up the stairs I'd gone straight to the mezzanine
because I wanted Zeb. I wanted Zeb so badly but he
wasn't there. I wanted to hold on to his big body, I wanted
him to stand there like a tree. But the door was locked,
so I couldn't even roll up his old paint-spattered shirt
and hold on to it, I could only lean my head against the
door and smell the inky smell of the keyhole then lift one

foot after the other up the stairs. I'd known fine well he wouldn't be there. The second-years had been gone days. But I still went there imagining he might be. Just shows how daft you can get.

I open my eyes. A little girl is crying. She reaches up to her mother, who lifts her on to her lap and strokes her hair. The little girl is flushed and tired and her mother soothes her. She curls up and puts her thumb in her mouth and her eyes flicker up and down, up and down.

I look out the window into the dark. We are in the countryside now, passing fields and hedges. The trees are black against the dark blue sky.

I'm so glad they came with me. I don't think I could have done it alone.

They must have met outside the lift where Rob was waiting for me, because when I came back downstairs Cecile was there too, and had been to fetch the jam jar for the flowers. She even brought candles.

It was Roberta who had asked in the police station where exactly it was they found him. That was one thing I didn't have the presence of mind to ask. I think Rob is right about the river; because I closed my eyes when I threw the flowers in, and my mind saw a river of light, even though it was raining.

We caught the bus there, and bought the flowers from the woman at the top of the Tube steps. I picked the free-sias out of the bucket. And we'd walked along the street by the river. It was a cold misty damp day and everything was dripping. There was no one there. It seemed like a miserable little alcove; a stone corridor leading to some steps. There was a piece of red and white tape lying on the paving stones, maybe the police had left it behind and I thought of dad there all curled up, and held him in my mind. We put the flowers in the jam jar and lit the candles and Cecile told us a Buddhist chant and the sound echoed off the walls. She said it would make it peaceful for him, and with the songs and the flowers and the flickering candles, I think it did. Rob said it was good it was by the river, because it was a holy river and it would take him home. We walked down to the riverside and I threw in some of the flowers and they floated along on the surface of the water to St Paul's.

And I was certain I could feel him with me; that feeling of being enfolded in something warm. He must have known we were trying to help the part of him that might get left behind, confused.

But I don't have that feeling now. I feel alone. Oh dad, I whisper to the cold window, now it's me who's left behind, confused.

When the train pulls into Penzance I step out on to the chilly platform and smell the sea air. I walk into the cold wind outside the station.

Magda is there, waiting.

She takes my bags, wraps me in a blanket, and puts me in the car. The red and black tartan blanket smells of cows. Straw and cows. We drive up the lanes and through the trees to her farmhouse on the hill.

Some people might say it was a coincidence she phoned when she did. I think it was a miracle.

She was so glad to get the letter from me, she said, and she was so sad to hear what I had to tell her. I could hear her sigh down the telephone, a long sad sigh.

When I get out of the car into the wind it's pitch black and I smell the slurry.

'There now,' says Magda. 'In you come.'

She sits me down in front of the woodstove, and it reminds me of being little, when I'd come into Magda's kitchen with my teeth chattering and she'd wrap me in a blanket so my arms were trapped and put me in front of the woodstove with the door open, and by the time she brought me hot chocolate I'd be warm enough to unwrap my arms. And that's what she does. She goes over to the stove and makes me hot chocolate.

'Thanks, Magda!' I say, taking the steaming cup from her.

'There now!' she says, and sits down beside me and pokes the fire so the flames flare up and sparks fly up the flue.

2

The day of the funeral is quiet and still. One of those days when you can hear the sea lapping at the bottom of the cliffs, and the sky is clear and the hills are lit up with sunlight.

I sit by the coffin in the cold dark and look at the twisted ropes that loop around the brass handles while the vicar, with his eyes closed, murmurs prayers.

I think of my dad lying inside it. I was surprised when I touched his forehead. Surprised by the cold. Magda waited outside the undertaker's when I walked up the long narrow room with dad laid out at the end next to an urn of false flowers, and when I leaned to kiss his forehead it was cold. Cold as marble.

The vicar is saying, 'He's at peace now,' and everyone is standing up. The sound of the organ fills the stone church. Magda looks awkward in her black dress, and we sing a hymn with words about finding rest, and peace at last, and I walk behind the coffin in a kind of trance and out the door into the light. I breathe in the scent of the flowers and feel like dad is holding me, as though I'm swathed in something soft. My mother's grave has been opened up for dad's coffin to be lowered into, and I realize his pain is over, the longing he always felt for her is finished, and I throw in a handful of earth that drums on the lid. I close my eyes and hear the skylarks and see the river of light.

Some people shake my hand and look solemn but I can't seem to focus my eyes properly. Magda says, 'Sit down on the wall.' I tell her, 'No, I'm all right, really, Magda, I'm OK.' But I can't get in the car, and have to walk along the cliffs with the waves crashing below and listen to the seagulls crying over the sea.

And as I walk along the narrow path through the tall yellow gorse I think, 'I'm glad it's over for you, dad.'

3

But for me, it isn't over.

In the next few weeks my thoughts don't fit together, and I walk around Magda's kitchen and the farmyard, trying to piece together my broken mind.

I felt it splinter apart when I walked into dad's cottage and saw the chaos of broken plates, empty bottles, piles of dirty clothes mixed up with books and letters and unpaid bills; and in the study, the stacks of paper that would never become a book.

I sit at the kitchen table feeling dislocated and unreal and no matter where I look I can't seem to find myself. There is an empty place where the colours used to be, and I look at the white page of my drawing book and the blankness says, 'There's no point to anything.'

I see puddles in the muddy farmyard that turn into faces and their eyes have the sky in them.

I go for a walk in the woods and put every feather I find in my hair so when I get back to the farm, my hair is so tangled and twisted into fifteen feathers that Magda has to cut them out.

I can't sleep at night and every morning I hear Magda crunch across the gravel under the window before it's light, on her way to milk the cows.

'Am I going mad, d'you think, Magda?'

'No, you're just exhausted. It'll work itself out,' she says, and sure enough I fall ill with a fever and feel like I am fighting a battle in my dreams.

I open my eyes a tiny crack and see a piece of light.

Where am I? I open them and see the window. Or is it a picture?

There is St Michael's Mount a long way away.

I reach out my hand to touch it. Maybe it's a picture. I lean back on the pillows and close my eyes.

I see dad's face under the sheet and the trellis of stories he wove across the room.

'There's his study to clear,' I say with a shock, 'and his face is so cold and so are his hands.'

Images keep swimming away from me like fish.

'Have a spoonful of soup,' says Magda's voice.

I feel sweat, clammy over my body and dripping down my neck, and a liquid heat behind my eyes.

'Did we bury him, Magda?'

'Yes, love.'

'Why's my hair short?'

'I had to cut the feathers out . . . Just a spoonful. It'll do you good.'

'I have to clear the cottage, Magda.'

I see the mess of broken crockery and the empty bottles on the floor.

'We've nearly finished it, Eve. I'll give you another pillow, then you can sit up.'

But I push her hand away. The sea of images crashes over me like waves; buildings that implode inwards, splintering bottles, dirty clothes, dark tunnels lit by yellow light. I am pressed down by the weight of the sea.

I want to tell her, underneath all this, deep down, there is a little sound. It is my sound, but I have to be quiet to hear it.

Then one morning I wake up and look out the window and see the sun rising behind the Mount, and the sea is pale yellow and turquoise and glows as though the sea itself is the source of light, and I lie in bed listening to the sound of the birds, and my mind is calm, pale blue and still.

4

'My God, Evie, it's been weeks! How are you? How have you been? I want to hear everything!'

'Oh, Cecile, it's so lovely to hear your voice!'

'We didn't know how to get hold of you, even Miss Pym didn't know. The number we had for you didn't work.'

'The phone was cut off, I know.'

'At your father's place?'

'Yes.'

'Where are you, then?'

'I'm at Magda's, she's got a new phone now.'

'Are you OK, Eve?'

'Magda's been amazing, Ces, I don't know what I'd have done without her. She helped with everything.'

'But are you OK, Eve?'

'Yes, well now I am. Think I went mad, Ces.'

'I'm not surprised. You've been through it, Eve. It was hard all that time he was lost, never mind the shock at the police station.'

'I know.'

'Was it OK, the funeral?'

'Yes. He's buried with my mum. It was quiet, you know.'

'How did you feel?'

'Dazed, really. But like he was there with me. It was afterwards.'

'What happened afterwards?'

'Oh Ces, d'you really want to hear all this?'

'Course I do, Eve! I'm your friend! I want to know what you've been through!'

I smile at her down the telephone.

'Well, it was after the funeral, really. I went to his cottage with Magda. Oh Cecile, it was a shambles, stuff everywhere. We took all the rubbish to the tip and loads of stuff to the charity shop, and Mr Tremethick's.'

'Who's he?'

'He's got the second-hand shop in town. He took most of the furniture.'

'D'you mean you had to clear out the house?'

'Yes, it's going back to the landlord.'

'Oh, I see.'

'Not till the end of the month.'

'Evie, listen, that in itself. Your whole childhood, everything going.'

'I know, I know, but it wasn't really that, it was when I went into the study. Oh Ces! I could just feel his despair. It went right through me. I couldn't breathe. The pain of it was horrible. I felt it somehow. Felt how he felt. All the pages of the book he'd never finish all scattered everywhere. I just couldn't think straight after that.'

'Look, Eve, it was pretty heavy what he was feeling, it's bound to leave an atmosphere, but he's free of it now.'

'I think he had lots of stories in him, Cecile.'

'I'm sure he did.'

'But I don't know, he got stuck somehow, then he just went down and down. I thought I had to find out why. Now I realize, I just have to know not to do that.'

'Well, it's good you know you don't have to follow him down there.'

'D'you know, Ces, I think that's what I've always done. Part of me got lost along with him.'

'And now?'

'And now I don't have to.'

'Well, thank goodness for that!'

'I think I'm free now, Ces.'

'Evie, I'm so glad.'

'I think he's been helping me somehow. I mean just knowing . . .'

'What?'

'I can't say it, it sounds daft.'

'Well, say it quickly.'

'There are two realities, Cecile, and one of them's invisible.'

'I know,' she says.

A silence falls between us.

'We went back down to the river, you know, Eve, and took flowers, me and Rob.'

'Oh thanks, Cecile, thanks so much.'

I look out the window and down over the fields to the bay and the Mount shrouded by mist, and the Lizard beyond, only just visible along the horizon of the sea.

'So where are you now? I want to imagine you.'

'Sitting by the window at the kitchen table, next to the stove.'

'Sounds nice and warm. What can you see out the window?'

'One looks on to the farmyard,' I say, looking out the rain-spattered window.

'Yes?'

'The barn, the big blue door to the cowshed.'

'What's the weather like?'

'Wet.'

'And the other one?'

'Down over the fields to Mount's Bay.'

'The sea? Can you see the sea?'

'Only just. There's mist today. But I can see it. Then in the far distance, there's the Lizard.'

'What colour is it?'

'Grey.'

'Have you been painting it, Evie?'

'I can't, somehow. Everything's gone blank.'

'Well, maybe it has to do that for a bit. But it'll be back, Evie.'

'How's your work going, Cecile?'

'Well, I like it. I've got into green. Everything's green. But the terrible tutors are just the same.'

'Oh no, how?'

'Honestly, I don't know. They all troop in and stand in front of the pictures and something in me just curls up and runs away. They don't even have to say anything.'

'Yes, I know the feeling.'

'But you stood up to Sergei.'

'Sort of, I was at the end of my tether, more like. It's funny, I can't really remember now. It seems like another life.'

'Well, it's like that, isn't it, when you've been through stuff. Eve, have you got friends down there?'

'Not any more. They've all moved upcountry now.'

'That's a shame.'

'What have you been doing today, Ces?'

'We were drawing with Karl.'

'Three-second poses?'

Cecile laughs. 'No, they're five minutes now.'

I feel a pang, remembering the classes, remembering charcoal and rubbers and dust and the struggle to put the model on the page.

'Will you say hello to the other two?'

'Yes.'

'And tell Miss Pym I'll be back soon.'

'Yes.'

'Otherwise they might throw me out.'

'Not with Miss Pym in charge.'

'Oh Ces, I'm so glad you're there.'

'Yes, I'm here, Evie, and I'm so glad you're there too. But I'd prefer you here.'

'I'm coming back.'

'Well, come back soon. Karl says he's going to get a shed in Regent's Park to store the materials, and do a painting project in the park now the weather's getting warmer. You have to be back for that, Eve, all the flowers will be coming out.'

'Oh Cecile, it sounds lovely.'

'Yes and we can have picnics, you know. It'll be fun. I miss you, Evie!'

'I miss you too, Ces.'

'Evie?'

'Yes?'

'I think you should burn all those papers. He doesn't need them now. It might set him free too, you know. Build a bonfire and burn them, Evie.'

'Yes, I will, Ces, I think you're right.'
'And give your sketchbook a chance.'
'OK, OK.'
Cecile laughs. 'See you soon.'

When I put the phone down, I take out my sketchbook to
face the blank page, but when I look at the white, I see the
white sky and the line of the horizon barely visible, and
the Lizard pale blue in the far distance along the horizon
of the sea. And within a few strokes the blank page has
turned into the sea, the sky and the far-away land.

5

The sack of potatoes is in the shed by the back door. The potatoes are muddy, and as I pick them out, the grit gets under my nails. I put them in the colander one by one. The sack is nearly empty and the potatoes have begun to sprout. I take them into the kitchen and wash them in the big square sink under the window.

I can still smell the smoke in my hair.

I did what Cecile told me, and burned the papers. I sat by the bonfire and fed the pages into the flames one by one, and watched them licked and swallowed by the fire, and the smoke coiled and billowed round me. All except a slip of paper that was whipped out my hand by the wind. It flew into my face so I caught it against my cheek. I want to keep it to show Cecile; it's a quote from William Blake.

I peel the potatoes slowly and plop them in a pan of cold water.

It was written in dad's handwriting so I felt like he was saying it to me.

'Everything in the Universe is lit by its own inner light,' and I folded it up and put it in my pocket. I look out the window into the farmyard and see Magda coming through the blue door in the corrugated iron barn that glows in the evening sunlight against the dark grey sky.

She opens the back door, bringing a blast of cold air into the room that makes the flames flicker in the stove.

'Well now,' she, says taking off her coat, 'there's quite a wind!'

She goes to the fridge and takes out the package of fish she bought from the fish van.

'All ready for tomorrow, then?' she says.

I dry my hands and lean on the kitchen table and watch her unwrapping the fish.

'I think so, Magda.'

'Come now, you can help me,' she says, lifting down the big black pan.

I place the pieces of fish in the pan; the white flesh is bluish, the skin is striped silver.

I spread them with butter and Magda pours the milk over. She lights the gas and lifts the pan on to the stove. The butter melts into yellow puddles in the milk, and simmers gently.

'It'll be a different place without you, Eve.'

I look up at her, but she is busy weighing out the butter.

'Now get the flour down for me, love.'

I take it off the shelf and weigh out two ounces.

'So you'll be going straight to your little flat?' she says.

'Yes,' I say. 'My friend Bianca's cousin has been staying there.'

'Well now, that's good.'

Magda puts the weighed-out butter into a smaller pan to melt and hands me the wooden spoon.

'There now, love. Mix the flour in and mix it so that it's smooth.'

I pour the flour into the hot yellow liquid and stir. The mixture smoothes into a paste and begins to change texture.

Magda pours the milk off the fish into a jug and hands it to me.

'Now you can add the milk the fish cooked in,' she says, 'but slowly, so it doesn't go lumpy.'

I stir the sauce round and round, adding the milk slowly and it thickens, turning smooth and yellow.

'And she'll still be there, will she?'

'No, Bianca said she'll be gone by tomorrow.'

'So you'll be on your own.'

'Not for long. I'll see them when I go in to college.'

Magda is carefully removing the cooked white flakes of fish from their silver skins.

'She's a good friend then, Bianca.'

'Yes, she is.'

'Well, that's good. You need people to help and that's that. I don't want you to feel alone.'

'I don't. And I can talk to you now,' I say, nodding at the new phone.

She smiles. 'I'll do for some things,' she says 'but you need your friends.'

'I'll get the parsley,' I say and go outside into the wind and pick it out of the stone basin at the back door where it grows along with the chives.

Back in the warmth, Magda is mashing the potatoes. Mashing and smashing and whipping them round. I wash the parsley and chop it small.

'Oh, wait now,' says Magda looking up. 'While I remember, I dug it out for you.'

'What?'

'Open the drawer, Evie, it's in there.'

I open the drawer and see a little black and white photo with a white rim all the way round.

'This?' I say, lifting it out.

'Yes.'

My dad is in the middle, squinting at the camera, holding my mother's hand. My mother has her hair up, with a far-away look in her eyes.

'She looks so young,' I say, looking closely.

On the other side of dad, a young Magda is holding me in her arms. The wind is blowing her hair across her face.

'Can I keep it?'

'Course you can,' says Magda.

I can feel something in me, something deep down, but I don't know what it is until it comes out of my mouth in a question.

'Magda?' I say, taking a deep breath.

'Yes,' she says.

'D'you think she didn't like me?'

She stops mashing and looks at me, and for a few seconds she is perfectly still.

Then she continues stirring the potatoes but more slowly.

'Your mother, you mean?'

I nod.

'She was just too young, love. She didn't know what to do with a little thing like you. That's all. But she loved you in her own way.'

I mix the parsley and the fish into the sauce and pour it into the square brown dish.

'That's all,' she says again, as she spreads the potatoes over the top and forks them into a pattern.

'There now,' she says as she puts the fish pie into the oven and closes the door. 'All we need now are the peas.'

I look out the window at the bay. The Mount is obscured. There is a dark cloud over the sea and the sun turns out like a light.

Magda looks up. 'Oh, my washing!'

'D'you want me to bring it in, Magda?'

'That rain'll be here any second, would you, love,' she says looking out the window at the Bay.

I take the basket from outside the back door, grey wicker from being left out in the rain, and walk to the washing line with the wind blowing against me. I pull the big stick down that keeps the line propped up, and take the washing off the pegs as quickly as I can. The wind is pulling the sheets out horizontally and billowing them so they're hard to get hold of, and I grapple with them.

Magda comes out the kitchen door.

'I'm going to give you a hand with this!' she shouts, because the wind is so loud. 'Didn't realize it was so bad.'

We pull the washing off the line and bundle up the linen, there's no time to fold it, and the sky breaks just as we've pulled the last one off the line. We run, crouching, into the house, being beaten by the rain and the wind.

'Thank goodness for that!' says Magda, wiping away a wet curl from her forehead. 'That washing would have been all down the valley if we hadn't got it in!'

She builds a fire in the big stove in the kitchen and we fold up the sheets between us.

6

We stand under the televisions waiting for the yellow writing to say Paddington. It is cold inside the station and I am jumping up and down to keep warm. When it says One, we walk through the gates, along the platform, into the wind. The train slides in and we look for my carriage and stand together at the open door.

'Oh, Magda, what would I have done without you?'

'I don't know at all,' she says and smiles. 'Now don't be a stranger!'

'No,' I say, 'I'll ring you.'

'Well, if you feel like it. I just want you to know there's always a place for you here.'

'Thanks, Magda.'

I climb into the carriage and open the window and lean out.

'Magda? You know with dad?'

'Yes, love?'

'What was the argument about?'

'What?'

'With dad. Why did you argue?'

'It was over the drink.'

'Really?'

'I told him he couldn't set foot in the house if he was drunk, and I meant it.'

She looks away and sighs, then looks up at me.

'But I never meant you,' she says, and pats my hand.

'Oh, Magda, I didn't know.'

'Ah, I thought you maybe thought I was interfering.'

'No. I was a stupid teenager. I took dad's side. But really all that time, my God, I wish I'd known.'

'Ah well, what's done is done.'

She nods and pats my hand again, and the train begins to judder and make moving noises.

'Now you take good care of yourself!' she says, and takes a few steps with the train, and I lean out the window and wave and watch her get smaller, and the train curves away from the platform, until I am sitting next to the Bay and I watch as the sea turns grey under the clouds, and the Mount slips behind the marshes at Marazion. I roll up my jersey and lay my head against the window and close my eyes and see Magda standing on the platform, waving, and imagine her getting in her car and driving back up the hill to the kitchen and the warm stove and the cowshed full of cows. And I imagine dad's empty house that I know I'll never go back to.

When I'd finished burning all the pieces of paper I'd walked back down the corridor to the study. There was only the green sofa and the desk left in the empty room, and I'd lain down on the sofa like I used to. The room had felt quiet then, and peaceful, and I'd remembered the trellis of stories dad had woven across the room when I was small. In and out of the dark alleys, along the river, and under the arches of the mysterious city, while I snuggled up beside him and listened, and the wind blew outside and the rain hit the window. We'd travelled backwards and forwards in time through golden coronations and music that echoed off the water, yellow fog and griffins with red eyes, and I'd seen the riots and the blue cockades. I'd seen the cherubs on the ceiling before the crowd fell silent, and the pigeons dropping out of the sky when the city caught alight.

And as I move through the evening towards London I sink into sleep to the rhythm of the train, remembering the stories that once flowed through him.

Part Four

1

It was strange coming up the stairs to the same hole in the carpet, the same chips in the paint, and letting myself into the flat.

Bianca's cousin had left a vase of red tulips on the kitchen table, and milk in the fridge. I had to turn the lights out and sit in the dark for a while and watch the car-lights from the street whizz round the walls. I didn't want to close the curtains and sit in the dark. I just wanted to feel what it was like being back in the city.

Feels like I feel everything, and I don't know what to do about that.

But when I got under the covers and lay in bed with the curtains still open, I felt glad about being back; glad of the honking sounds and the twinkling lights and the constant hum, glad of something else too; the feeling of hope, of possibilities that London exudes.

I didn't feel it when I got up, though. I felt that naked feeling again, and I biked along the side streets to avoid the vehicles with big wheels.

When I've chained up my bike, I walk across the quadrangle into the building. I smile at Stan, who raises his black eyebrows and nods at me. I walk straight into Cecile's studio, past a boy halfway up a ladder, painting an orange stripe on to his canvas with a wallpaper brush.

The music is blaring as usual and Cecile is sitting in the corner under a big green painting of tendrils and spiral patterns.

She is drawing a green labyrinth, and looks up.

'Evie! Oh, Evie, welcome back!' she says, getting up and giving me a hug. 'Sit down,' she says, pulling a stool out from behind the partition. 'How are you? How do you feel?'

'Like I've been all the way to the middle and fallen apart,' I say, looking at the green labyrinth.

'Well, now you can come back out again,' she says, 'and you'll be brand new!'

'I hope so, Cecile. Anyway, how are you doing? I like this green painting,' I say, standing up to look at the picture. 'Green is brave!'

'I'm discovering just how!' says Cecile, standing up and looking at it with me.

'On a good day I think, leaves, chlorophyll, on a not-so-good day I think pea soup, but on a bad day I think, well, mould!'

I laugh. 'That's the danger of green!'

'Yes, and everyone knew that except me!' she says, and laughs too.

'Oh, Cecile, it's lovely to see you.'

'You too! So what about the painting?'

'I'm in a muddle, Ces, I don't even know if I want to paint any more.'

'Well, I wonder that most days!' she says, and smiles. 'You'll be all right. You've fallen apart, and now you're a little shoot growing out of the rubble. Just take one step at a time.'

'I'm scared to go upstairs and even look at the half-finished pictures.'

'They'll be in the storeroom. I'll come with you,' she says.

So we take the lift up to the storeroom and collect my canvases and a bag of materials and I don't even look at the old paintings, or the half-finished paintings tied up with string.

'Thanks, Cecile,' I say when I walk out of the lift. She waves at me through the sliding doors. 'See you at coffee time,' she says as the doors close.

When I walk into the studio that I share with Rob there is a blanket over the window and one has been pinned over the skylight so the studio is dark but for candles, which flicker in jam jars on the floor. They light up the huge mud women that have been taped to every wall.

Their presence fills the studio with stillness and the smell of baked earth. I close my eyes in the flickering darkness, and wonder how Rob opened a doorway into another time.

I hear Rob walk in behind me. I open my eyes and turn round.

'Evie, you're back!' she says and hugs me. Her belly has grown big.

'How are you?'

'I'm OK,' I say.

'I'll take the blankets down I just wanted to see how they looked.'

'They're wonderful, Rob.'

We look at the figures in silence for a minute.

'Have you shown them to anyone?'

'Oh, I tried to get Tom to see the point of them but he just talked about the fire hazard. I want them to be like a cave wall, you know. Like you're deep down in the earth.'

We take the blanket off the window and fold it up, and

I stand on a stool and pull the pins out of the skylight so the other blanket falls down on me. I pull it off and light pours down into the space.

Rob looks up at me.

'You OK, Eve?'

'I feel a bit strange, Rob.'

'You're bound to.'

She untapes the paper so it rolls upwards.

'So the mud didn't crack?' I say.

'No, it's a good medium. It's holding it together, anyway. I'm glad you're back,' she says.

'Me too,' I say, and jump off the stool.

'Oh, I nearly forgot,' she says. I've got something to give you. Zeb left it for you when he went to Barcelona. It's in my locker. We didn't know where to send it.'

My heart beats. 'Have you heard from him? Is he coming back soon?'

'Yes, Mick knows when he's back, it's not long.'

'Really? Has he got friends out there, d'you think?'

Rob shrugs. 'Don't know.'

I follow Rob out on to the landing. She opens the locker and hands me the packet, and goes back in the studio. It has 'Evie, love Zeb' written on it in black marker, and I say his name Zeb, Zeb, Zeb, under my breath. I open it and pull out a box.

It is a big matchbox with a miniature battery attached to the base. I push it open and inside is a small tree made of gold wire, and on every branch is a tiny coloured bird, that lights up when the box slides open, and each one glows a different colour and I look at it under my jersey to see it glow in the dark.

*   *   *

When I walk into Bianca's studio at coffee time she gives a shrill cry and runs towards me with her arms out and kisses me twice on both cheeks.

'Evie, you look too thin! Almost as thin as me! You must come to Brixton and eat something!'

London spreads out under the white sky. There is a faint green mist over the trees. The new leaves are beginning to unfurl.

'I eat, Bianca. I do eat!'

I sit on the windowsill above the radiator and look around the room.

The work has grown larger. And sometimes a glinting person, just the shape, no features, shines from a corner, or a turquoise figure glows in the foreground on a background of gold.

Bianca sits on the chaise longue and crosses her legs. She is wearing floppy orange trousers. She hands me small boxes. 'These are just ideas for bigger ones,' she says, and I open their lids. Inside are strips of metallic paper and squares of ultramarine, green or rose, each like a doorway opening into a shrine.

'They're beautiful,' I say. 'I like them small.'

Bianca shrugs. 'Yes, maybe.'

I show her what Zeb left for me, and she slides it open and looks at it with her mouth open at the same time as smiling, because it is enchanting her.

'Ah!' she says and covers her head with a sheet so she can see it in the darkness like I did.

She is sitting with her head under the paint-spattered sheet saying, 'Bastard! Ingenious!' when Rob and Cecile walk in.

They laugh and want to know what she's looking at. So

we all get under the sheet and the coloured birds light up our faces in the semi-darkness.

'How is it, then, Evie, are you glad to be back?' says Bianca, pulling the sheet off us, her long hair gone electric and sticking to the sheet.

'I am feeling a bit weird.'

'Don't worry, we'll look after you,' says Cecile.

'Yes, we don't mind if you're weird.'

'Rob's always weird anyway.'

'Thanks,' says Rob.

'I'm glad to be back with you lot, that's for sure.'

'Me too!' says Cecile. 'Now I'm not the only one being referee!' and she points at the others with her eyes, and looks up at the ceiling.

'You know what we should do after coffee!' says Rob.

'What?'

'Stephanie's going to show a few of the first-year print-makers how to make pinhole cameras. She told me I could come if I want. There'd be space. We could always make one between us.'

'Yes, let's.'

So after coffee we walk down the stairs to the print room and sit at the high table looking over St Stephen's, and measure cardboard to the right measurement, paint it black inside when we've constructed the box, and pierce it in exactly the right place so when the light penetrates, it hits the photographic paper at the right angle to make an upside-down imprint. We make two cameras between us.

Stephanie hands out the photographic paper and sends us out to the sculpture yard to take photographs, and we pose for each other, trying to stay still for eight minutes, to take a clear picture, or move slowly, so an image is captured moving across the paper like a ghost.

We sit on the wall of the sculpture yard in the full light, in the shed in the dim light, and half-in and half-out, so the light is bright and the shadows are dark; then go upstairs and squash together in the tiny dark room to expose the pictures.

'Ces said you need a job, Evie,' says Bianca. Her lips are the same colour as her face in the red light.

'Yes, I do,' I say.

We stand in the corner, while the other two lean over the chemical baths and watch the photographic paper reveal its images. We are taking it in turns to drop the white glossy paper into the liquid. The chemical smell gets up our nostrils and stings them. Then we lift it out by the corner and hang it on the line to dry in a row.

'I've got some grant money left,' I say.

'Won't last long,' says Rob, looking up from the baths.

'I know,' I say, but I don't want to talk about it any more in this squashed space filled with chemical smells that make it hard to breathe.

'I'll ask Susie,' says Bianca. 'They often need people to waitress.'

'Thanks, Bianca.'

'Oh wow! Look at this one!' says Cecile, turning round. Even in this light you can see Cecile's lips are red.

'It's all four of us,' she says, picking it out of the bath with the tongs and hanging it on the line.

'It's nice!' and we look at ourselves in a row, staring out of the sculpture shed between sacks of plaster and a heap of wrought iron.

*   *   *

I lie awake. The curtains are open and the street light shines in. I listen to the cars passing and the sound of people walking along the street. The girl upstairs begins playing the violin and the music is gentle and sad.

'Dad?' I say, 'are you there? Are you there, dad?'

But I can't feel his presence, only his absence, and I look out the window at the night and feel a hollow feeling with no tears in it.

2

The window is open and I can hear the pigeons roo-cooing from the plane tree. Safi touches her fingers together and places them in front of her lips. They are long brown fingers and they make a pattern in front of her mouth. She is wearing a turquoise and gold sari. The gold is stitched into brown.

'It all seems too hard, that's all.'

'You've had a lot to deal with, Eve.'

'It's like the world is too much; it all seems too harsh, too noisy.'

'You are feeling vulnerable. It's only natural. You are grieving, Eve.'

'But there are so many other things to think about, I have to get a job for a start.'

'I'm sure you will find something.'

'Well, Bianca says she might know of one.'

'That's good, Eve.'

'But it's not even that, Safi.'

'What is it then, Eve?'

'Nothing makes sense. It just seems pointless.'

'What does?'

'Everything.'

'That's because you are tired. You will heal. Give it time.'

'I don't even know if I want to paint.'

'It won't be like this for ever.'

'Safi, I wish you'd tell me something.'

'What do you wish I would tell you, Eve?'

'I wish you'd tell me something beautiful, that would make it all make sense. It's just everything's gone blank.'

'That feeling is part of the grieving process, Eve.'

'What am I supposed to do? Just wait?'

'Trust in the process. Give it time. Don't expect too much of yourself, Eve. You will find your way.'

I look at the gold patterns on Safi's sari.

Then I look out the window at the plane tree and watch the breeze blowing through the newly unfurled leaves.

But I can't see the pictures when you speak, Safi, and the colours don't sing any more.

3

I sit in the studio in front of the white canvas. I feel afraid. The empty space blows a wind through me. It feels impossible to begin when my imprint is so faint I might disappear into the colours.

After the photos had dried, Cecile brought them upstairs and I was shocked when I looked at myself because it was a picture of how I was feeling; as though I had lost my edges; become insubstantial and see-through.

In one I could see the wood pile through me.

'What is that? It's spooky,' I said to Rob.

'It's because you moved,' Rob said. 'It's a very slow exposure.'

'But look, Bianca moved all the time and she comes out really distinct.'

'Well, don't move.'

'I told you I didn't move.'

'You must have,' she said.

'But I didn't.'

Behind the muslin curtain dotted with blue paint, I can hear Rob swearing under her breath. I look round and see her using her back and her splayed arms to unroll the big drawings on to the wall, but the corners keep rolling up. I stand up and go through the curtain.

'You daft idiot! Let me help you.'

'I can do it!' she says, staple-gunning the corner behind her head.

'Well, it's easier with two.'

We unroll the paper and staple the bottom corners and I look up at the new drawings. The figures are drawn in blue and their bodies are covered in pictures.

'Rob, they're great.'

'I think they're the Picts,' she says, wiping her hair away from her damp forehead, and a little out of breath. 'They were covered in blue tattoos.'

She unrolls the other two and staples them to the wall and the studio dances with the new figures.

'How's it going through there?' She inclines her head to my space.

I sigh. 'Don't know. I think I've lost my imagination.'

'Nonsense!' she says. 'Just have some fun!'

I shrug.

'Hey, I know what you need,' she says, squatting down on the floor. 'I got them in the market as an experiment.'

She empties everything out of her string bag and gives up squatting and sits down against the wall with her legs out.

'You're going to have to help me up, you know!'

'What are you looking for?'

'These!' she says, holding up a handful of triangular packets.

'What are they?'

'It's henna. You know, for drawing on your skin.'

'Where did you get it?'

'Southwark. Shall we try them? Look, you just tear the top off, it's like icing a cake.'

She hands one to me with the top torn off.

'What? Now, Rob? You mean ... oh look, it's coming out, I can't stop it!'

The henna is oozing out of the hole at a tremendous rate, and already making wiggles on the floor.

Rob sits down, lifts her skirt over her knees, and kicks her shoes off.

'Well, I didn't really mean now, but I didn't realize it was going to do that.'

You have to draw quickly at the speed it comes out the packet. I draw a climbing plant with tendrils, which wind round her calf and blossom at her knee, with leaves that turn into eyes, and faces that smile from the leaves.

'See! You haven't lost it!'

When the packet is finished I roll up my trousers and Roberta paints landscapes on my legs, the moon on my knee, and plants sprouting from my pores. She gets so carried away I let her do my hands and then my arms, which sprout wings, and birds singing, and animals, and people with the bodies of birds, and birds with the bodies of lions. We go to the bathroom to stick our limbs in the sink, and Rob has to stand still while I do her legs, and we wash off the earthy-smelling worms of henna, and the drawings are left behind in sepia, glowing from our skin.

'Let's go and show Bianca!' And we walk upstairs to the abstract floor.

Bianca wants to be decorated too, so she lies down on the floor of her studio, with her legs and arms stretched like a star and we kneel down on either side of her, an arm and leg each and continue our pictorial flow, while Bianca moans and sighs, 'Oh, this is ecstatic! Let's do this every week, I feel as if I am being transported,' and we laugh and tell her to be quiet, we're concentrating. Don't make us laugh, it makes the line wiggle.

We have become proficient and Bianca's decoration is a masterpiece of twirls and furls and laughing faces.

'My God, I am a walking mythology!' says Bianca, delighted, as she prances about after washing off the henna, with her trousers rolled up to her thighs, and in only her vest, stretching out her arms in elegant mudras to show us our skill, and pointing her feet this way and that so she looks like a painted Pierrot.

4

'Hey,' Bianca said, her painted fingers in an elegant posture. 'Susie needs someone to cover for a missing waitress on Sunday, says you'll be next in line for a job if you're any good. It's only £6 an hour, but the tips are good.'

'Thanks, Bianca,' I said, 'I'll do it,' but I've been dreading Sunday ever since.

As I walk along the street I take out the matchbox and push it open.

I need a new battery because the birds don't light up.

I look at the gold branches and imagine Zeb shaping them with his long fingers.

I asked Rob for his address. She said Mick would know it, or I could send it to the art school in Spain, and Miss Pym would have the address, but I said I'd prefer to wait and get it from Mick.

Bianca said, 'Zeb'll know you didn't get the packet straight away, don't worry, but send a postcard and tell him you've got it now.'

'He'll think I didn't care about it, it was weeks ago he left it, all that time ago.'

But Bianca said, 'Your father died, Eve! And it only seems that long to you because of what happened.'

I said, 'How many weeks is it, then?' and she counted them on her painted fingers and said, 'Seven.'

It seems unbelievable. Time doesn't always pass at the same rate, that's all, because I feel as if the whole of reality has been reconstructed, and isn't it amazing it can happen in seven weeks.

So I sat down at her table while she heated wax and resin, and filled her studio with interesting fragrance, and drew a picture on a piece of card of coloured birds flying across the blue sea to Spain. Seven weeks ago. He must have a girlfriend by now, and I said it out loud without realizing. Bianca shrugged. 'Maybe he does, but I think he loves you.' And I posted the card in the post box when I'd waited for Mick to come back.

I arrive at the corner of the road and wonder which way to turn. Bianca gave me a note with the address. I look at the numbers and follow them backwards.

There are plants growing up the walls around the door. You have to ring a doorbell.

'Hello,' I say to a tall man with blond hair. 'I'm here for the waitress shift. I'm standing in for someone.'

He nods at me, without smiling, and shows me along a corridor.

I am introduced to Susie, who shakes my hand. She has a beauty spot on her cheek.

'Come this way,' she says in a deep grainy voice. I follow her down a mustard-yellow corridor into the dining room panelled in dark wood. There is a long table in the first room, and tables of different shapes in the second room, and a conservatory that leads into the garden where there are benches among the flowers, and places to sit that are hidden behind trees.

'This is lovely,' I say.

She shrugs.

'For them!'

Susie has longer hair at the front than the back, so it hangs down either side of her cheeks like two telephones. When she leans forward she could speak into the receivers.

We go through the double doors into a large brown room with a billiard table and a fireplace and sofas and a bar, and Susie tells me she sings in nightclubs, and what she really wants to be is a singer. I say, 'You've got the voice for it' and she smiles and shouts across at the bar, 'This is the waitress today.'

'What's her name?' shouts the barmaid.

'Eve,' I say.

'Upstairs there are bedrooms where the members can stay,' she says, pointing up the staircase. 'I'll introduce you to the kitchen,' and we walk back down the yellow corridor into the dining room and through a studded green baize door into the kitchen.

The under-chef has grey hair although he is young, and a rough-looking red face. He looks up from his preparation and nods without looking at me.

There are some other boys working in the kitchen dressed in white, with dirty aprons.

'Where's Carlo?'

'Not here yet.'

'He's the head chef.'

We go through to the back.

'This is where you bring the dirty plates. This is Patrice.'

Patrice is African, with a closed face that opens into a smile.

He flicks his towel over his shoulder so it snaps.

'How do you do,' I say and smile at him.

Susie ushers me back through the kitchen where a tall bulky man is standing in a white coat and blue checked trousers. He has slicked-back hair.

Susie says, 'This is Eve, she's the waitress today.'

He nods upwards and looks me up and down.

We walk back through the swing door.

'Don't worry about Carlo,' says Susie. 'He's got the worst temper. He's a real pain in the arse.'

He bangs through the doorway, so the swing door slams against the wall.

'Susie, I want to see you!' he says. His black eyes have a closed-off look.

Susie looks at the ceiling. 'See, he's just showing off to you that he's the big boss. Honestly, he's such a child, don't get taken in.'

She winks at me and goes through into the kitchen. I am left in the corner looking at the empty tables and wishing I could go home.

A blonde girl slides in, undoing her coat.

'Oh thank God, I thought I was late. Haven't even eaten yet. Look, this is where the cutlery is, I'm Edna.'

Susie and I put white cloths on the tables between us and lay the tables in all three rooms, after we have eaten our roast beef and yorkshire pudding cooked by the under-chef. The light slants in through the windows and Susie tells me she's in love with someone who comes here with his wife. They are having an affair and each time she sees him it's agony.

'He'll come today,' she says.' He always comes on Sunday.'

Carlo opens the door and blares, 'Susie, come here!'

'See, he's doing it again,' she says, smiling. 'He just loves being in charge and manly!'

People begin to come in and sit down at the tables. Susie comes back through with a biro behind her ear.

'You can take these tables here, all right?'

I must look alarmed because she says, 'Don't worry, we're not open yet, I still have to tell you what to do!'

She shows me how to take an order, how to put it on the nail through the hatch in the kitchen, and where to collect the plates.

'Carlo or someone will put it through and call it out. Then you take it to the table, all right?'

'OK,' I say.

'He's here!' she says, suddenly blushing and pointing him out with her eyes.

The man she is in love with has a reddish face and black curly hair and eyes that are in a smile, that isn't really a smile. He slides a glance at Susie while he pulls the chair out for his wife.

'Oh, he makes my heart race!' says Susie.

'But he's revolting, Susie.'

'Oh no, you don't know him,' she says. 'He's just wonderful.'

'I don't want to know him.'

Susie takes me by the arm.

'See that woman with dyed black hair, see over there in the blue?'

I look over to the corner and see a woman dressed in bangles and jewellery and feathers, with bright red lipstick and long false eyelashes.

'She's about seventy! Well, she's going out with the under-chef.'

'Is there any service?' a woman calls out.

'We've only just opened!' says Susie.

Suddenly it seems all the people arrive at once, the dining room is filled with the noise of people talking. They are pulling the chairs out and sitting down and shouting across at each other.

I take my pad and take the order for the first table, and put my order on the nail inside the hatch.

'Hey, come back!' says the under-chef. 'What's that?'

'Two roast beef.'

'Well, you have to write it, 2, number two, *times*, understand, or I don't know what the fuck you mean, geddit?'

'OK,' I say.

I go back and forth with orders and starters.

People are sitting down at all my tables.

I take the dirty plates from the first table's starters through the swing door and through the kitchen, where there is a frenzy of cooking and Carlo growls 'Get out the way!' as though I am a dog. I go into the back kitchen where we put our dirty plates, and smile at Patrice.

He receives them with a towel over one shoulder.

'Do you want to sleep with me?' he says.

'I . . . er.'

'Do you want to sleep with me, yes or no?'

'I don't even know you.'

He takes the dishes and clatters them in the sink. He whips his towel off his shoulder.

'You English girls, you're all the same. Yes or no! I say Yes or NO! I am just asking.'

'I, er, well, no,' I say.

'Thaaankyou,' he says. 'A straight answer, that's all I am asking. A strrraight answer.'

He has an African accent.

'Did he ask you if you would sleep with him?' says Susie, when I come back into the dining room.

'Yes.'

'He asks all the girls.'

'He didn't ask me!' says Edna.

'You haven't got the tits!' says Susie.

'Maybe someone should tell him it isn't exactly the best approach.'

'Oh, you'd be surprised,' says Susie.

My two other tables are full. I approach with my note-pad and pen. I still have the faded henna on my fingers.

'Oh, very exotic!' says the young man. 'Are you exotic?'

'No,' I say. 'What would you like?'

'You look rather exotic to me,' he says.

He speaks sideways so I can see up one of his nostrils. Someone should tell him not to do that.

'Are you,' and his eyebrows flick up, 'painted all over?'

'No,' I say. 'Can I take your order?'

'And how long have you been a waitress?' he says.

'This is my first day. What would you like?' I say.

'Oh, first day! I see, how splendid! I say, Mummy what d'you want?'

Mummy proceeds to order in French. The menu is written in English with a translation in French but she has to order the whole thing in bloody French.

I hesitate. 'Is that the calves' liver?'

She says it again in French and looks at me with a blank look.

'Thank you,' I say, trying to memorize what she just said so I can look it up. I collect the menus.

'Oh, I haven't finished yet,' says the young man, his nostril pointing at me, and pulling the menu towards him. 'Does the *marmite dieppoise* come in a white wine velouté?'

I have no idea, and I'm still trying to memorize what Mummy said.

'I'll ask in the kitchen,' I say.

'Well, it says it does here,' he says. 'And I'd like to change mine for a *confit de canard.*'

'Yes. OK.'

'You might need to do a bit better than that,' he says, 'if you're going to stay longer than the first day.'

When I walk through into the other dining room Carlo opens the kitchen door.

'Look, you idiot, your beef has been waiting here five minutes! It'll be COLD!'

'Sorry,' I say, and take the beef and hurry away.

'WAIT!' shouts Carlo through the hatch. 'You have to serve it at the same time as the sea bass. Are you an imbecile?'

Susie comes up behind me.

'No, she's not. Leave her alone, she's doing fine.'

'Don't you worry,' she says. 'It's OK.'

'I've got two more for that table.'

'Don't worry,' she says, winking at me. 'I'll bring them through.'

I manage to get all my orders in, but then I collect some main courses that belong to someone else and serve them, so Carlo goes spare and starts banging on the hatch table.

How does he know they're for another table?

How do I know?

The rest of the afternoon seems to be a blur of coming and going and shouting and Susie running about picking up all the orders that I can't manage. When there is a lull I say to her, 'Oh Susie, you're a gem!'

'S'alright darling, oh, if only someone else would say that to me!'

Mummy wants brandy and the nostril wants a whisky and soda so I go through to the bar with a tray.

'Do they want them on the tab in here, or are they going to be put on the bill?' says the barmaid.

'I don't know.'

'Well, you'd better find out. We can't be short at the end of the day.'

A man sitting at the bar whispers something incoherent into my neck.

'Get off me!' I say, pushing him away.

'Oh,' he groans, 'be friendly, can't you?'

She finishes putting the drinks on the tray. I lift it up and the man gets a hold of my buttock and squeezes it. I slam down the tray with the shock.

'What the hell are you doing?' says the barmaid. 'You want to break my glasses?'

'Don't you dare do that to me!' I snarl.

The man slams down his hand on the bar. 'Can't anyone get a drink round here?'

'Well, tell me what you want?' says the barmaid.

I pick up the tray and walk down the yellow corridor.

Outside the dining-room door, Susie's lover has his leg in between hers and his hand up under her white shirt.

Susie is looking blissful.

I squeeze past them into the clattering chattering dining room.

At last everyone is ordering coffee and some tables are getting their bills. Susie is doing the adding up and the dining room begins to empty. When we've cleared away the cutlery and plates and glasses and wiped down the tables, Susie brings out the cash box and opens a bottle of white wine and all the waitresses sit down at the end of the long table and have a drink.

'Oh, I don't think I've got the hang of it,' I say, putting the glass to my forehead. 'I really don't think I'm cut out for this job.'

'You did fine,' says Edna.

Susie shares out the tips. 'You got good tips, though, Eve.'

I walk out into the cool air and take out the matchbox and for a few seconds the birds light up, then flicker and go out. I close the box and put it in my pocket and walk along the street with ringing in my ears.

5

'He should have told us we were meeting there, I could have got the 159 from Brixton all the way.'

'Yes, instead of leaving a stupid note on the board.'

'He must have left it on Friday.'

'I thought we were going to Regent's Park.'

'That's the painting project, and it's not till next week.'

'Better than the bloody National Gallery, all those boring old paintings.'

'They're not boring.'

'No, they're all Italian, I know.'

'That's got nothing to do with it.'

'And there'll be loads of people.'

We are walking towards the bus stop, with our bags of sketchbooks and charcoal. Karl is meeting us at the National Gallery for the drawing class.

We wait under the tree.

The 22 comes along the road and Rob and Bianca decide we'll get it to Piccadilly and walk down the Haymarket. Cecile is busy looking in her bag, wondering if she's left her purse behind. We climb up the stairs and sit in the seats at the front.

Bianca sits down beside me.

'Hey, what was it like?' she says. 'Sunday lunch?'

'Pretty horrible,' I say.

'I spoke to Susie, she said she liked you.'

'Yes, I like Susie, but everyone else is so bad-tempered.'

'Oh, it's always like that in restaurants.'

'And everyone's having an affair with everyone else.'

'Sounds fascinating!'

I shake my head.

'Oh, tell me the gossip, what's Susie's boyfriend like?'

'Revolting.'

Bianca laughs. 'She says he's really handsome.'

'He's having an affair right in front of his wife.'

Bianca shrugs. 'Well, people do, you know.'

'I didn't like him.'

'You are a bit of a prude.'

'Maybe I am. I don't know.'

I look out the window and watch the shops flashing past in clashing colours.

I close my eyes for a moment, so only the light and shadow flicker on my eyelids. When I woke up I just wanted to stay under the covers; lie in bed and be very still listening to the quiet, because it seemed like there was too much noise, and too much to feel.

'Well, maybe you are an idealist,' she says, thinking better of it.

'Maybe that too,' I say.

'You have to live in the real world,' she says.

'I know I do.'

We clamber down the stairs and out into Piccadilly. People are gathered at the traffic lights and move along in a body. Cecile holds on to my coat through the crowds and we follow Bianca and Rob along the road, past restaurants and banks and cinemas and stairs going underground.

'You're a bit far away, Eve,' says Cecile.

We walk along the grey street in silence for a while.

'So you didn't like the waitress job much?'

'It was horrible, Ces.'

'Why?'

'Because everyone is so mean and I'm useless at it.'

We pass the *Evening Standard* news-stand and photographs of women crying over men killed in the war.

'Don't you think it's all too much sometimes, Ces?'

A car door slams and two men begin shouting at each other in an alley.

'Sometimes it's all too much, don't you think?'

Cecile nods. 'Look, I know what you mean. I feel like that sometimes too.'

'Everyone is so mean, I can't stand it! And the thing is, Ces, you just have to feel it all.'

We pass a woman huddled in a doorway, holding on to a dog.

'That's why people paint, Eve, why they write music or sing or make films. Because they can't stand it either.'

'Is it?' I say, feeling helpless.

I look up at the roofs of the buildings where the pigeons are flying and Cecile puts her hand in my arm and guides me along the street.

'Don't forget the good things,' she says as we cross Trafalgar Square between the huge lions.

We walk up the stone steps and into the building. He said he'd meet us inside but Karl is nowhere to be seen.

'Are we late?' says Bianca.

'It doesn't matter, you know he's just going to tell us how composition leads the eye round the painting and all that stuff. Come on, let's find some paintings to draw,' says Rob.

The floor squeaks as we walk through the galleries. The huge rooms are almost empty of people.

We walk past Titian and Goya, Velazquez and Rembrandt.

Cecile says Titian could make ugly people beautiful, he paints them with such tenderness, and Bianca tells us that the flesh colours are painted over green to make them glow like real skin.

We look at how Titian paints velvet and Goya paints brocade and Rembrandt's portraits glow out of the darkness.

And Rob groans, 'Old *masters*' and Bianca says, 'Idiota' in an exasperated voice.

We look at the Duke of Wellington in his medals and pink sash, and Bianca starts calling Rob 'Dona Isabella' after Goya's portrait, because of the resemblance.

We look at Van Gogh, and Cézanne, Monet and Pissarro.

'Oh Evie, you'll like this one!' says Rob. 'Montmartre, it's like the one you did when the robber ran past.'

'If only,' I say, and the night glows in beautiful colours, reflected in the wet street.

We walk through the huge rooms on the creaking floorboards, looking at the centuries pass by in moments that are captured in layers of oil paint, depicting beautiful and wrinkled faces, naked bodies, light on water, landscapes, and sunflowers and holy families.

Bianca says she wants to draw *The Baptism of Christ* by Piero della Francesca, and Rob says, 'Bianca, you are secretly religious!' But Bianca says, no, she isn't, she likes the man taking his clothes off behind John the Baptist.

Cecile says, 'But d'you know he worked out the composition mathematically, and that's why if you look at it, it makes you feel tranquil?'

Cecile says she's going to try Philip of Spain's brown and silver brocade, and Rob says she'll go and draw *Diana and Actaeon* because the women have real bodies, instead of the spindly things you see in magazines.

Cecile changes her mind and decides on Van Gogh's *Long Grass with Butterflies* in spite of Rob shaking her head, saying, 'How are you going to copy all those grass stalks, Ces? You must be mad!' and I walk back to *The Baptism of Christ* and draw the tranquil composition and it's true it makes me feel more peaceful.

After the stillness of the pictures we come out into the bustling noise of traffic and rushing people. Someone is handing out leaflets for an anti-war march. Bombs are dropping across the page. The date is written in a fluorescent explosion.

As we walk across the square, the pigeons are flying all over the place, and the police have arrived because some men are fighting and there is blood on the pavement.

'Eve, this is all you need!' says Cecile, but I shrug, and smile at her, and we all catch different buses to go home.

I climb off the bus before home and walk down the street to the river. I cross the road on to the bridge.

I walk out into the middle of the bridge. Even the trees in the park look dirty.

The light has gone out of the sky and the evening is grey. I lean over and look into the water. It is dark green, and feels magnetic as though it is pulling me in, and I imagine falling.

A man walks towards me from the other direction. He has a long coat on but the sleeves are too short. He stands beside me and leans out over the water.

'It's bad, isn't it?' he says.

I can smell the alcohol and I feel sorry for him.

'Life is bad,' he says. 'It's rotten.'

I look into the dark water.

'A person could be tempted to throw themselves in,' he says.

'I know,' I say.

'There's not much to live for,' he says.

'No,' I say.

'Go on!' he says. 'Jump! I'd like to see the splash!'

I turn to him and he looks at me with mad eyes.

'It's extraordinary how quickly a person can go under!' he says, 'like he's been grabbed by invisible hands.' He fingers the air in front of my face.

'No!' I say. 'No!' as I walk backwards away from him. 'No!'

I turn round and run back to the Embankment, and I can still hear him laughing even above the traffic noise. I don't stop running till I'm two streets away from the river, and when I get home I write a list of things that are good about life.

6

'He might have been an angel,' says Cecile. 'You never know.'

We are sitting on two blocks of stone in the sculpture yard, while the other two roll out the paper.

It was Cecile's idea to paint a picture together, but Bianca and Rob took over, and went to Green and Stone to buy the roll of Fabriano, and split it four ways so it cost £5.77 each.

'He seemed more like a devil to me,' I say, watching as Rob puts a tin of paint on one of the corners so it doesn't roll up.

'Are we using the whole roll, Rob?' I call out.

She looks up. 'Why not? Don't you think?'

'It's just . . . it's massive, all twenty-three feet!'

'Liberating!' she says

I shrug. 'OK.'

'Yes, but look what you were about to do!' says Cecile.

'I wasn't going to throw myself in, Ces.'

'But you were miserable enough to!'

'Imagine how horrible that would be,' I say.

Bianca is telling Rob to pull her end along a bit, so the rest of the roll isn't in the shed. The day is sunny and their shadows fall across the white sunlit paper.

'Loads of people do, you know. Maybe it's comforting to join all the other people who've done it.'

'I don't know about comforting, Ces, sometimes you have funny ideas.'

'Is that really what he said, about how quickly a person can go under?'

'Yes, like they'd been grabbed by invisible hands! And I'm telling you he'd seen it, Ces, I'm sure he had. It gives me the shivers.'

'So it should! Apparently someone was found in Wapping who'd jumped in, and they had shrimps coming out their eyes and their nose and their mouth.'

'Oh Ces! Where d'you get these facts?

'I read it in a book.'

'You're making it up.'

'I'm not! It's in the book, I'll show you.'

'Look, it's ready,' says Rob, the paper is rolled out. 'Let's go and get our stuff!'

We take the lift up to our studios and meet back in the lift with our boxes of materials.

Roberta has brought potatoes.

'What are those for?' says Bianca, pointing.

'Printing,' says Rob. 'We do it with the kids.'

We take our baskets and boxes and bags through the sculpture department and outside into the yard to our huge piece of paper; six feet wide and twenty-three feet long.

We lay our materials out alongside the paper, on the ground. There are jars of acrylic, tubes of printing ink, rollers and brushes and squeezy bottles of poster paint. There is charcoal and oil pastels, oil sticks and chalk, and some silver aerosol car-spray that Mick had left over. Bianca has brought sheaves of gold and metallic paper, and Cecile some corrugated cardboard and the bits and pieces she picks up off the street for collage.

We have empty jars and buckets full of water, and plastic egg cartons for mixing the paint.

'And if we don't have every colour that exists,' says Cecile, 'we can make it!'

'Well, I think we've got enough,' says Rob.

It is a warm day and Bianca ties her hair up in an old piece of cloth and looks fetching, and takes her shoes off. We decide to copy her so we can walk across the paper and stand in the middle of it if we need to. The henna tattoos that have faded on our fingers are still bright on our legs, and I like watching the decorated feet walking over the white surface.

Roberta starts straight away, rolling a colour on to the white with a printing roller. Bianca crouches down and begins to smooth gold leaf on to the surface, and Cecile starts painting a big green labyrinth.

'Don't feel inhibited!' says Rob, from the other end of the paper. 'If it isn't any good we can always go over it.'

'Thanks,' I say, sitting in front of the big white space.

'I'm just saying,' she says. 'It'll be easier when we get going.'

I try painting a crow, but it looks lost on the empty paper, so it turns into a black oblong that might be a door, and I decide instead to paint nothing in particular.

The paper begins to fill up with colours and I move around the paper putting dots on to coloured shapes and tendrils in the spaces between. I forget myself as the painting begins to have its own life.

We move round and in and out of each other's pieces of work, sometimes covering them or letting little parts of them show through, in layers of paint and collage. The colours are dark and light, ugly and beautiful, drab and glinting.

We become absorbed and silent, and sink into an exhilarated painting trance. Time stops passing and stands still, and in the long moment the picture moves and pulsates with spirals and curves, and explosions of dots.

The henna paintings on our legs get splashed too, as we walk across the paper, and seem to become part of the painting.

I watch Bianca as she crouches down on the paper, getting her knees covered in paint, printing faces and eyes and hands, with potatoes cut in half, and magenta and turquoise printing ink. Cecile's huge flowers blossom in unexpected colours, and through them, and among them wind Rob's mysterious pathways. She has brought her dried earth to mix with medium, so among the sprouting flowers some earth-caked women are squatting.

Suddenly I see something. I paint an undulating line that changes colour along the length of the painting, meandering between Rob and Bianca's feet from one end to the other. It is the edge of the river, and the buildings and their reflection in the silver, sometimes copper, water.

'It's the river!' shouts Cecile.

The picture has turned into the wildest painting of London you've ever seen. London with its ancient history, with fireworks, with its wild spirit and primeval beginnings, with fields of marigolds in Pall Mall and Mesolithic ancestors, and frenzied atmospheres and flashing neon, and places of unexpected pale blue peace. I paint Tower Bridge and Lambeth Palace and a flaming angel with jewelled eyes, and Bianca adds patches of different-coloured metallic sky.

Rob starts painting the outlines of buildings. Huge flowers are sprouting from Westminster, Big Ben is splashed with fluorescence and the outline of St Paul's contains a labyrinth.

By the time we have finished, our feet and hands and knees are covered in paint. We have streaks on our faces and paint-spattered hair, as Bianca took to flicking fluorescent pink over the paper so the dots of light would glow on the dark colours.

The sun has gone behind the buildings and the air has become cool.

'We've been at it four hours!' says Bianca, picking up her watch and putting it back on. 'Can you believe that?'

We stand together and look at the painting.

'It's amazing, don't you think?'

'Yeah, don't know how we did it.'

'Let's put it under cover,' says Rob. So we drag it into the sculpture shed, and Bianca fetches traffic cones from the bike shed and we leave it to dry, and go through the sculpture department and up in the lift with our bags and baskets, suddenly so exhausted we can hardly see.

7

I lie in bed under the covers. I don't want to move.

There is traffic outside the window and the cars are honking and hooting. I get up and close the window and put Nina Simone on the player and climb back into bed. I feel like a snail outside its shell. I can't even go through to the kitchen and make a cup of tea.

I don't want to think about the studio and the mess I've left on the canvas.

I was so glad after the wild painting we made together, because it didn't feel pointless any more. I thought, 'Now I know what I want to paint,' and I'd gathered all the colours, even gold. I'd tried painting the city, the beautiful river and the ancient past, under the metallic sky, that shines dark and light at the same time, with the mad men and the sad men and invisible hope; but the picture turned into a dirty mess. And when Andrew, my new tutor, came through the curtain to introduce himself I was sitting on the stool holding my head, next to a canvas of muddy chaos.

I liked him because he knocked on the partition when he came through the curtain, and blushed when he said hello.

'Are you all right?' he said.

'I'm making such a mess!' I said.

'Maybe you're trying to do too many things at once,' he said, and I took him out on to the landing where we'd put our painting on the wall, beside the stairwell.

'See, it has them all, the beautiful and the ugly colours,' I said.

'But it's twenty-three feet long!' he said. 'There's more space for all the colours! You can't paint all the paintings at once!'

I stood there looking at it, and knew what he meant.

'It's all right,' he said. 'You'll get there!'

But it isn't because of the painting that I want the covers over my head.

I listen to Nina singing:

'My father always promised me that we would live in
    France,
We'd go boating on the Seine,
I would learn to dance, we lived in Ohio then,
He worked in the mines,'

and I think of my dad and I lie in bed and draw my knees up to my chin, and pull the covers round me because there are too many feelings to feel, and my senses are too raw for the outside world.

8

'Come on! Let's have one more go,' says Cecile.

'But it's so nice just lying here,' I say.

'I know,' says Bianca. 'I want to live here.'

I am lying with my eyes shut. When the water splashes it echoes against the tiled walls.

'How long have we been here?'

'Three hours, I should think.'

'Bianca!' calls a voice from downstairs.

'Coming!' she says, and gets up off the bed and pads downstairs, wrapped in a towel.

It was Bianca's idea, of course. As soon as she saw me she said, 'You're miserable, you look ill! You need a treat!'

I smiled and said, 'What like?'

She said, 'Come on, I've got an idea!'

Cecile was nodding, but Rob said, 'We're supposed to be drawing with Karl, we can't just not turn up!'

'Yes, we can!'

'Come on, he'll be livid.'

'Who cares!' Bianca said. 'Eve's ill!'

'I'm not ill.'

'You weren't in yesterday,' said Cecile.

'I'm OK, honestly.'

'Anyway, we can draw in there,' said Bianca.

'In where?' said Rob.

'I'll tell you when we get there.'

So we took the Tube and next thing you know, we were walking up the stairs into the huge, warm room and the sound of splashing.

A small lady with dyed black hair brought us piles of towels and said, 'Here you are, darlings,' and Bianca started talking to her in Italian. After she'd shown us into two cubicles as big as bedrooms, hung with red curtains, we undressed and wrapped ourselves in the warm towels.

Rob said, 'But we can't draw in here!'

'Yes, we can!' Bianca said, and she was right.

The oil pastels melt in the heat and slide over the paper. I drew a picture of Rob lying on her back, her hands on her big stomach, sitting in the wooden chair in the hot room, and Cecile lying on a bench with her legs stretched vertically up the tiled wall.

Cecile and I tried drawing in the steam room and two women with long dark hair said, 'Draw us, we don't mind,' but then the paper got so damp it wrinkled, and began to tear, and it was hard to see through the steam.

We have spent the afternoon sweating in the hot room, lying around in the steam, and plunging into the icy water by turns.

'Come on,' says Cecile, 'just once more.'

'OK,' I say, opening my eyes and sitting up.

We slip through the red curtain into the huge room where women wrapped in towels are lounging among the tiled pillars, having tea, and walk down the stairs by the cool air of the plunge pool and through the double doors into the tropical heat. There is a smell of soap in the wet air, and a faint scent of pine in the steam.

Bianca is lying naked on a marble slab being soaped all over with a bristly brush by the Russian masseuse.

Through the open door of the hot room we can see Rob, who is still talking pregnancy with two old ladies. Cecile and I walk into the steam. The walls are dripping. The air is wet. We lie naked on our towels and sweat trickles down our arms, behind our knees, between our breasts, and down our necks.

When we come out Cecile is pink all over.

We pass Bianca again, who is being hosed down and pummelled. She mouths 'Help me!' as the masseuse presses down on her shoulders so her cheek slides up and down on the soapy marble slab.

We laugh, and watch her make open-mouthed and shocked expressions as the muscular masseuse cricks each vertebra all the way up her spine.

The plunge pool is ice cold. Cecile stands at the side and slowly dips her toe in. I draw her quickly as she steps into the water.

I put down my sketchbook when she is fully submerged and leap in. I gasp at the sudden icy cold. When I step out of the water my whole body is warm and tingling, and we walk upstairs and lie down.

'Feel my skin!' says Bianca, coming in and climbing on the bed. 'It is scrubbed smooth.'

'There were three in the bed, and the pregnant one said, move over! move over!' sings Rob when she comes through the curtain, and we join in until a curt 'Shsh' from the next-door cubicle makes us quiet.

So we push the beds together and lie top to tail, and look at the gold ceiling, and listen to the whirring sound of the heating system that hums downstairs.

'I don't know what we're going to tell Karl,' says Rob, 'and we've got Regent's Park tomorrow.'

'You worry too much,' says Bianca.

'Well, he's still pissed off with us because we went to the National Gallery instead of the National *Portrait* Gallery,' says Rob, looking pointedly at Cecile.

'I told him it was my fault,' says Cecile. 'I read it wrong.'

Bianca laughs. 'Don't worry!' she says, languidly hitting the air.

It was obvious he didn't believe we'd even gone to the National Gallery until we showed him the drawings; though Cecile's didn't prove anything as it was a thicket of black lines.

'What's that?' he said.

'*Long Grass with Butterflies*,' she said, surprised he didn't recognize it, 'by Van Gogh!'

He just started laughing and said, 'There's no one quite like you, Cecile.'

But when he saw *Diana and Actaeon* and *The Baptism of Christ* times two, he believed us, and said, 'OK, girls, you're forgiven,' and tapped Bianca's drawing and said, 'You've got to use your pencil as a measurement, or you'll never get it in proportion!'

'You're not really worried, are you?' I ask Rob.

She shrugs. 'Oh, who cares!'

'You know, I don't want to be a mother,' says Cecile out of the blue. 'My mother frightens me,' and Bianca says, 'Let's not get on to mothers!' and Rob says, 'Ahem! I'm just about to be one!' and Bianca says, 'But I didn't mean you!'

Rob looks at me and says, 'My God, Eve, you're an orphan!' and I feel the empty place in the world they've left behind.

'But I've got Magda!' I say, and for a moment I think of her on the farm among the cows, and the blue sea and the Lizard far away in the distance.

'And you've got us,' says Ces.

Then we talk about who wants what in a boyfriend and Rob says she just wants Mick and Bianca says, 'That's lucky!'

Cecile says she likes her husband, he's kind, and Bianca says she wants someone with a sense of humour who's maybe a bit dangerous, and Rob nods to herself as though she knew it all along. And I look at my feet next to Bianca's closed eyes on one side, and Cecile's pink cheeks on the other that make her hair look more orange than usual and think, 'I want a man with dark eyes who wants to make sculptures out of light, and says that reality's 80 per cent invisible.'

'I think we should order tea and toast,' says Bianca and all of us agree it's a good idea, but our limbs feel so heavy, and the drowsiness so pleasant, none of us can bear to get up and we continue to lie there thinking how nice it would be.

'We should be drawing,' says Rob.

'We've done a few,' says Cecile.

'I'll do mine later,' says Rob languidly.

'D'you think the baby likes it?' says Bianca.

'He's gone quiet,' says Rob.

And we hear each other's voices along with the whirring and the humming and before long we have all fallen fast asleep.

9

It was while I was sleeping I decided to go. I must have dreamed the idea because when woke up I had the place in my mind. Cecile said she'd come too, when I told her on the way to the Tube. We stepped out into Queensway in time for the rush hour, and walked through the traffic feeling delicate and clean.

'I'll come if you like,' she said, but I said, 'No, thanks, Ces, I think I'll go on my own this time,' and she nodded and gave me a kiss goodbye.

I'm glad somehow that I'm all clean; as though I'm sparkling. Doesn't make any difference of course, and anyway he's under the earth in Cornwall, but it's where he left his body and that must mean something.

Ces gave me her water bottle and I bought candles from the cobbler by the station, and when I walk up the steps from the Tube on to the pavement by the river I buy a bunch of freesias from the same woman as before.

I walk along by the river, up some steps and into the alcove. Today there is sunlight and it shines right into the dark places, lighting them up. I put the bottle in the lit-up corner, and the yellow and pink freesias glow in the sunlight. The other corner is dark and I light the candles and leave them in the shadows.

Sometimes you think something is over and suddenly it takes you by surprise.

All at once I see dad. I imagine him lying here, crying. It is déjà vu, or the vague memory of a dream. I feel pierced by his sadness and I crouch down by the flowers and start sobbing so uncontrollably that an old lady stops and strokes my hair as she passes, and leaves a pound coin by my feet.

Then something peaceful happens. It comes over me, and fills me through and through, and I feel sure this happened to him too.

And when I go out of the alcove and walk along by the river, I have to stop still, and hardly breathe. The sky is so blue and the light is so clear and the sunlight is on the water; and I feel the invisible reality of dad's presence spread through me; and the promise, and the hope, and the longing, fill the whole sky from deep within me, and glitter on the water, and spread out into the clear light.

10

'Well, we were showing him pictures of us naked if you think about it!' says Bianca, and starts laughing.

We are lying on the grass in the sunlight in Regent's Park, while Bianca unwraps boiled eggs, pears and ciabatta bread folded in tea towels.

'You know, I never even thought about that!' says Cecile. 'We were stark naked!'

'Cecilina!' says Bianca. 'Well, it's the first time he hasn't criticized my proportions!'

Rob laughs.

'It's because you drew us lying down, so we were fore-shortened,' says Cecile.

'Whatever you say, Ces,' says Bianca.

When we showed the drawings to Karl he shook his head and said, 'You four are something else.' But he said it was an original alternative.

'He didn't really mind,' I say.

'No, I think he thought it was quite funny,' says Rob.

When we'd arrived in the Park in Karl's van we'd walked through the green heat and cool shadows, weighed down with easels and canvases, and bags of paint and brushes. We'd walked along paths, by hedges, across sloping lawns, and down a grand avenue, past fountains and flowerbeds laid out in colourful symmetry, that scented the air with lilies.

We walked until we came to the lake, the weeping willows dipping their new leaves into the water.

Roberta sat on a bench to paint, and Bianca walked across the grass to draw the fountain, and Cecile and I had settled by the water to paint reflections. Cecile sat under a tree because of the sunlight and her pale skin. She wanted to paint the water through a curtain of green, and we've worked all morning.

'At Goldsmiths they're making a dove,' says Bianca, putting little twists of salt next to the boiled eggs, and a jar of capers, and Parma ham wrapped in greaseproof paper.

'A dove, what for?'

'The anti-war march.'

'Are you going?'

'Of course!'

'What are they making it out of?'

'Willows.'

'And what?'

'Oven-proof paper painted with PVA.'

'Why oven-proof?'

'They want to light it up inside.'

'With candles?'

'Don't know. Might be bulbs.'

'But they can't plug it in!' says Cecile, and Rob starts laughing.

'There are batteries, you know, Ces,' she says.

'Must be candles,' says Bianca.

'I'd like to see that.'

'Does the march go on till dark?'

'There's a candle-lit vigil after.'

'In Trafalgar Square?'

'Westminster. Outside the Houses of Parliament.'

'All night?'

'Don't know.'

'We should make something,' says Cecile. 'What shall we make?'

'Are you joking?' says Rob. 'Look at me! I'm hardly gonna manage the march with this!' she says, pointing to her belly, 'let alone carrying some bloody bird!'

'Keep your hair on! I was just thinking.'

'And Bianca gets tired, you know, she's not going to want . . .'

'OK, OK.'

'Hey, this is a fabulous picnic, Bianca!'

We eat our picnic and fall silent, and the bees buzz among the flowers.

'Look, Karl's coming,' says Cecile. 'We better get back to work.'

I walk back to my easel and sit by the lake, looking at the surface reflecting the trees, and the sky and the sunlight; and butterflies flit about behind my head, twirling round each other in shadows across the canvas.

Before long a mandarin duck with a bobbing quiff swims through the water I am painting. I try to paint him into the picture as quickly as I can. He has a red streak in his feathers and yellow eyes.

11

When we gather in Hyde Park behind the long trail of people that stretches up to Park Lane we are glad we have nothing to carry. Especially Bianca, who is dancing around, talking to everyone.

We are standing behind a group of men in long white shirts and white trousers with beards and skull-caps who have posters written in Arabic in green curly letters.

The men begin to sing a mournful and beautiful song, led by one who calls out the chant.

Around us are the green summer trees of Hyde Park, the birds are singing and the bees are buzzing in the long grass. It is a clear sunlit day. The march is taking time to begin.

Cecile and I wander away towards the trees.

The anti-war march looks like a colourful carnival from here.

'Oh look, I can see it!'

'The neck's a bit long for a dove.'

'Silvia said they tried to make it a dove but the willows were too long.'

'It made itself into a swan.'

It's near the head of the march and there are four people carrying it.

The bird rises up very slowly on poles, the wings begin to flap up and down, and we realize the people are beginning to move.

Though when we get back to our little crowd it's still at a standstill, and Rob is lying on the grass on a shawl that one of the bearded men has gallantly spread down for her to lie on.

As the people begin to move she stands up with a little help from Cecile and folds up the shawl. The man bows to her when she returns it to him.

We begin to move. But Bianca wants to join the dove, so we walk briskly alongside the slowly moving people towards Speakers' Corner.

We pass a crowd of travellers in rainbow jerseys drinking cans of lager and singing about a new world, and a crowd of little girls in tie-dyed frocks doing cartwheels on the grass. We pass people holding banners and placards, people laughing and people looking bored.

Silvia and Carlotta are standing under the big white bird, along with a crowd of South Americans. Bianca is greeted with warmth and laughing and they all begin to talk at the same time.

We begin to walk down Park Lane behind the Gays Against War, some of whom are twirling about on roller blades, wearing pink tutus.

The South Americans and the Gays Against War begin to mix together and the tutus begin twirling around the big white bird so that by the time we reach Hyde Park Corner and come to another standstill they have devised a choreographed piece which they perform to the delight of the tourists in a roofless tourist bus, who all stand up on the top deck and applaud.

We move slowly along beside Green Park, and a group of serious-looking people dressed in black and grey, who do not smile, push past us, carrying posters of dead soldiers.

Maimed and swollen faces, bloody limbs, bounce off the placards into my eyes. 'The unpublished pictures,' 'the real face of war,' say the placards. Then come several posters of death tolls and statistics and a truly horrifying picture of dead children, which Rob looks away from with her eyes shut and her mouth open.

Bianca doesn't see them; she is busy wobbling unsteadily on roller blades five sizes too big, holding the hand of a huge man in a pink tutu, who walks along barefoot past the Ritz. She is screeching with laughter.

There begin to be more and more policemen standing in the roads leading off Piccadilly; some are on horses.

The tall buildings of the Royal Academy and Fortnum & Mason seem to close in on us. I begin to feel claustrophobic. There is a scuffle with the police in Piccadilly Circus, when the people with dyed black hair and black eye make-up, with chains in their clothes, decide to sit down in the road.

We walk down the Haymarket. There are red and white barricades at the mouth of all the roads, and police with riot shields. The march gathers in Trafalgar Square. It is crammed. People are talking on a stage. Their voices echo off the walls of the National Gallery. Placards are being raised up and down. An unquiet feeling throngs the air. I can see people climbing up on to the lions. Rob says, 'D'you know they're made from. . . .' 'Melted down guns,' I say, nodding.

I am surprised she isn't affected by the violence in the air. Cecile looks like a frightened rabbit. We catch each other's eye.

'Let's go into the Underground!' she says. Bianca feels it too, and we push our way through the seething crowd.

A pole smashes through a window. There is a surge forward. People are throwing stones. I see a policeman hiding his head. I see a girl in a green skirt being pulled into the back of a van. The air has become strange.

I look round to see where Bianca is, and a crowd of people dressed in black are pushing past, raising their placards and shouting.

I am separated from the others. I can hear Rob shouting, 'Eve!' I see Cecile's red hair slip between the people, and the crowd surges away from the centre of the square. I am pulled along in a mass moving up St Martin's Lane. I am squashed in the press of bodies. A bang explodes behind us. The crowd begins to panic and run. I run along with them, and slip down a side street and run up an alley, away from the noise. I see a pub. I push the door open and fall in. I close the door, and stand against it, breathless, my heart pounding.

The landlord comes out from behind the bar and looks over the frosted glass window.

'What's it like out there?'

'Mayhem,' I say.

He locks the door, and we watch through the back-to-front 'Beer and Ale' etched into the window, as the people run past in both directions.

I buy a half of cider and my hands are shaking when I lift the glass. I hope the others are all right.

I look round at the dark brown pub, crimson flock velvet on the benches and stools. It is dingy and smells of smoking. An electric organ instrumental of 'Danny Boy' is playing on the jukebox.

'Were you on the march?' says a girl in a rainbow jersey.

'I got separated from my friends,' I say.

'You poor thing.'

I walk over and sit down.

'I hope they're all right, one of them is pregnant!'

She pats my shoulder reassuringly. 'Doesn't do any good to worry.'

We discuss the march, and how it had begun so peacefully. It turns out she's from Cornwall too, and we talk about missing the sea, and the stupidity of war and my hands stop shaking and outside it grows quiet.

'Are you going to the vigil?'

'We were planning to,' she says, inclining her head to the boy beside her.

'Looks like it's getting dark outside.'

He gets up and begins to feed money into the slot machine.

Suddenly she turns to me and says, 'You look WOW!' and puts her hand up to my face. 'It's like, geometric!'

'Are you on something?' I say.

'I think it's just kicked in!' she says, looking about her slowly with an open mouth. 'Sometimes he just slips it in my drink,' she says, nodding towards the boy, 'and I say to him, "No, you haven't, you *haven't*," and then I realize, "Yes he has!"' and she starts giggling. 'He most certainly has!'

This is all I need, I think to myself.

'Well, it's quietened down out there,' I say, standing up and nodding.

'Far out!' she says, stroking the air around me as though it is soft.

'Nice to meet you anyway.'

When I walk out into the evening I see the damage; shop windows are smashed and I crunch through the glass strewn over the road. I pass a scaffolding pole smashed through a windscreen of a car, surrounded by police tape. There is hardly anyone on the streets.

A neon cockerel says 'Take Courage.' Maybe the others will be at the vigil.

Flyers are being blown across the road by the wind or plastered to the tarmac by the drizzle. I walk over the bricks and cans on the paving in Trafalgar Square and the photographs on the discarded placards are covered in footsteps.

The square is deserted after the riot, the traffic lights change colour even though there are no cars. There is an eerie feeling, as though the buildings are listening to me. Watching me.

The placards have been chucked in the fountain and photographs of dead soldiers look up from under the water that reflects the orange sky.

There are strips of police tape flying about. I walk between the fountains. I turn to look at the National Gallery and to my horror it shouts at me. It shouts so loud I put my hands to my ears in case they bleed, but the sound is still overwhelming. I scream and can't hear the sound. Then I realize it's my own thoughts which are loud and the sound is echoing off the buildings.

I collapse on the rim of the fountain and put my hands in the water. The sound subsides.

'Maybe he spiked my drink, too,' but the thought does not shout back.

Then I look in the water and see dismembered soldiers calling to me through their own thin red blood. Their hacked limbs are waving and running.

'Oh God, oh God.' I put my head in my hands and the water cools my hair. I put my face up to the light of the moon that has come out from behind an orange cloud, and the light touches me.

I am blinking my eyes, seeing the ripples of reflected moon.

'Please don't let me see anything else.'

There is a terrific boom. I look up at Nelson's Column and the air throbs. The sound evaporates into the enraged sky and the lions begin to melt back into guns.

I run between the fountains of blood, and men with green faces spew water from their mouths.

The silver angel from the *Evening Standard* is flying about above the steps down into the Tube, which seems like the mouth of hell.

There is a face down there in the dark, his hair is long and matted, his eyes glint at me. I hurry past. Lion-headed, claw-fingered creatures with scary roaring mouths have jumped on to the lamp-posts. Winged children without legs look down from a pillar. I run away down Whitehall towards the river, past a cloaked man high up on a horse, but he is no help.

People have left empty clothes hanging on a plinth. They have turned to stone. Their emptiness reminds me of death and I smell the musty stone smell of a tomb that echoes when you whisper. I stop running and walk along the pavement.

The feeling of the night changes and becomes desolate. The wind makes an eerie sound along the hollow

pipes of the scaffolding like many sad singing voices.
The grief-stricken wind blows through me and tears
pour down my cheeks. I feel burdened by the pain in
the world. I walk past a huge poster of a dry river bed.
Skeletons lying on the bank, with their skin still on, open
their mouths. Their eyes revolve upwards and swivel in
fear.

I reach Westminster and Big Ben looms up.

I cross the road to be by the water. The river is high and
laps against the walls.

A brick-red shadow steps out of me and slips off into
the darkness and I realize I've been looking through the
eyes of despair.

There is a crowd of people standing outside the Houses
of Parliament. I can see the dove but it isn't lit. I look for
the others but they aren't among the crowd.

The people are humming and the sound has pictures
in it; I feel them changing the atmosphere as they rise
up into the night. A breeze blows from the river into my
face.

Then everything stops. No noise. The water does not
flow. The trees make no sound. There is no movement.

The world is passing through a still point.

The stillness is like a prayer. The air is potent.

I stop breathing and listen, and out of the silence I hear
a beautiful sound. I open my hands and raise them to
touch the air it passes through. It lights up every atom
and makes my breathing sweet. It hums in my ears and
glows behind my eyes with gold light.

All at once there is a dong. It is Big Ben.

Big Ben stops booming and little lights are being lit
among the crowd. I see the dove being lit up from within

and carried over and placed on Boudicca's chariot so it looks as if she's riding a bird.

I cross the road and pass through the luminous people. The sky is dark blue. An angel is looking out of my eyes, and everything is made of coloured light. A man gives me a night-light to hold. People begin humming again and the sound is soothing. I feel washed with relief.

A small girl looks with longing at my candle and I give it to her, she smiles shyly at me, and I decide to go home. I walk away from the humming people past the tall stately buildings and through the plane trees that hang over the river.

A Japanese man with black-rimmed glasses walks up to me. 'Excuse me, Downin' Street?' he says, adjusting his glasses. I can't think what he wants there at this time of night but I point him in the right direction.

Then just before I step on to Lambeth Bridge I seem to hear the leaves tinkle together in the night breeze, and look round.

There are birds here, small and lit-up. They glow with colours and emanate their coloured light. They are turquoise and rose-pink and orange. The songs they sing into the vast London night are complex and beautiful melodies. They fly up and about from branch to branch as birds do, never interrupting their song. Then they rise up in a swift synchronized motion and swoop up into the night. They leave the echoes of their harmonies and change the dark into something that is alive, that touches you and wants to open you, and I walk back along the river all the way home.

12

The birds flit about in my mind as I walk into college, and fill me with stillness although they are moving.

I walk up the stairs and meet Bianca coming down.

'Hi, Evie, were you OK? We lost you. Did you go to the vigil?'

'Yes, what happened to you lot?'

'We went down into the Tube.'

'All of you?'

'Yes. Cecile went home with Rob, she was a bit shaken.'

'I'm glad. I had visions of her being trampled or something horrible.'

'What about you?' says Bianca.

'Oh blimey,' I say, 'I was in a stampede.'

Bianca nods.

I open my mouth to tell her what I saw, but can't fit the words together to describe it, and instead I say, 'The birds are flying round my head.'

She looks at me with a frown. 'Are you all right, Evie?'

'Sort of.'

I want to tell her what happened but I can't.

'Come to the print room with me,' she says. 'I've got to finish my etchings, and I'll show you how to do mono-prints, you missed that.'

All the images and feelings are in me and I can't speak about them, so maybe I will make them into pictures, and I nod, 'Yes, yes, that's a good idea. Monoprints. Show me how.'

The sun is slanting through the tall windows of the print room, cutting the room into triangles and rectangles of light and shadow. The big room is empty and all the tables are washed clean.

The window next to the etching press looks in the same direction as Bianca's studio but two floors down, so we can't see over the tops of the trees, but into the leaves and among the branches.

'Here! I'll show you,' says Bianca, pulling out a piece of plastic-coated chipboard from a box under the table and two rollers and some ink from the shelf above.

She sits down on the stool and leans over the chip-board palette and squeezes some black ink on to the shiny white surface.

'Did they light the bird?' she says, looking up at me.

'Yes, it was beautiful. Everything was so . . . surreal.'

'Did you see Silvia?'

'No.'

'She must have come home. OK, you take your roller.' I smile because she lifts up the roller to show it to me.

'And you smooth the ink out like this.'

She makes a rectangle of ink with the roller.

'Make sure it's not too thick, and it's evenly spread out.'

'Let me try.'

She gives me the roller to roll the ink. It makes a sticky sound.

'Did you get home all right?'

'I walked along the river.'

'At that time of night?'

'I just felt like it.'

'OK, now you take a piece of card,' and she starts drawing into the oblong of ink. The lines are white.

She gives me the card and I draw into the ink.

'I like this.'

'Then all you do is put the paper on top and roll the clean roller over it.'

I lift my hands to let her do it. Then she nods at me to peel the paper back; the white lines and shapes glow out of the black ink.

'Wow.'

Bianca slips off the stool and goes to the other side of the room to cut paper, and soak it in the paper bath ready for her etching, and I sit down to work.

I make pictures of the frightened faces, the dismembered bodies and the lions melting into guns. I peel the pages off the palette and tape them to the shelves.

I draw the clock and the bridge over the water. I print the shining swan, and a figure in the dark, and people lit from within. I make the river of black ink in the background, or leave it white so it shines in the foreground, and as I work the birds begin to fly outside my head and out the window.

I lose sense of time as I draw into the ink, one after the other, the images pouring out of me like dreams. And as I print I see the paintings I will paint emerging from them, of someone in despair who remembers hope, and know that now I've found my own way of working.

'My God,' says Cecile bursting through the double doors, 'I've been looking everywhere for you two.'

'Cecile!' says Bianca.

'It's Rob!' says Cecile.

'What?' we both say together, standing up at the same time.

'The baby's coming!' says Cecile. 'It started this morning; her waters broke!'

'Oh no!' Bianca's hands cover her mouth, she doesn't like thinking about things like that.

'Where is she now?' I say.

'She's in hospital, with Mick.'

'Oh, I'm glad Mick's there.'

'So are you coming or not?'

'Where?' says Bianca.

'To the hospital! She's just about to have it!' says Cecile, holding the doors open.

'O Dio, I hope we don't have to watch!' says Bianca, covering her eyes at the thought.

I take her arm and glance back at my prints taped to the shelves; they'll be all right. 'Come on, Bianca, let's go.'

We fetch our coats and run out into the road. Standing on all three corners to make sure we get the first taxi that comes. Bianca calls out and whistles and we all clamber into the back of a cab.

'Where to?' says the cabby.

We look at Cecile, who tells him which hospital.

'Our friend is having a baby!' says Bianca through the glass.

'I'll get you there quick!' he says, doing a U-turn so we fall against each other, and putting his foot down so we zoom along the road.

'He's not joking!' says Cecile.

'Is she all right? I mean, it's not dangerous, after yesterday and everything?' says Bianca.

Cecile shrugs. 'They don't know. They were asking her all sorts of questions when I left.'

'Oh God. I hope it's all right.'

We arrive along with ambulances and climb out of the cab and through the big white doors into a turquoise hall. We run along a green corridor following signs and down a moving stairway.

'It's like a bloody airport!' says Cecile.

'I hate the smell of hospitals,' says Bianca, holding her nose. 'I hope she's had it,' she whispers to me.

Every desk we come to, and think we have arrived, we get directed somewhere else.

'Go up two floors, and turn right, and then left,' says the nurse with the telephone next to her ear.

We have to take a lift along with a man attached to a drip, and a bandage round his forehead.

'That's 'cos of the bump,' he says, pointing to his black eyes. 'I haven't been in a fight or anything,' he says.

'No,' says Cecile, shaking her head, then nodding so he knows she wouldn't have thought it.

We get out the lift and walk along a violet corridor past collages made with real flowers, and through double doors with oval windows, and ask another nurse at another desk, who tells us to wash our hands, please, and go along the corridor and turn left. No one has told us yet if Rob is all right, but when we walk along the corridor and turn left, the lilac curtains of the end cubicle are drawn back and there is Rob sitting up in bed, with Mick leaning close to her, both looking at a bundle with a furry black head.

'Oh my God, she's had it!' squeals Bianca, running along the corridor. 'Oh, we should have brought you flowers!' she says.

Rob looks up, and down again as if she can't bear to look away.

'Hello, you lot!' she murmurs, her eyes glued to her baby.

We gather round him and admire his little pink fingers and tiny ears. Rob looks down on him with a gentleness I've never seen before, and I lean over to look into his blinking mystified eyes, and smell his sweet baby fragrance. His presence has a stillness that fills the room and the corridor, so we fall into a quietness and just watch his ancient newborn face move slowly through emotions and then fall asleep. We look at each other. 'He's fallen asleep,' we whisper, while Rob and Mick continue to gaze.

'I hope you'll be well in time for my birthday,' says Bianca, breaking the spell.

'Well?' says Rob. 'I'm not ill!'

'Up and about, I mean,' says Bianca. 'We could have been twins,' she says into the baby's ear.

'Of course I will,' says Rob, looking up for a brief second.

'Good! I want to go to tea at the Ritz!'

'Trust you!' says Rob.

'You can bring Mick,' says Bianca.

'Thanks,' says Mick, smiling. 'I'll carry the baby.'

'No, you won't,' says Rob.

'Zeb'll be back then,' says Mick.

'I will invite him too,' says Bianca.

'Don't you want to be alone with a horde of women?' says Rob, looking up at Mick.

The rhythm of my heart has changed pace.

'Is he back soon?' I ask.

'He'll probably be in college next week,' says Mick, gently rubbing the fluffy head of his son.

I look at the floor, then the lilac curtain. I want to find a place to look so I can repeat the words and still breathe. Next week! Zeb will be back next week!

13

Every day I come in, and look through the window in the door of the mezzanine studio, expecting to see Zeb, but he isn't there.

Today is Friday and I rush up the stairs and look through the window in the door. But the studio is empty and dusty and I walk up the stairs, disappointed.

If Zeb isn't back by the degree show I won't see him till the autumn. By the time I've reached my floor, he might not come back at all.

The studio has become spacious without Rob and the canvases I have stretched and sized for the new pictures are lined up round the wall. I have mixed the primer from titanium pigment and rabbit-skin glue, and as I kneel down and begin to prime the surface in layers, I look into the white with Zebedee on my mind.

But when I tape the prints to the wall, and draw them out in charcoal on the canvas, and flick off the dust with a rag so only the line remains faintly visible, when I begin to imagine them in colour, and which colour, and what tone, his dark eyes begin to fade, and the white surface shows me other pictures.

At break time Cecile comes through the door.

'Oh, I like these new pictures, Evie!' she says.

'Well, they're only ideas so far.'

'I can see them as paintings. They're like London and dreams mixed together.'

'I don't know what they are, but I'm enjoying it, Ces!'

'About time!' she says.

I laugh. 'I know.'

'Shame I have to pack them up so soon, before they've even been painted,' I say as we walk up the stairs.

'You know we can paint in the annexe over the summer?'

'Can we?'

'Yes, as soon as the degree show goes up; in the studios above the ballet school.'

'Are you going to?' I say.

'Definitely. I used to go to that ballet school,' says Cecile, looking wistful, as we reach the abstract floor, and I imagine Cecile as a little girl in a tutu doing a plié, with her red hair tied in a bun.

The abstract studios are hot in the sunlight, and Bianca is sitting in the corner, wearing a hat she has made out of newspaper.

'Bianca, you can make a paper hat look elegant!' says Cecile.

The windows are open and the day is still.

Cecile takes the coffee pot out the door to fill it with water.

'Still no sign of him?' says Bianca.

'No,' I say, collapsing on to the chaise longue. 'He's probably decided to stay.'

And I think of Zeb all brown with a Spanish girlfriend.

'Oh, he'll be back,' says Bianca.

'Who you talking about, Zeb?' says Cecile, coming through the door.

Bianca nods.

'He's back! But they've put him in the sculpture yard because of the explosions!'

'He's back?' I say, standing up suddenly.

'What explosions?' says Bianca.

'Oh, I don't know, stuff like fireworks, coloured smoke, you know him. It's a new dimension to his work. I only spoke to him for a minute when he came through our studio with all his stuff.'

'A new dimension?'

'He'll have all eleven soon,' I say, aware of the blood rushing in my veins.

'Well, we can take him some coffee,' says Bianca.

I swallow and look out the window and suddenly don't know what to do with my hands.

'Yes, let's,' I say.

So after we have brewed our own pot we brew another for Zeb and take it down in the lift along with the sugar while I struggle with my heart rate, trying to calm myself, because he didn't write back to my postcard and he made the matchbox of birds ages ago, and anyway that was because he knew about dad. He didn't come and find me, but then I was in late. Anyway, he's bound to have found someone else by now.

Bianca keeps glancing at me, while Cecile scrapes the paint off her fingers, unawares.

Why do I feel like this? It's just stupid, I mean what good does it do? I think to myself as we walk through the big studios on the ground floor and through the sculpture studios.

On the other side of the sculpture yard, under the corrugated roof, I see his figure in the dark shed.

278

He is kneeling on one knee, the other leg square, his arm on his thigh, leaning over something he is lighting. His body makes a beautiful shape. The sleeves of his dark blue shirt are rolled up and his black hair falls down his back, tied in a plait like an Apache. I don't want him to look up.

There is a smell of gunpowder.

He kneels on both knees and sits back on his heels.

POW! A blue flame explodes with pink sparks, and momentarily lights up the interior of the dark shed, followed by a plume of smoke.

Bianca puts down the coffee pot and claps.

He looks up.

'Zebedee!' she cries.

'Hello, Bianca!' he says, getting to his feet and putting out his arms to greet her.

'Here! We have brought you coffee!' she says and hugs him, and I suddenly feel absurd, holding the sugar.

He looks at me. 'Evie, how are you?' He puts his arms round me and hugs and I feel the warmth of him on my skin. We pull apart quickly.

'Have you seen the baby?' says Bianca, pouring the coffee for him.

'Not yet,' he says. 'I got back yesterday.'

His face is brown. He smiles and nods at Bianca as she hands him the coffee and I see his asymmetrical dimples.

'His dad is happy, that's for sure,' he says, sipping the coffee.

'Mick is over the moon!' says Cecile.

We sit down on the dirt floor of the shed and talk about Barcelona and Miró and the Gaudí mosaics.

Bianca talks about the gold mosaics in Ravenna and I

look at his face and his hawk nose and his black eyebrows and for a moment he looks round and catches my eye and I look down. When I look up he is still looking at me. It makes my heart turn over.

Bianca asks him about the fireworks, and he tells us it's just an experiment, and he wants to make sculptures out of sunlight that disappear when the sun goes in.

We stand up and brush the wood chips and plaster dust off our clothes.

'See you later,' says Bianca. 'Come to my birthday tea!'

'I'm coming,' says Zeb. 'Mick already said.'

We are standing in the shed and I can't speak, I feel as if there is a force that pushes me away from him like a repelling magnet.

Then just as I turn to leave, he catches me by the arm.

'Evie,' he says.

'Yes,' I say, suddenly breathless.

'I'm so sorry about your dad.'

I shake my head then nod. 'Yes,' I say. 'Thanks, Zeb, it's OK now, and thanks, you know, for the beautiful tree,' and again I pull away too quickly.

'He likes you!' says Bianca as we leave Cecile in her studio on the ground floor and take the lift up together.

'But maybe it's because he feels sorry about dad,' I say.

'Oh, for God's sake, Evie.'

'He might just feel … I mean, I know he's a good friend.'

'Bollocks!' says Bianca in a high-pitched voice. 'I could ask him for you!'

'Oh, don't do that, Bianca, please don't do that,' I say as the doors open to my floor and I step out.

But Bianca's expression doesn't convince me that she won't, so I step back in before they close.

'Don't! Will you, Bianca, please?'

'All right, don't panic!' she says, 'but don't be such a wimp.' The doors open and she steps out.

'Just grab him, Evie! What do you really want?' she says as the doors close, and the lifts moves down again.

I want to look into his eyes, I want to break through this awkwardness, I want to hug him and kiss him and feel his heart beating, I think to myself, and find I've missed my floor.

14

'No, it's because your baby is wrapped in a tablecloth, and they thought you were a gypsy!' says Bianca as we walk up Piccadilly.

'It's not a tablecloth! It's from Morocco,' says Rob.

'Well, it might have been because of my gym shoes,' says Cecile.

'Or the paint on your trousers! It doesn't really help that you're wearing them under a dress!' says Rob.

'They would have let the boys in,' I say. Mick and Zeb are walking on ahead.

'That's because the doorman fancied Zeb,' says Bianca.

'Well, he certainly didn't fancy us!'

'He couldn't keep his eyes off him!'

He's not the only one, I think to myself, as I look down at the pavement, or up at the tall buildings of Piccadilly, trying not to look at Zeb all the time; but I can always see where he is, like a blue light in the corner of my eye.

'We've all got paint on our clothes somewhere!' says Cecile, and Bianca looks round at herself to see if it's true.

'You could have managed it, Bianca, you look like you've stepped out of some bohemian version of *Vogue*,' says Rob.

Cecile comes up beside me and says in a low voice, 'I

do actually think it was Rob's Doc Martens with socks and a skirt.'

I start laughing. But whatever the reason they wouldn't let us in to have Bianca's birthday tea at the Ritz.

'Oh poor Bianca!' I say, walking up beside her and putting my arm in hers. 'We'll get dressed up and come back another day.'

'There would be no point,' she shrugs. 'Anyway, the cakes are better at Patisserie Valerie.'

Zeb and Mick have stopped on the pavement and are pointing at the RA.

'What?' Bianca calls out.

Mick is looking at his watch.

'D'you want tea at teatime, Bianca, or shall we treat you to Picasso on the way?'

She lifts her hands up. 'I am in the hands of the gods!'

'Good!' says Mick, lifting up his hands and Zeb's too. 'They're good hands!'

When we walk through the archway some of the RA students are outside, painting. Mick knows two of them and we talk to them in the sunlight.

'Why don't you take our passes,' says the girl with a long plait, who is painting a tree. 'If you're going to see the Picasso, you might as well.'

'But don't they know you?' says Bianca.

'They don't know us at the ticket desk. As long as you look like painting students.'

'Sometimes it helps to have paint on your clothes,' says Cecile as we walk into the exhibition for free. 'We're like the band of raggle taggle gypsies-oh,' she says, as we walk behind Rob with the baby in a bundle, Zeb and Mick, and Bianca talking to everyone in a loud voice.

In the first room Picasso looks at us through close-together eyes from a gentle boyish face, wearing a white shirt, and painting his own portrait with black and white and Indian red on his palette.

'I'd quite like to try that,' says Cecile, 'paint with those three colours.'

We walk around and stand in front of the pictures.

The picture of his studio is filled with shapes, turning the painting into a room with far-away places in it.

'He's brave, isn't he? Black and white and all the colours,' says Rob, pointing to the picture.

'Then all the shapes and stripes,' says Cecile. 'Sometimes it's all curves.'

'I think he's curvy, really,' says Rob, moving along to look at a woman whose blue profile kisses her own face with gentle violet lips. 'He's just playing with the squares.'

'He's playing with everything!' says Zeb.

A blue woman reclines with her legs stretched vertically on a red and white cloth. It looks like Cecile in the steam room.

'Wish I'd seen this before we went to the Turkish baths,' I say. 'I'd've painted you blue, Ces.'

Cecile is busy in her sketchbook, copying a figure in a red coat who has a pattern for a face and holds a blue feather in a feathery hand.

'God, everyone starts looking like a Picasso painting!' whispers Cecile, glancing at a man near us, with big eyes and long stubble and black eyebrows that meet in the middle.

'Here's someone who knows how to copy the "old masters",' says Bianca, collecting Cecile and me by the elbow, one on each side, and steering us into the next room to look at his copy of Velazquez's Infanta in her square dress. In the foreground the outline of a figure steps out of the sunlight.

'What would Karl say if we had a go at copying them like that? Bet he doesn't measure!'

Cecile laughs. 'You should try it, Bianca!'

'He's called Lump, you know,' says Bianca.

'Who?'

'Picasso's dog!' says Bianca, pointing at the long white dog in the picture, 'called Lump!'

Suddenly Bianca draws her breath in. 'Oh my God, no!'

'What?' we say together, looking round.

'Not in the gallery!' says Bianca, closing her eyes.

Rob has sat down on the black square bench, and opened her shirt and begun feeding the baby, who sucks loudly and makes little squeaking sounds.

'She could at least have chosen the room with the naked women in it!'

Cecile and I laugh. 'Come on, Bianca!' says Cecile.

'Next thing it will be puking!' says Bianca, walking away into the other room, saying, 'No! I really can't bear it!'

The guard looks confused, and pretends not to notice, and eventually moves into the other room, too.

Cecile shrugs and we follow them.

Zeb and Mick are standing together, looking at a painting.

Between them I see a skull and a black lamp, and sea urchins on a white plate in diagonals of light, but I can't help looking at the figure in blue who stands with his weight on one leg, and his hands in his pockets, with a long black plait falling between his shoulder blades.

Rob comes in, doing up her shirt. Mick turns round. 'I'll take him now, love,' and Rob hands him the bundle tied in the red and white shawl, and he holds him easily against his shoulder with one big hand.

'Come on,' says Cecile, putting her hand in mine and drawing me through the doors. 'Look! It's the picnic!'

Bianca is standing in front of the picture of a blue lake in a green forest. Clothed and naked people sit among the trees having a picnic.

'He's copied Manet!' says Cecile.

'And did you know Manet copied Raphael?' says Bianca.

'Oh well, that's the way to do it!' says Cecile, taking out her sketchbook to copy Picasso.

'Let's go on a picnic!' says Zeb, coming behind us, and looking at the picture between me and Bianca.

'Yes, with Evie and me!' says Bianca, pointing to the naked woman and the other bathing.

Zeb smiles and blushes slightly, and we look at each other for a second and the light from his eyes seems to jump into mine, and dances there when I look back at the painting.

'Come here!' says Cecile, holding my arm. 'I want to show you *The Rape of the Sabines.*'

'Do you have to?'

Bianca is laughing at the funny little man who is lying with his feet in the air.

'Isn't it wild?' Cecile says, taking out her sketchbook and frantically drawing the women and their mounted captors.

Bianca turns to the picture of a woman who falls backwards off a horse.

'Look! You can see its arsehole and its bollocks!' she says, pointing at the horse.

'You like that word!' says Rob, coming over to look and patting the baby, who is now tied diagonally over her breasts.

The man holds a carving knife next to the flaring nostrils of the horse.

'You shouldn't show him such violence at such an early age,' says Bianca, smiling and patting him too.

When Mick and Zeb saunter over we decide it's time for birthday tea.

So we go to Patisserie Valerie and have pyramids of strawberries and chocolate éclairs, and custard tarts and Bianca gets mesmerised by a couple who start kissing outside the glass door. They keep trying to part and kissing again, pulled together like two magnets, and get so carried away they put their hands under each other's clothes.

Bianca claps and the shop assistants watch them through the shelves of cakes, and even the manager goes to knock on the window and then shrugs in a French way, and says to the café, 'That's what French cakes can do for you,' and leaves them to it.

'It's my birthday,' says Bianca.

'Bon anniversaire!' he says, and brings her a cake gratuit with caramel icing, and a candle burning on top, and we sing 'Happy Birthday', and the manager sings in French, and some of the other customers join in.

15

The floor has been painted grey and all our spots of paint have disappeared.

The muslin curtain has been taken down, and the doors are open to the landing.

The technicians are putting up partitions and there are the sounds of hammering and sawing in the studios. They are transforming the college into an exhibition space.

The third-years are running about, calling questions to each other up and down the stairwell about, 'Where is this?' and 'How much?' and 'Can you get mine done at the same time?' in a frantic rush to get their work mounted, framed and hung in time for the degree show.

The first- and second-years have to pack up paintings and put them in the storeroom, and gather what we need for the summer, and transport it to the annexe.

'When do we need to be out, then?'

'Five o'clock, I think, but the van is going up to the annexe this morning.'

'D'you know who is going?' says Cecile.

'Only us lot from our year, and some second-years,' I say.

We are putting Rob's materials into boxes to load into the van.

'Is Zeb coming?' says Cecile.

And I remember yesterday, when we were hidden behind the crowd.

'Yes,' I say, 'he is.'

We'd all walked along Shaftesbury Avenue after the birthday tea to catch our buses, and waited at the bus stop among a crowd of people. I stood next to Zeb on the steps of the Casino, and heard the dringing sounds of the slot machines, the mini sirens and ding-dong of the pinball, and he'd leaned over and said, 'Are you going to the annexe?'

'Yes,' I said. 'Are you?'

He nodded and his eyes looked at me like sunlight.

'We've got the whole summer,' he said.

'I'd like to hear about Spain,' I said.

'I'd like to tell you,' he said.

And then his eyes had turned dark and deep.

'And you, I want to hear about what happened with you, all of that, Evie. I want to know.'

His eyes had reached into mine, and I had to hold on to his arm; tears were pricking the back of my eyes.

'I know,' he said. 'I'm sorry, Eve. Not now. It's not the place.'

And I dropped my hand, and he caught it and held it, and I heard him say, 'Evie,' close to my neck.

Then all the people were moving at once. Cecile was shouting through the people, 'It's our bus, Eve!' and grabbed my free hand through the crowd, and I'd looked back at him and he'd squeezed my hand before he let it go, and I felt the pressure all the way home.

'What about the fire hazard?' says Cecile.

'What?'

'Zeb. The fire hazard.'

'Oh, it's all right, he's going to work on the roof,' I say. 'Trust him!'

When we've finished the boxes we take them downstairs and pile them up with the rest. And when I've swept the studio and emptied my locker, I go up to Bianca's studio, and she is lying on the chaise longue with a hand over her forehead.

'Oh, it's unbearable!' she says. 'I can't bear to leave! I don't want to pack anything!'

'But we can unpack it again today,' I say. 'We can start painting again tomorrow.'

'Oh, it's so traumatic!' she says. 'I can't bear to leave my lovely space!'

Cecile comes upstairs and we sit down together and help dismantle Bianca's studio into boxes, and take it downstairs in the lift.

When the van arrives, everyone packs in their paintings and Karl flicks his eyes up to the sky when Bianca comes through the door of the college carrying the chaise longue upwards, with her hands round the middle as though she's dancing with it.

'Bianca, do you have to?'

'Yes,' she says. 'Yes, of course. I can't do without it!'

So when the big canvases have been tied to the roof rack and we are sitting in two rows next to a stack of materials and smaller paintings piled up behind Karl's seat, he and Bianca lift the chaise longue into the van and lie it along our knees.

I am wondering where Zeb has got to when a second-year comes out of the door with a big box and stands at the door of the van.

'Another box?' says Karl, scratching his head.

'Zeb's not coming,' he says, resting the box on the step, filled with an assortment of copper tubing, rolls of wire and plugs and metal shapes. 'But could you take this for him? He says he'll bring the rest later.'

'OK,' says Karl, pushing the box into the van so we have to lift up our feet. He closes the door and we are jammed together in the back. He starts the engine and we judder forward.

I am disappointed that Zeb isn't coming. But when I look back at the college my heart sinks and my breath quickens as I see him in the corridor, having an intense conversation with Suzanne.

We arrive at a tall red-brick building and the studios are on the top floor. We walk up flights of stairs, and the green tiles on the walls make our voices echo. We can hear the sounds of the bouncing muffled feet of little ballet dancers, and the plink-plink of the piano keys behind the closed doors, as we carry our boxes and stretchers up the stairs.

The studios have tall windows that look over the trees and houses all the way to Putney and Wandsworth.

We sweep the floor and choose our spaces and Bianca finds a good position for the chaise longue.

'Let's go back and pack up the pictures now,' says Bianca. 'I feel homesick!'

'I'm going to stay here a bit,' I say.

So everyone troops out of the double doors, and I hear their footsteps echo on the tiles of the stairwell.

I unpack my pictures in the silence and arrange them on the floor around the walls. I take out the photograph Magda gave me and put it on the windowsill next to the palette.

I look at the faces of my mum and dad, looking so young and unsure, and decide that somewhere I will put them in the paintings, maybe surrounded by blue.

I unpack my paints and put them on a table and unwrap my brushes so everything is ready. I look at the pictures again and imagine the colours. I am ready to go back.

Before I reach the door, I turn around and look at the big studio, with the boxes of materials stacked in the corner; tubes of paint, rolls of paper and canvas, tins of media, primer and glue, and in the quiet I can feel something is waiting; an invisible reality more vast than this one. That's why Bianca wants the glinting colours, and why Zeb wants the exploding light, and Rob the presence of her ancestors caked in mud; because part of us is from there, and longs for there, and we want to touch that place, and let it through somehow.

I close the door and walk down the stairs, and try not to think too much about Suzanne.

When I get back to college the ground floor is already a gallery with pristine white walls and work on display. Upstairs, our studio space has been divided by white partitions.

I walk up to the top-floor storeroom and find Bianca wrapping her work in bubble wrap.

'I'm scared it will get nicked, actually,' she says, 'but it needs protecting anyway. Here's a good space for yours, Evie. Let's put them together, safety in numbers!'

She looks up. 'Did you start painting?'

'No, I was just unpacking.'

'Oh, Zeb was looking for you,' she says, moving her eyebrows up and down quickly.

'Was he?' I say.

'Yes, he said to tell you he'll see you at the degree show.'

I look at her for a minute.

'Why didn't he come?'

'Oh, the third-years finally decided it wouldn't steal the show but enhance it to have his fireworks, as long as he didn't attach them to his sculptures, so he had to sort them out. Suzanne was making a song and dance about it, though.'

'I saw them talking in the corridor,' I say.

She looks at me for a moment. 'Did you think he was getting back with her?' She smiles. 'You idiot, Evie!'

And I look into the dark corner at the back of the storeroom and shake my head at myself.

16

'Come and get ready in Brixton with us,' Bianca said. 'Silvia is coming too, it'll be fun!'

So I went back with her on the 137, clutching my dress for the degree show in a plastic bag, and watched the sun slip over the water from the top deck while Bianca took the dress out the bag and told me not to wear 'that old thing'.

After we'd climbed the stairs through the glass-stained sunlight, Bianca made fennel tea and we went and sat in the scented bathroom where Silvia was in the bath, washing her hair. I tried on the dresses from the rail, and Bianca gave her opinion from the armchair, and every now and then Silvia turned round to look. By the time Silvia had rinsed her hair, and was stepping out of the bath with the towel wrapped round her, I'd decided on the dress with roses on, that I'm wearing now.

We took it in turns to sit in the armchair and after another pot of fennel tea, everyone had decided what to wear.

We caught the bus and teetered down the road to college, Silvia in a deep red dress with a blue-black boa around her naked shoulders, and Bianca with feathers in her hair, in a Chinese dress of gold silk.

We turned the corner, and people were spilling out of the glass doors and standing around the Henry Moore sculpture with wine glasses in their hands. 'Fine Art Degree Show' was written in red letters on the glass wall, and the quadrangle was bedecked in bunting made of white-fringed flags, printed with red and black drawings.

The tutors looked strange in their smart clothes. Paul was gleaming in a silver suit with a yellow tie and long shiny shoes, which looked like crocodile skin.

Bianca said, 'Oh my God,' and made a face behind her hand.

We walked through the doors and into the noise of people talking and I noticed Miss Pym resplendent in turquoise, and Terry wearing a tie.

Bianca wanted to go upstairs to her space, but Silvia said, 'I'm going this way,' pointing to the sign that said 'Sculpture Department'.

'I'm looking for a strong sculptor!' she said, flicking the feather boa around her neck, 'not a wimpy painter!' and she kissed the air with her eyes closed.

I didn't think about it then, when I watched her cross the hall. I don't know why. It's only now as I look over the banisters, through the crowds of people, that I think of Zeb.

We watched Terry catching sight of her and following her with a wine bottle and an empty glass. I even said, 'Will she be all right with the terrible Terry on her trail?' and Bianca flicked the air with her hand. 'Silvia? She's from Sicily!'

It was when they both disappeared down the corridor to sculpture that I began to think about how everyone loves Silvia.

'Come on,' says Bianca. 'Let's go upstairs to the abstract floor.'

'D'you think Silvia's got anyone in mind?'

'No, she just likes flirting!'

We pass Geoff, wearing a Hawaiian shirt, and Bianca whispers, 'I am a born-again Christian looking funky!'

I smile at her, and decide to put the whole thing out my mind.

I look through the crowds of people at the paintings we have watched emerge, and the spaces without their grime suddenly make the paintings stand out, cut clean of their beginnings.

Maria Ines and Anna are on the landing and they greet Bianca in a shower of Italian.

'Come through!' she says. 'I will show you where I have been working. Ah, my beautiful space!'

Bianca's old space is filled with people and hung with blue paintings that belong to Mona, the third-year student. Bianca takes no notice of the paintings or the people and points out the window, showing Anna and Maria Ines the view of London. Mona is hovering round her space with a wine bottle, introducing her friends to each other, and looks a little ill at ease.

I walk upstairs and find the colour harmonies I once saw in a sketchbook, turned into paintings as long as the wall.

They fill the room with clear colour sounds and I stand and look, and listen to them sing.

I wander through the unfamiliar spaces, partitioned into corridors and alcoves, looking at the paintings in between the crowds. The third-year students, with wine bottles in their hands, talk very fast, smile a lot and hand out their cards.

I look over the banisters and see the top of Cecile's head and walk downstairs to the next floor with relief.

'Oh I'm glad to see you!' I say. 'All these people!'

Cecile looks elegant in a green dress.

She puts her arm through mine. 'Me too. Let's wander about! Where's Bianca?'

'Upstairs in her space.'

'Her space!' Cecile laughs. 'Poor Mona.'

I shrug. 'You know what she says about the paintings?'

'I know,' says Cecile. 'Dishcloths. Isn't she awful!'

We walk downstairs to the figurative floor and the sounds of people talking echo up the stairwell. On the landing are paintings of a man with a cow, and chickens in a farmyard. The paintings are colourful and splashy.

I see Sergei wearing his same old jacket, walking round the pictures, eyeing them up close, with his hands behind his back and the strange quivering sneer on his lips.

But as I pass by I notice his hair is all fluffy on the back of his head, like he's been sleeping on it, and hasn't brushed it out. It reminds me of a little bird.

'Cecile, I feel sorry for Sergei!'

'Quick, let's get away, that sounds dangerous,' she says.

We walk around the figurative floor, past the model painted from many angles lying on a blue curtain, through landscapes and cityscapes and portraits, discussing the pictures we like, and every now and then I take a look out the window to see if I can catch a glimpse of Zeb in the sculpture yard.

'You like him, don't you,' says Cecile.

'Yes,' I say, smiling at the floor.

'Let's go down,' I say, looking up.

'Come on then,' she says. 'I want to see the sculptures, and they're doing a piece of performance art in a minute.'

We meet Rob on the stairs with Mick and the little bundle, who is now called George. She smiles a tired smile.

'It's mayhem here!' she says, and Mick puts his arm round her shoulders. 'I'm beginning to feel claustrophobic!'

'Come outside with us,' I say.

So we all walk downstairs, and I meet Safi coming up, dressed in a brown and silver sari.

'Eve, how glad I am to see you!' she says, folding her hands over mine.

Around her the air feels less crowded and more peaceful.

'You look very beautiful today, my dear,' she says. I love the melody in her words.

'Thank you, Safi,' I say, and I walk down the stairs to join the others, feeling very beautiful today.

A crowd of dishevelled students pass us as we cross the hall, talking about 'Our sculpture department is better equipped! And aren't the studios dark', and Rob and Cecile look at each other and say, 'Royal College'.

We meet Bianca in the doorway. She is talking to Giacomo and Cesar, and everyone is getting a bit drunk.

'There's going to be music outside!' says Bianca, looking excited and flushed. 'I want to dance with you!' she says, putting her arms round Giacomo, who lifts her off her feet.

We walk through the studios; past sculptures made of glass and mirrors, carved wood and plaster figures, and metal geometry in three dimensions, through Suzanne's space, past the wobbly sculpture on a plinth, and Suzanne in a rubber dress talking to two men in sunglasses, and out into the sculpture yard.

In the back of the shed I see Zeb in a red shirt, busy with some boxes. Cecile looks at me, smiling, and I wish that she wouldn't.

We watch a piece of performance art involving a large rusty metal wheel, and two people make gestures that are sometimes in synchrony and sometimes not, but none of us can work out what it signifies. Everyone claps, except Rob, who says, 'Performance Fart!' in a loud voice.

Then someone tinkles a glass and Paul gives a speech about the third-years and Zeb punctuates it with fireworks with pink tails and unexpected colourful explosions in the dark shed, which make everyone laugh with surprise.

Afterwards I watch him as he moves around the shed with a bucket, kneeling down to collect the spent fireworks. He must feel my eyes on him, because he looks up and smiles.

People begin to disperse or linger and someone turns on the twinkling lights that are threaded round the yard, and music starts playing through the speakers that are hidden in the piles of wood and bags of plaster.

Cecile says, 'There's my husband!' and goes to join a man with grey hair who greets her with kind blue eyes.

People begin to dance where they are standing, and I don't know if it's the dimming light, but the air feels charged and vibrant, as though something secret is happening under the music; and the sculpture yard slowly changes its atmosphere and becomes intimate.

I look above me and the sky has turned violet.

When I look down I see Silvia leaning against the wall, talking to Zeb.

Her feather boa is flung around her naked shoulders and her hand slowly strokes her other arm. She blinks slowly at him and smiles with her mouth open.

I look down. I look away. Everyone around me is talking and the music confuses me. I walk through the people into a dark corner. What if he likes her more than me? I stand there, breathing. They're just talking, I say to myself. For heaven's sake, Evie! and just as I turn round I feel the warmth of him, and he is holding both my hands.

'Hello,' he says, drawing me towards him and away from the dark corner. 'I've been wanting to talk to you all evening,' he says.

'Hello,' I say, looking up at him.

His face is in shadow but I can see the light in his eyes.

'Shall we dance, d'you think?' he says.

'Yes,' I say, 'I feel like dancing.'

'So do I.'

I put my arms round him and it's like holding a tree that sways in the wind.

Stevie Wonder is singing sadly about an empty well.

'Come on now, Stevie, cheer up!' says Zeb, smiling down at me.

But Stevie goes on to shattered dreams and we start laughing at how miserable the words are. I feel his body trembling with laughing next to mine, and he holds me just a bit closer.

'Now it's worthless years!' I say, looking up at him. He shrugs and looks down at me and that's when it happens. Something slides down between us and collapses; a wall that has kept us apart. It crumbles, and suddenly we are in the same world. It is glowing. It must be one of Zeb's dimensions that you slip into, and he looks at me with naked eyes, that say, 'Here I am, this is me,' and the look is so beautiful I cannot look away. Then my cheek is touching his cheek and my arms are circling his neck and I feel his breath by my ear. He holds me close to him so we are almost one person, and a river of light slips through us. Then his lips are on mine and we are kissing, and Stevie is singing, 'it will be for ever,' and circles of coloured light are exploding behind my eyes, because the world is being born.

ACKNOWLEDGEMENTS

With special thanks to Marigold Farmer, for helping me to finish this book, and to Richard Farmer, both for their kind hospitality.

Many thanks to Alexandra Pringle, as always, for her amazing ability to see the final book in the first chaotic draft.

Thanks also to my agent Victoria Hobbs, and my editor Victoria Millar, to Barbara Turner, Katy Noura Butler, Oonagh Harpur, Angel Green, Erica Jarnes, Audrey Cotterell, and everyone at Bloomsbury.

Many thanks to Buz de Villiers for helping me through the book's darkness.

Thank you to the Hawthornden Foundation, the Royal Literary Fund, the Author's Foundation, DW Gibson and Ledig House USA, and Arts Council England.

And thank you to Peter Ackroyd for his two wonderful books, *London – A Biography* and *Thames – Sacred River*, both of which feature in this book.

A NOTE ON THE TYPE

The text of this book is set in Berling roman, a
modern face designed by K. E. Forsberg between
1951 and 1958. In spite of its youth it does carry
the characteristics of an old face. The serifs are
inclined and blunt, and the g has a straight ear.